DECORATIONS IN A
RUINED CEMETERY

DECORATIONS IN A RUINED CEMETERY

JOHN GREGORY BROWN

HOUGHTON MIFFLIN COMPANY

BOSTON   NEW YORK

1994

For information about permission to reproduce selections from this book, write to Permissions, Houghton Mifflin Company, 215 Park Avenue South, New York, New York 10003.

Library of Congress Cataloging-in-Publication Data

Brown, John Gregory
Decorations in a ruined cemetery / John Gregory Brown.
p.   cm.
ISBN 0-395-67025-X
I. Title.
PS3552.R687D4   1994
813'.54 — dc20   93-13295
CIP

Printed in the United States of America

BP 10 9 8 7 6 5 4 3 2 1

Text design by Anne Chalmers

The author is grateful for permission to quote from *Collected Poems* by Wallace Stevens, copyright 1936 by Wallace Stevens and renewed 1964 by Holly Stevens. Reprinted by permission of Alfred A. Knopf, Inc.

*For Carrie
and in memory of Frances*

If ever the search for a tranquil belief should end,
The future might stop emerging out of the past,
Out of what is full of us; yet the search
And the future emerging out of us seem to be one.

— Wallace Stevens

DECORATIONS IN A RUINED CEMETERY

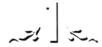

THE DAY WE LEFT my stepmother, the Lake Pontchartrain Causeway collapsed, and the new life my father had imagined, spiriting his children back to his childhood home, fell away from us as quickly as that bridge, the whole world thrown off-balance like a gyroscope hammered into the wrong shape, the lake coughing up our family's secrets in the form of an old bent-backed black servant.

Today, twenty-five years later, my father is dead. He died while sitting on the back porch of the house we'd tried to get to twenty-five years before, looking out over what had been my grandfather's garden, three acres of trees and shrubs I had recently, on my weekend visits, resurrected. The afternoon sun would have just crossed beyond the line of oaks at the western edge of my grandfather's property, and the chill my father must have felt beginning in his arms and legs could just as easily have been a sign of that autumn's first cold evening than what it was, the diminished circulation from a stroke that two minutes later would kill him.

My father did not like to talk about our leaving. He would mention the causeway's collapse in conversation as though it were one of a million benign recollections, an eccentric and amusing detail of New Orleans history that we happened to have witnessed. He'd laugh and say to me, "That was something, wasn't it?" as though our presence on the bridge were nothing more than a bit of great good fortune, a Sunday lark that, the moment the causeway collapsed, became transformed into something magnificent.

Once, toward the end of his life, I asked my father again about that day and the weeks that followed, about what he thought it had meant in the course of his own and his children's lives. We were sitting in the garden at a cast-iron table I'd bought for twenty dollars at a garage sale a few weeks before. Pineapples and cornstalks were woven into the tabletop's green iron grid. My father kept his hands on the table, lifting and lowering his fingers into and out of the holes formed by the grid as though he were sitting at a keyboard and slowly trying to compose what he could not say.

"I want to talk about this," I said, and my father let out a long breath, raised his hands from the table, and pronounced my name as though he were set to begin some version of the story he had never told, one that — in that instant of his exhalation — I dreamed would stretch on for hours and hours, for days and days, the two of us trading our memories until we had found a true measure of our hearts.

"Meredith," he began, reaching over to touch my arm, but then he shook his head and just looked at me.

That was it. He wouldn't go on.

"Please," I said, but my father looked away from me. I watched his eyes trace a path across the garden, along the line of oaks, and then up to the sky. What could he have been thinking — that the past was too much, even then, to talk about with his daughter?

"Please," I said again, but my father pushed himself up from his chair, his entire body straining with the effort, and walked back toward my grandfather's house. He died before I had the chance to ask him again.

❧

Catherine, my stepmother, remarried. That was years ago. She sends me pleasant letters from North Carolina on pastel-colored paper, her writing as leisurely now as her life seems frantic, caring for her husband and teenage children, volunteering as a docent at the art museum in Raleigh, taking literature classes at the university. We love each other well enough still that there is a melancholy to our correspondence. Unable now to gain an apology from my father, we apologize to each other, though we keep to small regrets. We are sorry for missing birthdays, for forgetting to call, for not getting around to the visit we absolutely must, sometime or the other, plan. Secretly, I prefer the letters Catherine sent when we left her. I reread those, not the recent ones, when I long for her company.

But I am glad for the letters she sends now, and I am sure that she is glad for mine, too. I suspect we will carry on this way for the rest of our lives, moving no closer to what it is that prompts these letters than any other mother and daughter, divided, would.

✤

My brother Lowell, although we see each other quite regularly, is lost to me in the comforts of his own life. When I visit him, I step through his door, his children gather around me, and he looks at me with a sort of startled curiosity, as though I were a Benedictine monk who had been roaming the cold stone halls of the monastery just down the road from his Covington home and had mistakenly wandered over.

At dawn, the monastery's leaden bells summon the monks for Mass, seven bells playing hymns at one quarter speed, a ringing that blankets Lowell's neighborhood in somber Catholic grace. Lowell says he no longer wakes to the ringing.

I do not know what to make of my brother, of his polite reticence toward me. Today his life is much like his blindingly white clapboard home: spacious, well built, well positioned. It is enough for now, since that's not my story, to say that my own life is not.

More than any other moment, I remember the two of us, twelve years old, sitting frozen in the front seat of my father's maroon Checker. I am looking over at my father, not at his face but at his left hand gripping the steering wheel so hard that his fingers are white and pressed flat against it. I hear him whispering "Jesus Christ" over and over, again and again, not as if in prayer or even in terror but in the way you would whisper a person's name when you want him to come see something quickly, before the moment is gone — a rare and beautiful bird perched on a nearby tree, or a child quietly singing to himself in his sleep.

I look away from my father, to see what he sees. A single concrete section, sixty feet of the twenty-four-mile bridge, has crumbled into Lake Pontchartrain directly ahead of us, halfway between New Orleans and Mandeville. The falling concrete has stirred up so much mud in the lake that within moments of the collapse the blue water has turned brown for miles around, and the twisted metal coils that were buried in the bridge now stand up above the water's surface like the tops of gnarled tree branches rising out of a giant flood.

A blue station wagon, driven by a man whom Lowell and I thought we recognized when his car passed my father's, has swerved and then sliced across the railing, plunging down into the water. From my father's car, through the Checker's great curved windshield, we see the blue station wagon's bent frame bob back up to the surface like a fishing cork, empty.

I remember the shape and size of my body and Lowell's as we sat there in the car, my bird legs and bony knees, Lowell's dark blue jeans, his too-large feet, the forward curve of his shoulders that made his plaid shirt, with dark blue and purple bands, fold in just below his ribs. And my father, his body pressed deep into the black seat, his arms thick, his face creased, his wire glasses pressing against his temples.

It is our physical presence there, our solid weight in that car, that has stayed with me, as though it was only then, when the causeway collapsed, that I began to untangle myself from my father and brother. It was as if my own shape had emerged out of what was not Lowell and was not my father and was not, because of her absence, Catherine.

I looked at my father and brother, and I was — my body was — whatever was left over. Their features were rough; mine were smooth. Their hair was straight; mine was curly. Their skin was fair; mine was dark. Their frames were solid; mine was slight. I did not know what this meant, if it even meant anything at all, but I recognized the difference that morning and wondered what it was exactly that I had discovered.

It is twenty-five years later, yet I still need to remind myself that my father was a young man then, that he knew his own mind no better than I know mine now. Today I am the same age, thirty-seven, as my father was when we left Catherine. Of course, I have wondered if it is that fact which has enabled me to begin this story.

I have meant to do this for a long time, though.

So why have I begun now? I can say, although it is just the sort of romantic notion my father would have blindly, secretly embraced, that it has simply taken three nights of drenching weather, New Orleans' streets running with ankle-deep water, to push me toward a sort of blank distraction, one that allows the past to accumulate and regain its shape.

It is more than that, I suspect, although for the life of me I cannot say what it is.

~❦~

As improbable as that morning's coincidences seemed, through the years I've considered that of the hundreds of cars stalled by the fallen bridge, wasn't it likely that one would contain a man who moments before had left his wife, had set out on what he'd decided was the only means of preserving his own and his children's well-lived, well-ordered life? No matter that this life was in truth not so well lived nor so well ordered as he believed. No matter that in trying to save his life, he lost it.

And surely there must have been, for good measure, tragedies averted by the causeway's collapse, quarrels and foolish missions suddenly interrupted by this disaster, a contrite husband looking over at his wife to offer an apology for past unfaithfulness, a father resolving to understand rather than condemn his mysterious, rebellious son. Do such conversions persist beyond the moment? I'm not sure.

Also this: Once, in college, at Tulane, I met at some party a boy who had also been on the bridge that morning. It was, I discovered, nothing to him. The boy — a fraternity friend of Lowell's? His architecture school classmate? An athlete? — said that his family, headed somewhere he no longer remembered, had simply turned around and gone home. Hadn't it been raining that day? Hadn't someone died?

The boy smiled and said he'd like to know what I remembered. Now, if I'd found myself in love with him, would I have answered? Would I have pulled him into a dark corner or outside to the street or to some quiet bar and said, *Let me tell you what I remember, I will tell you*? Or did I in fact find this boy handsome, intelligent, apparently kind, and so not answer him for that very reason, for the dim, unlikely possibility of love? I was capable of responding, of failing to respond, for such a reason, but I don't remember the exact circumstances.

In truth, I can't even talk to Lowell about it now. He has acquired family, friends, and career with such swift and pleasant ease that I wonder how he managed to avoid what I have not: the sense that the world cannot be put right, that its spinning will forever be wobbly and uneven.

Lowell has developed, these last few years, both the fondness and the means for elaborate vacations during which he photographs his wife and three beautiful children in front of great architectural triumphs, most recently the Sistine Chapel, the Musée des Beaux Arts in Brussels, Saint Stephen's Cathedral in Vienna. *See here, Meredith*, these photographs protest when I slip them from the fold of Lowell's letters, *it is not so difficult after all, is it?*

Well, it is. Like my father and my grandfather — or at least this is how I understand them — I am saddled with the secret compulsion of considering, as one poet put it, the odd morphology of regret, its brittle bone and skin, its peculiar shape.

Regret is always, I've decided, a long and complicated story, as this one is. While I now realize that my own regret begins not on that morning, November 7, 1965, but much earlier, long before I was born, I will begin with that morning nevertheless and slip, as my memory slips, both forward and back.

That's a fine way to do this, I think.

We make sense of the world, some philosopher once said, only through its rearrangement, through a constant shift in perspective coupled with a slight movement of this or that here and there and then here again. In that manner, in the imperfections such movements reveal, the truth becomes apparent.

The causeway's collapse, then. Once the first moments of fear had passed, all the men, including my father, climbed out of their cars and stood in tight circles, smoking cigarettes and shaking their heads. Their wives and children leaned out of the car windows for a glimpse of what was going on, worried that more of the bridge might go down.

Soon enough the police appeared, young officers running up through the line of cars, their blue uniforms dark with sweat. They began turning back the miles of traffic that had accumulated on both sides of the bridge, while above us black helicopters circled in the sky like ugly moths, dropping divers in wet suits to search for the body of the man who had been driving the blue station wagon.

Lowell and I both thought we knew who the driver had been: Murphy Warrington, the old black man who had worked for my grandfather for years and years but then, a few months after my grandfather's death, after he'd come to live in New Orleans but had quickly returned to my grandfather's house in Mandeville, had simply disappeared.

When he pulled the station wagon beside my father's Checker to pass us, the man had turned his head and smiled, raising a hand to the brim of a worn gray hat, the sort many men had already abandoned wearing except, it seemed, with long double-breasted wool coats in winter, when businessmen marched down Canal Street from one office building to the next or rode on the streetcar in the mornings, their heads bowed over the *Times-Picayune.* Actually, I could say here that the man in the blue station wagon was dressed like the black men who had begun to appear at just this time in newspapers and magazines, standing in front of swelling crowds to make inspired speeches, but I knew nothing of that then. I knew that the president had been shot and killed two years before, within weeks of my grandfather's death. I knew there was a war. Beyond that, I knew practically nothing of the world; my father created the peculiar boundaries of our lives.

From my father, we learned about New Orleans, the proper French pronunciations of its streets and neighborhoods, its parks and canals. We learned my father's version of the city's history, from which I'm sure I will never extract the truth. And we learned, Lowell much more than me, about the music that had begun in this city, how a group of black men called the Razzy Dazzy Spasm Band, led by Stalebread Charley, used cigar-box fiddles, old kettles, and cowbells to create the cacophonous music that ended up as jazz.

My father would recite the names of New Orleans musicians as though he were speaking of well-loved friends who had passed away: Joe Oliver, Kid Ory, and Sidney Bechet, Henry Allen and Buster Bailey and Johnny Dodds. He would pull out the old records he had bought at secondhand shops and sit Lowell and me down in the living room. "Just listen," he'd say, smiling. "Just listen to this."

My father closed his eyes while the music played, and Lowell and I looked at each other and quietly laughed.

"He's crazy," Lowell would whisper, although eventually he grew to love this music, too, letting his eyes drift closed while listening the way my father did, opening them again only when a song was done. "That's something," Lowell would say, just like my father, and I'd be left wondering what that something was and why I had missed it.

On the causeway, my father looked straight ahead and so didn't see the car next to us, but Lowell and I smiled back and waved.

Just like Murphy, this man wore thick black-rimmed glasses, and he had two buckteeth. His shoulders sloped forward, and the hand he raised to the brim of his hat was long and thin, a skeleton's hand. He was wearing a dirty white shirt and a black tie. The window was rolled down so that the tie blew back over his collar, flapping and flapping the whole time like a dark cloth left out on a clothesline in the middle of a hurricane.

For a few seconds he kept his car even with my father's and we smiled at one another. Just as my father turned his head to look, though, the man leaned forward and the blue station wagon shot ahead and pulled in front of us.

"Who was that, Meredith?" my father asked.

That was one of my father's habits, always asking me questions instead of asking Lowell. He thought of me as a silent, sullen child. He called me his lonely only begotten daughter, his quiet mouse, his lost little lamb. I didn't think I deserved it, but my father was always trying to get me to speak. Even when he did, though, it was usually Lowell who piped up.

"He looked exactly like Murphy, only dressed up for church," Lowell said.

"He did," I added.

My father nodded his head and smiled. He seemed to think that Lowell and I were setting him up for what was his own favorite trick, concocting an elaborate, unbelievable story from an obvious lie, one embroidered detail after the next until, as if by magic, the story suddenly seemed more plausible than not.

That morning, once we'd pulled away from our house, my father had acted as if we were simply off on an enjoyable Sunday drive, the sort he'd take us on after Mass, when we'd stop at home to pick up Catherine and then drive from one neighborhood to the next, my father pulling the car up in front of old houses so he could tell his stories about the people who'd once lived there: an exotic Cuban dancer, the brother of a famous French painter and his blind wife, the pharmacist who'd arranged for Napoleon's death mask to be smuggled to New Orleans in a wooden crate filled with aspirin powder. We never believed the stories he told, but we knew that we weren't meant to. My father simply wanted us to enjoy, as he enjoyed, the sound of his voice, the emerging story, his sense of irony, his flashes of humor.

"Tell me," my father said to us on the bridge.

"Tell you what?" Lowell said. "It was Murphy."

"Meredith?" my father asked.

"It did look like him," I said.

The truth, though, was that we hadn't seen Murphy for two whole years.

Murphy had lived in the basement of my grandfather's Mandeville house for nearly forty years, since before my father was born, helping to mix and pour the concrete for the garden statuary my grandfather made, the saints and Virgin Marys and Jesuses that people liked to put on their lawns, a display that might be considered gaudy and trite in other cities but in New Orleans was a symbol of genuine and modest devotion. In some neighborhoods, these statues were so abundant that they seemed to have marched in like a troop of missionaries and taken over. Spotlights were buried in lawns and trained on them so that at night they shone like sentinels of God protecting their owners' lawns and foliage from desecration. On Bienville Boulevard, the street where we lived, there were twelve Virgin Marys just on our block. Even the old bar two blocks down had one, the neon Dixie Beer sign in the bar's window casting a green glow over the statue all night.

When my grandfather died, my father didn't know what to do with Murphy. Over the years, my father said, Murphy had practically become family, standing beside my grandfather through his long life, the two of them enduring all manner of disaster, hurricanes and floods and neighbors so angry they made it clear they'd be happy to see both men hanging side by side from a tree like dead rabbits meant to scare away all others. My father liked to say with half a laugh that my grandfather had the skill of finding the worn thread in every silver lining.

"You've gone and hitched yourself to the wrong horse," my father used to tell Murphy, but Murphy always shook his head and laughed.

"That horse is a mule, Mr. Thomas," Murphy would answer. Although they were about the same age, Murphy called my grandfather "Old Mr. Eagen."

Murphy never married. He lived with my grandfather until my grandfather died. He carried his body into the house from the shed out back where he'd collapsed, then called my father with the news. "He's gone," Murphy said as soon as my father picked up the phone. "We'll leave now," my father said, and he hung up.

So after the funeral, after my father spent an evening sorting through my grandfather's things — thumbing through old account books and letters, flipping through dusty photograph albums — he brought Murphy to New Orleans to work for him. My father's office was on Magazine Street, on the first floor of a dark green Victorian house my father had bought from a dying man a month before Lowell and I were born.

My father liked to say that he'd bought the house for a song, and when I was a child I thought that was what he really had done. I pictured him standing over the bed of a yellowed, bone-thin old man and singing with his fine deep voice some song the man was desperate to hear, maybe a big-band tune like the ones my father sang in the mornings while shuffling through our house, "Lady Be Good" or "Sweet Lorraine" or "Embraceable You." I thought my father did have the kind of voice a dying man would long to hear, deep like a calm blue ocean. He would sing every word of "Autumn Leaves" in French, and it was enough to make me cry. It made me think of my mother, of how much my father must have missed her, of the catalogue of songs I imagined he had placed in his memory, each attached to some particular feature of my mother's. I could just imagine an old man giving up the house he wouldn't need anymore, holding a pen in his shaking hand to sign a crumpled sheet of paper, if only my father would keep on singing.

Of course, my father had actually bought that house with

money. It was money my grandfather had loaned him, money saved bit by bit over years of selling his statues. My father had just finished his orthopedic residency at the Touro Infirmary, where he'd only been paid fifty dollars a month. He had a wife and two children on the way, though he thought it was only one.

You'd think that ten years later, when my grandfather died and my father brought Murphy to New Orleans, there would have been more money than my father knew what to do with, but there wasn't. Murphy, though, didn't seem to mind. He helped my father cut away old casts from people's arms and legs, and he washed all the clinking, shiny instruments in the sterilizer. He carried the heavy stacks of x-rays to and from my father's car and did whatever else my father asked.

I don't know what my father was able to pay Murphy, but he did let him move upstairs, to the rooms on the second floor above his office. I like to imagine that together Murphy and my father mourned my grandfather's death, trading stories between them of my grandfather's kindness and quiet devotion, sharing whatever memories of him seemed most profound.

I am not sure, though, that any such conversations ever took place. My father and Murphy dealt with each other in much the same manner Murphy and my grandfather had, standing side by side as though they shared a secret understanding, one that did not require any words. More often than not, my father and Murphy greeted each other in silence, simply nodding or shaking hands. When they did speak, they pursued a sort of joking banter that, while confirming the intimacy between them, also somehow denied it.

Eventually, I came to understand some of what was at work between my father and Murphy. Unable to meet each other on equal terms, they chose not to meet at all but to orbit around each other like two separate planets of entirely different composition. It was, I realize now, the way my father dealt with just about everyone, including his wife and children.

It was only a few weeks after my grandfather's death that Catherine's mother died, too. Catherine didn't take anyone with her to North Carolina for the funeral. We'd only met her mother once, one summer when Lowell and I were seven and we'd all gone up there for vacation. But I'd liked her, and she'd liked me. We'd spent one evening sitting out on folding chairs in a giant field to look for shooting stars, the earth and sky stretching out all around us the way it couldn't do in the city, and Catherine's mother had welcomed me into her lap and hugged me as if we'd known each other for years. Her dress smelled of chlorine bleach, I remember.

Once we got home, I wrote her a letter, just a few scribbled lines, and she wrote me back, describing how autumn had come on and the trees had all changed color, something we didn't see in New Orleans, where almost every bit of vegetation stayed green the whole year and winter lasted maybe three weeks at the most, never lining up with Christmas or promising snow the way cold weather did up North.

Catherine read me her mother's letter, and it made her cry because it was so beautiful. "Even for an old woman like me, these are days of grace," the letter began, though in fact Catherine's mother was not yet fifty years old when she wrote those words. I meant to write her my own letter again but never did.

The week Catherine was gone to bury her mother, Lowell and I took the streetcar to my father's office after school, and Murphy looked after us while we waited for my father to finish with his patients. On one of those days, Murphy walked over dressed in his white cotton coat and asked me to go upstairs.

"You look like a doctor," I told him, pointing to the white coat.

"That's regulations," Murphy said. "Mr. Thomas runs a tight ship." He laughed and shrugged his shoulders and stuck his hands in the coat's pockets, as though he were embarrassed to be dressed as he was.

"Come on," he said. "I've got a gift for Miss Meredith." He waved his arm and started marching up the stairs in his dusty black leather shoes.

I'm not sure I had ever been up to the second floor before then, but I followed directly behind Murphy. The steps were creaky, with the wood polish worn off down the middle. The whole house looked like that, dilapidated and a little unkempt, and it made me wonder sometimes how anyone thought my father was a respectable doctor. In fact, most people — those with money — didn't think he was, although I didn't know that at the time.

I followed Murphy through a long hall and into his living room, which had a bay window looking out over the street. Murphy had furnished the room with a sofa and three easy chairs that he must have picked up from the secondhand shops that ran for blocks along Magazine, every piece upholstered in a different floral design, the whole room a jungle of faded orange and red and green. Even the dusty curtains had a floral pattern over a background of giant, olive-colored leaves lined with spidery gold veins. Murphy walked over to the window and picked up a shoebox that had been sitting on the windowsill.

"Your grandfather wanted you to have this, Miss Meredith," he said. "I'd be honest to say I would have preferred to keep this myself as a reminder, so to speak, of old Mr. Eagen, but he insisted his granddaughter have it."

Murphy stretched his arms out to hand me the box, and I took it. Inside were old black-and-white photographs of the statues my grandfather had made, hundreds and hundreds of statues he'd placed in front of the magnolias and azaleas in his back yard so he'd have pictures of his work.

When we'd visited my grandfather, Lowell and my father had spent most of their time across the street, sitting on the sea wall trying to catch fish, dropping their lines in the water and usually coming up with nothing except dirty catfish and tiny croakers. I wanted nothing to do with that, so I'd go out back and watch my grandfather and Murphy work. I'd watch them mix the slurry or peel the tin molds off the dried plaster and run steel wool over the surface until the statues were as smooth as silk and skin. I'd liked those statues since I was the tiniest little girl.

Although he did not ever say so, I know that my grandfather appreciated my interest in his work. He understood, I think, that my fascination was a child's version of his own, how the process of pouring this coarse mixture of sand and water and stone, of watching it take on its human shape, was nothing less than a confirmation of belief, of a faith so elemental that the statues were not merely a representation of what is sacred but were sacred themselves.

"Surely the good Lord is smiling down upon us today," my grandfather would say when he'd completed a statue with which he was particularly pleased, and I'd wonder if that were true, if each of my grandfather's statues somehow gained him a moment of recognition from above, entitling him to some apparently lucky but actually heaven-sent turn of events — a lost object found, a pleasant meal, a profitable last-minute purchase by a hesitant customer. I decided once that my grandfather's reward for each of his statues might well be another day of happiness and good health, imagining that if he simply kept at it, kept turning out one statue after the next, he would live forever.

My grandfather kept the finished, unsold statues spread out across the garden, and when there weren't people looking to buy, I'd stand in front of them and pretend they were talking to me, like Saint Francis telling me the story of how God had said to build a church all by himself, one stone at a time. His own father and everyone else decided he was crazy, a holy lunatic, which my grandfather said he probably was, this craziness being what made him so special in God's eyes.

On the back of each photograph, scrawled in my grandfather's fancy script, was a date and the name of the statue, including saints like Patrick and Bartholomew and Ignatius whose lives I knew from the books my grandfather had given me, books that were usually beyond my understanding but that included artists' illustrations of the saints' lives, ones where they stood surrounded by children or alone on battlefields, a light as from heaven cast down on them. I went through my childhood half expecting to come upon someone cast in such a light, as though God might already have given a signal as to who'd been chosen in this life.

There weren't only pictures of statues in the shoebox. There were also photographs of other objects my grandfather had made, birdbaths with strands of ivy and grapevine carved along the base, giant urns and tiny Greek columns and even gravestones, with names like Jackson and Jones and Davis, which I pretended were the names of famous men but were actually the names of those headed for the cemetery over in Covington, just beyond the monastery grounds.

When I was a child, that cemetery was identified, by whites and blacks alike, as the nigger cemetery. It was reserved by the Catholic church not simply for its black parishioners but for all other blacks within fifty miles of the spot, in the fear that if those families did not have a cemetery, they would be forced to lay their dead in the earth wherever they might find the room to dig — behind their rented houses or hidden in the brush on the side of the road.

Even as a child I knew, because my grandfather had told me so, that most people's gravestones were made of marble or granite, not cement, and only the poorest of the poor settled in their grief for something my grandfather had made. Once the blocks had dried, though, my grandfather smoothed the edges and carved them with his own hands just as though they were marble, all those names and dates and whatever Bible verses people wanted beneath them. He told me it was a shame that what he'd taken so much time to carve wore away from the wind and rain sometimes before a wife was even ready to join her husband in the earth. Sometimes, without anyone's even asking, my grandfather would drive his truck over to the nigger cemetery and carve an old stone over again. He said he thought it might be some small comfort wherever those people were to watch their names fade away together.

Though he could have afforded better, my grandfather's own gravestone was cement, too, which was only right, considering how he'd spent his life making them for others. He'd made the stone himself and included not only his own name but his long-gone wife's as well, leaving Murphy to carve the date he died: September 29, 1963. There was no date for his wife, my grandmother Mollie, who just like Murphy had disappeared. But that was long before Lowell and I were born, when my father was still a boy.

The other thing my grandfather did was to make arrangements to be buried not in the white people's cemetery near the courthouse in Mandeville but in the nigger cemetery in Covington.

It was Murphy who told my father of the arrangements. "I guess he'd talked about it a time or two, Mr. Thomas," Murphy said when we arrived in Mandeville, shaking his head and handing over a brown paper envelope that must have contained whatever documents my grandfather had thought to gather. Lowell and I were standing behind my father, Catherine between us, holding our hands. My father slapped the envelope twice against his leg as if to shake off whatever dust was on it, and I felt surprised that my grandfather, no matter how old he might have been, had let his thoughts turn to his own death so much that he had already carved his own stone and decided where he'd like to be buried.

Only once had I seen the grieving come to my grandfather to request his services. It was a Sunday, and the whole family arrived, a woman, whose face I saw only when she lifted her torn black veil to run a gloved finger under her eyes, along with her three children, all of them older than me and dressed as if for church.

"We're in need of a stone, Mr. Eagen," the woman said. "Nathan's passed."

"I'm sorry, Gertie," my grandfather said, and he took the woman's arm and led her out through the back door. Along with the three children, I stood on the back porch and watched my grandfather and the woman walk through the garden and then step inside the shed. The children did not speak to me or cry or even acknowledge my presence. They stood in silence and watched until, a few minutes later, my grandfather led the woman back to the house.

"I'll be done tomorrow morning," my grandfather told her. "I'll deliver it to the cemetery and then come by the house. I'll see you then."

"We're grateful, Mr. Eagen," the woman said. "God bless you."

After he had seen them out the door, my grandfather took a notebook from his coat pocket and wrote in it. I asked what he was writing. "A verse from the gospels," my grandfather said, "from the Gospel of Saint Mark."

I asked him what the verse was, and he told me: *When the evening had come, he saith unto them, "Let us pass over unto the other side."*

"The other side means the nigger cemetery?" I asked.

My grandfather laughed for a moment, then looked at me. "I'm afraid it does, my dear girl," he said.

~ ❦ ~

The nigger cemetery was a rundown place, full of overgrown weeds and an iron fence that sagged in spots as if too many people had climbed over it, though who knows why anyone would. For my grandfather's burial, Lowell and I had gotten dressed up in black — Catherine had to take us both out to buy those clothes — and we held my father's hand while a priest from Saint Alphonse's read from a prayer book.

After the burial, my father let Lowell and me look around while he and Catherine stayed by my grandfather's grave, both of them with their heads down, my father saying silent prayers the way he did every Sunday until Mass began.

Lowell and I made our way through the cemetery, pointing out all the gravestones and decorations we guessed my grandfather had made, sleeping lambs sitting on top of children's stones, angels and open Bibles and flower bunches carved on square blocks that didn't have names. Everything was in disorder except for one or two neat rows, as if after a short while the cemetery owners knew they would run out of space and so started putting the graves wherever they could.

Looking through the photographs Murphy had given me, I

saw some that were taken right there in the cemetery, weeds already growing up around the stones as though they'd been there a hundred years.

"You take care of those pictures," Murphy told me. "That's not a ten-year-old's toy. That's a good man's life."

"I will," I said, and I looked up at him. He looked back at me through his thick glasses, his forehead wet and shiny the way it always seemed to be. "You want some of these?" I asked him.

"I already took my favorites, Miss Meredith," he told me. "I'm grateful. I don't think your grandfather would mind."

"I don't mind either," I said, and we went back downstairs. I showed the shoebox to Lowell, and he nodded and looked at a couple of the pictures. When my father was finished with his patients, I showed him, too. He flipped through the photographs and smiled. "That's something," he told me, and he looked over at Murphy as if he'd known Murphy had this to give me, which I guess he did. "That's something special, Meredith," he said. "What do you think?"

"They're nice," I told him.

"Well, we'll make an album for them," my father said, and he put his hand on top of my head the way he always did, just his fingers touching my hair, as if he were afraid I might get hurt.

I figured Murphy didn't like working for my father or maybe didn't like living in New Orleans, but whatever the reason, after a few months my father sent him back to Mandeville, to take care of my grandfather's empty house, opening the windows and preparing the beds whenever my family went to visit.

I thought Murphy might go back to making statues as a way to get more money than my father could give him, but he didn't. I didn't know what he did. With Catherine, he acted as if he were a butler dressed in bow tie and tails, though in fact he wore the same dirty brown pants and stained white shirts he'd been wearing for years, his black leather shoes worn down so much that I was sure the soles of his feet went straight through to the ground. For Catherine, though, he held the door open and said "Yes, ma'am" and "Indeed," and he took an interest in everything that came to Catherine's mind — how the broken window sash needed fixing, whether or not this or that piece of furniture could stand repair, how the back garden could use some shaping up.

Murphy only talked about those things, though. He never actually did them. But no one seemed to mind, not Catherine or my father, and not Lowell or me, both of us preferring that he spend his time leading us on walks through town, which seemed his favorite and near-only occupation, saying hello back to whoever said hello to him, leaving us to kill time on porches or swinging on tree ropes while he went into this or that house for a quick glass of water, a quick bite to eat, a quick conversation — none of which was ever quick but instead stretched to near and sometimes beyond an hour. Lowell and I felt we'd been set loose. The neighborhood children stood back and watched us with wide-open eyes as we jumped off porch rails or climbed trees or swung so high on the tree ropes that the branches sagged and we felt as though we were floating above the world.

It wasn't long after moving back to my grandfather's house that Murphy just disappeared. When we went to Mandeville one weekend, we found his clothes rolled up in paper bags in the kitchen cabinets along with his few other possessions: a leather toilet case with an old-fashioned razor and shaving soap; one of those King James Bibles with red ink whenever Jesus speaks, although nearly half the pages had been torn out; and a glass box with gold cufflinks and miniature versions of the statues my grandfather had made. Unlike my grandfather's statues, which were always white, these were painted in crazy colors, the Virgin Mary's robes canary yellow, Saint Francis's raised arm and face royal blue, a lawn jockey in a pinstriped suit. I asked my father if I could keep the statues for myself, but he said he thought that he ought to keep them. "He'll want them back, I suspect," my father said.

I couldn't find the photographs Murphy had said he kept, though I looked for them. I wondered if Murphy carried them around in his wallet like a father with photographs of his children, showing them off to whoever he thought might be interested.

Lowell and I decided right out that Murphy was dead, that he'd been killed in some kind of fight. My father laughed at that and said Murphy would be the last man in the world to end up in a fight. So instead my father tried to find him, spending hours walking up and down the lakefront in Mandeville and talking to the black men who threw their crab nets off the sea wall. He took Lowell and me with him to Sharp Street, where Murphy used to take us on his walks. My father talked to the families sitting outside on their rotted porches or stood in doorways and shouted through the screen doors to whoever was inside. Nobody had seen him all week, they said. He hadn't talked about leaving. He hadn't been drinking.

Murphy's mother had been dead for years, but we stopped at the house where she'd lived and asked the man there if he knew anything. He said he didn't know any Murphy Warrington and wouldn't tell us if he did. We could hear the man cursing as we stepped away from the door.

For a while my father ran an advertisement in the *Times-Picayune*, offering a five-hundred-dollar reward, but nobody called. My father didn't say so, but after that he decided that Lowell and I were probably right, that Murphy was more than likely dead.

⁂

So of course my father didn't take us seriously when we told him that the man in the blue station wagon had looked just like Murphy. The station wagon moved further and further ahead of us, and my father didn't speed up. He drummed his fingers on the steering wheel and went back to singing with the radio.

Even though it was November, the air was summer damp and salty, and we had the windows down. The three of us were crowded in the front seat because the back seat was piled high with our clothes, which Lowell had handed out to me at dawn through the laundry room window. I'd carried the tall, unsteady stacks out to the car, leaving our lawn littered with the shirts and socks that slipped through my fingers while I walked. I tried to go back to pick up what I'd dropped, but my father told me to get in the car. He didn't want Catherine waking up in the middle of our leaving, as if it were one thing to leave your wife and a completely different thing to get caught in the act.

As we drove across the causeway, with the whole city of New Orleans disappearing behind us, I kept imagining Catherine waking up and looking for us, walking from room to room like someone who'd woken up after what she thought was a single night but was actually a thousand years, everyone she knew and loved a long time dead and gone. I figured, though, that once Catherine opened the front door to check for my father's car, she would see the clothes there on the lawn and know we were gone.

The night before we left, I tried to write her a letter. I wanted to leave it someplace where she would find it. I started one on a piece of her own stationery but didn't get any further than "Dear Catherine." The truth was, I didn't know what to tell her. She and my father had been married for seven of Lowell's and my twelve years. She'd taken on the task of raising someone else's babies without any of her own. She was as much a mother to Lowell and me as anyone could be.

Even so, it was as if the wrong sort of miracle had happened to her, as if she'd expected one glorious thing but gotten another. I could tell just in the way she touched me or held me in her arms, the way she pulled the covers up or sang me to sleep. It was as if she could never get the right sort of love going with us, and it just broke her heart.

So when my father decided he was leaving, we didn't have a choice. My father said that we did. He sat us down in Lowell's bedroom and explained that this marriage, which he said had been a good one full of love for many, many years, was not a good one anymore. He was going to move to Mandeville and maybe start a new practice there. Maybe he'd give up on being a doctor and find another way to live. He said he didn't really know. We could go with him if we wanted, he told us. He said he'd understand if we decided to stay.

The whole time he talked, his eyes were red, and he took his glasses off and rubbed them. Then he looked down and ran his hands over the bedspread, the same motion time and again, as if he were trying to rub it smooth.

I couldn't say anything, but Lowell asked my father what Catherine wanted, if she wanted us to stay with her. My father looked up and said they hadn't yet had a chance to talk. "There are some things adults have a hard time discussing," he told us. "This is one of them."

He told us we should talk about it between ourselves, just Lowell and me, but we didn't. We couldn't bring ourselves to do it. We both felt, without a single word passing between us, that we had not truly been offered a choice. We felt that my father, by confessing that he meant to leave, by telling us this secret, was telling us something else as well — that he was our father, while Catherine had never been, no matter how we all had tried, our mother.

Our real mother had died, we'd been told, of pneumonia, a few months after Lowell and I were born. We took flowers to her grave every August 1, on Lowell's and my birthday. Her gravestone was in the Old Metairie cemetery, which had a grand spiked iron fence around it that someone had decided would look better painted blue. Her stone was marble, with only her name carved into the pale pink surface.

Every year we took magnolia blossoms with us and left them in the concrete bowl next to the grave. We filled the bowl, which my grandfather had made, with water we'd brought with us in milk bottles and carried over from the car. We said a prayer, and my father touched his hand to the stone just under her name. He told us this was a kind, thoughtful way to celebrate our birthday. We kept going every year, even after my father married Catherine. She'd go with us but would stand back a short distance, not sure what to do.

Eventually, I found out the truth about my mother's death.

She had really died right after giving birth to Lowell and me. No one had realized she was carrying twins, and the delivery took longer than expected. I was first, and Lowell was second, but he was turned the wrong way and the doctor had to reach in and turn him around. My mother died of bleeding the doctors couldn't stop and an infection that set in because of it. I'd learned the true story from my grandfather, who'd gotten himself tangled up trying to tell the same story my father had told us.

Once I'd found out, I told my father I knew. He looked at me and frowned. "You're a smart girl, Meredith," he said, as though that were cause for regret. He didn't try to explain why he'd told the lie he had. He just said there'd always be times in my life when I'd need to decide what to do with the things I knew. "There are some secrets worth keeping for all concerned," he told me.

I wasn't sure, but I thought I did understand what he meant. So I didn't tell Lowell or even Catherine. I just kept it to myself.

And maybe I had not written Catherine a letter to tell her that we were leaving because I'd believed my father about keeping secrets, about how that might be better for all of us.

Driving across the causeway, I kept thinking that I should have gone to her, let her sweep me up in her arms, let her hold me so that my head rested on her shoulder. "Make him stay," I could have whispered, and she would have heard me. That would have been enough. She'd have known.

While my father drove and I looked out across the water, I decided that I would write a letter to Catherine. I would tell her that Lowell and I would visit her as often as we could, especially in three years when we turned fifteen and got our driver's license. I'd tell her she should keep our rooms exactly as they were.

I had no way of knowing then that Catherine wasn't about to wait for us. Instead, she would pack up and leave New Orleans and go back to her own father in North Carolina, which as far as I was concerned was a million miles away. I thought that after seven years of taking care of us, of being almost if not quite our mother, the feeling would have stuck a little more. But it didn't seem to.

⚜

It was just when the station wagon disappeared in the distance ahead of us that the bridge went down. All of a sudden, we saw a thick white cloud of dust rise from the lake. By the time my father pulled to a stop, the white dust had begun to settle on the windshield of the Checker. It kept falling and falling until the windshield turned the grainy white of a movie screen the moment before the movie begins.

My father stopped the car, keeping his right hand on the hand brake that had been installed because of his bad right leg, which he'd hurt as a boy. He sat still for a few moments but then ordered Lowell and me to sit tight while he got out to take a look. I watched him pull himself out of the car, one hand on top of the open door and the other on the roof, dragging his bad leg out behind him. He shook the white dust off the hand that he'd put on the roof, and he closed the door. Because of the open windows, my lap was covered with the white dust, too, and so was my arm and part of my right leg.

Lowell started shaking, which scared me, and he kept saying, "What happened?" But then he reached over to the radio and turned it up even louder, as though he were trying to drown everything out with noise. Every one of the black buttons on the radio was tuned to WWIW, the Way It Was, big band and hot jazz and Dixieland, the only station my father listened to except for sometimes at home, late at night, when he'd switch to WWL for the recitation of the rosary from Saint Louis Cathedral.

Then I found myself shaking, too, and I wished I had the rosary that my grandfather had given me on my first communion but I had never used. I grabbed Lowell's hand and held it, but Lowell pulled it away and said he wanted to take a look. He slid over behind the steering wheel and turned on the windshield wipers.

▪ 25 ▪

The white dust brushed off the glass like fine, dry snow, and we saw the groups of men standing there in circles. Every once in a while, one of them would point down into the water and they'd all turn and take a look, but then they'd go back to hanging their heads and smoking their cigarettes.

Soon the police officers started running up past the line of cars and the black helicopters appeared overhead. The police talked to the men for a while and then must have told them to go back to their cars, because they all stepped back and turned around.

As my father walked toward us, I looked at him for some kind of sign as to how I should feel. He'd rolled up his shirt-sleeves, and he was drenched with sweat, but he seemed calm. He put his hand in front of the windshield and motioned for Lowell to slide over, then he swung himself back in the car. He turned the radio off and said, "This is probably going to take a while. Everything's fine. A car ended up in the water. They'll look for the driver and get these cars turned around. We're safe."

I didn't ask, but I wondered what my father would do now — if he would take the causeway's falling as a message that we ought to turn around and go home. That's what it seemed like to me: a sign from God that what we were doing might be wrong. What would my father say to Catherine if we did go back? That he'd been wrong? That he'd been shown this was not the time to leave? That whatever differences there were between them were ones they could overcome?

I tried to imagine a celebration, all of us shaking our heads in amazement at the way things had worked out, the causeway's collapse suddenly a miracle instead of a disaster.

But there was another way to get to Mandeville — by driving around Lake Pontchartrain instead of across it. That was the way my father had traveled between Mandeville and New Orleans when he was a boy, riding in the back of my grandfather's pickup to deliver statues to families in the Garden District or Old Metairie or the Faubourg Marigny, neighborhoods where everyone had brick patios with wrought iron tables and chairs overlooking the most beautiful gardens. My grandfather wrapped his statues in old blankets and tied them with rope and then laid them on top of an old mattress he kept in the back of his truck.

Once, after a week in Mandeville without my father and Catherine, when they'd gone on their honeymoon to Mobile, my grandfather had taken us back to New Orleans the old way — along the Industrial Canal, which had been dug to connect Lake Pontchartrain with the Mississippi. We drove along miles and miles of the Chef Menteur Highway, which cut through swampy land with tin-roof fishing camps built on stilts and a coffee factory you could smell long before you saw it. Although my grandfather said he preferred it, that drive took close to two hours, which was why the causeway had been built in the first place.

But my father didn't say if that was what he intended to do, to swing back around the lake once we'd gotten off the bridge. When we were all calmed down, he just turned the radio back on, starting the Checker's engine every once in a while to keep the battery going.

Lowell asked my father if he'd been able to see why that part of the bridge had collapsed, but my father shook his head. "One of the supports just gave way, it looked like," he said. "It must have been a problem just waiting to happen."

Then he tried a joke to make things easier, telling us that now they'd probably have to use the drain on the bottom of the lake again. Lowell and I both did our best to laugh. We'd heard the story a thousand times, about the giant drain down at the bottom, one that was covered with seaweed and old tires and sunken pirogues. According to my father, when he was a boy an old drunken captain had once mistakenly steered his ship, which was filled with sugar, from the Mississippi through the canal and over to the lake. When the ship ran aground and split its side, the sugar spilled out and turned the entire lake into heavy syrup.

My father told us he'd stood on the sea wall and watched the water gradually disappear for three days. He said that on the third day, when all the water was gone, he figured he'd walk out across the muddy bottom and look around. But as soon as he took that first step, his leg sank down into the mud up to his knee. "Your grandfather had to pull me out," he told us. "And when he did, both my shoe and sock were gone."

My father said you could still tell where the drain was because of the way the sun reflected off the water at just the right spot. For years, whenever we reached the middle of the causeway, where you couldn't see land on either side, Lowell and I would put our faces to the Checker's side window and wait for my father to say "Right there!" and point his finger. I never saw anything, of course, and neither did Lowell, but he pretended that he did. "I saw it!" Lowell would shout, and my father would smile.

"What about you, Meredith?" he would ask, and I'd have to admit that I didn't see anything.

I didn't know why my father kept up with stories like that, never actually admitting that he'd just made them up but laughing in a way that showed he knew we didn't believe him.

When the line of cars behind us was finally gone, my father started the engine and curved the car backward until there was room for him to turn around. The helicopters had flown off after an hour of searching, and my father stopped by the policeman directing traffic and asked if they'd found the man driving the station wagon.

"Swollen up like a whale," the policeman said. "The poor bastard couldn't swim."

Lowell nudged my father, and I knew what he wanted. He wanted him to tell the policeman that just maybe we knew who the driver was. My father ignored Lowell, but when the policeman waved us ahead, he stopped and yelled out the window, "You get a name? The drowned man?"

"No idea," the officer said, "but he wasn't drowned." The policeman pushed a button on his radio, held it up to his ear, and listened for a second, then he looked back at my father. "He was bloated like a whale, I heard, but still breathing. That's all I know."

"Thanks," my father said, and we took off, headed back to New Orleans. I could feel Lowell's knee bumping up against my own, and I knew he was wondering the same thing I was. I bumped him back and got him to turn his head. "Ask him," I whispered. "Go ahead."

Lowell looked at me for a second and then looked over at my father. I looked out the windshield at all the cars ahead of us, a slow procession of people heading back to wherever it was they'd been coming from. Finally, after what seemed like an hour, Lowell said it.

"Are we going home?" he asked, his voice trembling a little.

"I'm sorry," my father said, and he didn't turn to look at us. I could see in the way his head hung forward and in the way his eyes seemed as though they were squinting into the sun though they weren't that he didn't want to say it, that he was having trouble saying anything at all.

"I'm sorry," he said again, and he reached out and touched Lowell's head and then reached across Lowell and touched mine. "We can't."

2

MY DEAREST MEREDITH,

I hope you are thinking of me as much as I am of you. I realize as I start this that before now I never had a reason to write you anything more than the briefest note. Now that I have a real letter to write, I don't even know if you'll ever get it.

I'm in North Carolina, five states away from you, looking out of what was my own childhood's window, facing south across the pond to your Grandfather Reynolds's old alfalfa and barley fields, which are now lying fallow. A nearly full moon and a hundred stars are in the pond tonight, and something is making the water ripple. The stars jump from one spot to the next, and the moon gets folded over and then straightened out again. Sometimes I think there's nothing so important as letting your heart wander out across a beautiful view.

Actually, right now I'm simply feeling helpless. What if these words end up in your father's hands rather than your own? I've got no way of assuring they won't, and I've got good cause to suspect they might. Your father had a habit of opening my own private mail, of hunting it out from every secret place I could find. (Maybe you're the one reading this now, Thomas. Damn you to hell if you are, but at the least be honest and pass this along to your daughter.)

Not much of the mail I got, Meredith, was anything important. It was mostly just small-chat letters from family and old friends. But I did believe those letters were private, meant only for me. I came to learn, though, that your father read every piece of mail I received. He rooted it out from wherever it had ended up, at the bottom of my desk drawer or inside a zipper pocket of my purse or in a cookbook I'd been paging through when the mail arrived.

Not that there was anything earth-shattering for him to discover, but once I'd learned his habit — I'd noticed how my letters were turned a different way in their envelopes — I started hiding them anywhere I could think of, crazy places like inside cereal boxes or taped under drawers, and finally even in a dark corner of the attic. I swear to you I crawled on my hands and knees in the pitch black up there just to find a place to put those scraps of paper so I could feel like I had something that was my own. Of course, it made me feel I was the one, and not your father, whose mind wasn't right.

Still, your father found those letters. I could tell he had.

And what in the devil did he expect to find written in them? I had half a mind to put some shocking made-up story down into words just to teach your father a lesson.

What I should have done, I know now, is make him face up to what he was doing. I should have confronted your father straight out, Meredith, but I never did. It's as simple as being too embarrassed, which may not seem to make sense, but you'd be surprised the things people can feel ashamed about, even things that are another person's doing.

Anyway, at first I decided that it was just a game for your father and he wasn't truly interested in what the letters said. He just wanted to know he could get to them, I decided, and maybe even show me that he could, purposely turning the letters in the envelope or placing the pages out of order as if to say, *Everything about you is mine, Cathy Reynolds, so don't you try and hide.*

I now realize I was half wrong in my conclusions. While it's true your father didn't give a damn about what my family and friends had to tell me, I finally figured out he must be searching in those letters for something else, something that had to do with him and not anyone else. You might as well know, if you don't already, that your father is a man who, once his neck has been grabbed by even the slightest delusion, can't manage the strength to get himself free but instead chokes and chokes until he suffocates.

I don't say all this because I'm angry with your father. What's important is not that I'm angry with him and hurt by him, as much anger and hurt as anyone could be expected to bear. He will tell you someday, when he gets his own version of the story complete in his head, that it's the hurt and anger I caused him that made him do what he's done, running away like a coward rather than standing up and looking his own wife directly in the eyes and trying to set his world straight.

Ask your father how he manages to look at the world such that happiness gets turned on its head and winds up as sorrow. I'd like to know.

You know what I'm thinking now? I'm thinking of how your father reminds me of this man named Melvin whose butcher shop was near the town square in Pittsboro. When I was a girl, my mother would take me with her on her errands. We'd go to the butcher's to get our Sunday meat, and my mother would stand in front of the glass counter and say, "It's a beautiful day, isn't it, Melvin?" She said that on purpose, knowing she'd get a laugh at Melvin's reply.

"It's foolishness to trust the weather one mile to the next," he'd say, the same response every time, pulling his apron strings tighter around his waist and then putting his hands up on the counter as if to let my mother know all he wanted was for her to get on with her order.

"But it's so gorgeous out, Melvin," my mother would go on, goading him, smiling at him and then looking down at her grocery list like her mind wasn't yet made up on what she'd get. "You ought to step out and take a look."

"Probably a storm brewing in the mountains," Melvin would say. "What can I get you, Elizabeth?"

"Go on," she'd say. "Go take a look."

And they'd go on and on like that, my mother getting Melvin so upset that finally he'd be stomping around and pulling those strings tighter and tighter and slapping his hands on the counter like they were the meat she'd ordered. "What can I get for you, Elizabeth?" he'd demand.

Well, that's your father, Meredith, always letting his concern over what's coming next stand in the way of him finding a moment's peace and enjoyment. I can't tell you how many times I had to say, "Thomas, just calm down. Calm down, and maybe you'll give the world half a chance to catch up with your thoughts."

Then your father would take off his glasses and run his hand over his brow and say something like "What do you know, Cathy? You're just a girl." And I'd glare at him so.

But sometimes, and I'll give him this much credit, he would smile and pull me into his arms. Once he even said, "You're an angel child," whispering it into my ear when he held me, like it was a secret he'd just uncovered. You should have heard how his voice shook with sorrow, though.

"Thomas," I said back to him, holding on, "what's wrong?"

But he didn't answer. He just let go of me.

The truly sad part is, all that looking beyond the moment, all that fearful anticipation, never did your father any good. He never managed a clear mind as to where he was heading because he never stopped to take a good look at where he was right then. That's an awful truth, and it's one that this time has worked itself through in about as mixed-up and confused a manner as it possibly could.

Your father told you, I know, that leaving was a big secret, something you and your brother had to keep from me for my own sake, taking cover from darkness, slipping out the door just before dawn while I slept. Well, it wasn't a secret. That's the difference between your father and me. I didn't ever need to go snooping around to discover what he was up to.

I didn't know exactly *when*, I'll admit, and so those last few weeks I slept like a snake or a hyena or whatever animal it is that keeps one eye open the whole night. So I was out of bed before you all were so much as out the driveway. Yes, I was standing just behind the living room window when your father slipped that car of his into neutral and let it roll backward down the driveway just as quiet as could be.

As hard as it was to do, I stood there because I wanted one last look at you and your brother and even, I'll admit, your father, not just because I wanted to remember the sight of him in his cowardice, but because he was the one man I'd loved with all my heart, whatever he goes and tells you to the contrary.

But it was you, dear Meredith, I kept my eyes on as the car rolled back and jerked to a stop before your father turned on the engine and headed off. I've told you a thousand times that there is no child so sweet as you, and I'm sorry for what I saw in your face with that last look. I saw the fright that had made your face as white as bleached cotton. That was a child, I told myself, who needed her mother to tell her some story of what a beautiful place this world can be, how there is such a thing as love.

I looked at you in the car and made myself remember what we sometimes did when I put you to sleep at night when you were a little girl. Do you remember? I would switch off all but the candlestick lamp in the corner, then I'd lie down at your side and snuggle up close. You'd ask me to name everyone in the world who loved you. It was a long list, and if I am right it always will be.

We'd start with your father and your brother, then go on to your Grandfather Eagen and Grandfather and Grandmommy Reynolds and your aunts and uncles and all their children, most of whom you'd never met but who loved you nevertheless because they were my brothers and sisters and nieces and nephews, family to you as they were to me. When we ran out of people to name, we moved on to animals, Lizzie the beagle and Zephyr the cat and the finches and mourning doves and cranky grackles with their silver-sheen black feathers who flocked to the feeder out back and sometimes got themselves tangled in the vines along the fence, searching out those hard-as-nails berries that grew there. And when we were done with the animals, you wanted me to name the trees in our back yard and then the names of all the stars in the sky, names we made up at night looking out your window. They were crazy names that would be impossible to spell, names I have to admit I no longer remember. Then you'd go through the list of your favorite saints, which I didn't and still don't know much about, and by the end of it all you were as sleepy as a breastfed baby, your eyes closed before I'd turned off that final lamp, which left a faint glow on the walls for a few seconds before your room went completely dark.

You were so sleepy by the end of that I wouldn't even know if you were still awake when I stood in the doorway and told you that I loved you as much as anyone, as much as the stars and sky and everything else in the universe.

It's still true. I've got a picture of you here, one I sent my parents the summer you turned six, before they'd even met you. In the picture, you're sitting on the sea wall in Mandeville, wearing a flowered sundress I made for you, with a ruffled neck and a matching hairband. Your hair was still straight then. Nobody would have guessed how curly it would get to be. You're smiling and looking over at Lowell, who is not in the picture but who'd found, I remember, a dead crab he was making dance on its claws. It's clear just from your smile how much you love your brother.

What I see about this photograph now, something I can't remember ever noticing before, is all the bumps and bruises on your legs. It's not that they're frightful-looking; they're typical for any six-year-old. But looking at them now makes me remember how much tending you needed — not because you were fragile but because you were not. You didn't seem to have much of a sense for danger, and you bore every injury in virtual silence, like it was something you deserved. So I watched you much more closely than I watched your brother.

I once realized that whenever I looked up from what I was doing, sewing or cooking or just reading a book, my eyes landed on you first and only after that on your brother. I worried for a while that I was playing favorites. When the two of you walked in the door from going somewhere with your father, I tried to make myself look at Lowell first, see to him before I saw to you. It wasn't right, I told myself, to give you special attention if it might hurt your brother.

But my eyes were drawn to you, Meredith, the way our eyes are drawn in a black night to the quick flicker of a firefly, and I finally made my peace with that fact. I told myself that there was something at work I didn't fully understand, maybe a woman's understanding of her own kind or just some special kind of love that had managed to join us in a way that your brother and I would never be joined.

Even so, it pains me to say it. There is something about raising twins, even ones as different from each other as you and your brother, that calls for equal measures of attention, a constant balancing of affection and discipline and every other part of being a parent. So if there is ever the chance for you to tell your brother how much I love him too, I wish you would do it. It really is true that I've got no less of a feeling for him than for you, but it's a different feeling, different in ways I couldn't explain even to myself. So be it.

Well, after the three of you drove off down the street, I went to the front door and stepped out onto the porch. The air was sticky, and I felt my nightgown stretch across my body. I could feel it tugging on my breasts and hips and bottom with every breath. I crossed my arms and shivered, but I stood there feeling huge and awkward, like there was no way my lungs could get enough air into my body. I was sure I was going to suffocate.

I won't forget my whole life the feeling of being a woman left by her husband and children. In one way that morning seems like years ago, even though it's been less than a week, but in another way all I have to do is shut my eyes for a moment and I'm standing again on the porch, looking at the clothes scattered across the lawn. How is it that this came to be my fate, a woman with more mother in her than most who lost her two children and her husband in the time it takes to pack up a car, the time it takes to wake up and walk from the bedroom to the living room window, not even pausing to throw on a robe?

There are women who make much worse choices than the ones I made who don't pay that kind of price. In your short life you've lost a mother twice, Meredith, and maybe that's as bad as what I feel. I'm sure it is. But I can't help being angry at you for letting your father do this. Lord knows that even in your quiet way, you've got more sway with him than a wrecking ball on a house of straw. Didn't you think to tell him that you just wouldn't go?

Sometimes I think I hurt more from your leaving than from his. Of course, if that's the case, then he was right to leave. He'd be right to think I didn't love him enough. Maybe I didn't. And maybe the story he ends up telling you, whatever it is, will be truer than my own. I admit I've sometimes asked myself if your father, with his crazy dreaming, has a more direct line to the substance of things, the root cause of all our behavior, than any ordinary person would ever hope to possess.

Well, that's surely what he wanted me to believe, as if his staring day in and day out into the bodies of all those patients, the layers of skin and muscle and fat peeled back like so many colored veils, gave him a sure path to wisdom. I don't really believe it, of course. As one whose own body was wrecked at an early age, your father should understand that substance doesn't reside in the body but somewhere else, somewhere where you can't just peel back a few layers of skin and muscle and take a look. It's harder than that.

I understand your father's need to think as he does, though. Old farmers like my father can pick up a handful of dirt, let it run through their fingers, and believe they're watching their own souls. Politicians, I guess, hear their own voice, and it sounds to them like a choir of angels. What have I got to compare with that? I had the notion of being a wife and mother, of feeling like the smallest of my children's triumphs was a clarion call proclaiming peace and justice in the world. I had the love of a man to make me feel my body and spirit were heavenly blessed.

What have I got right now? I could say nothing and kick myself over and over and head off to bed — it's late right now, by the way, and I can't stop myself from wondering about the smallest things, how you're sleeping, what sort of dreams this last week has given you, whether you've dragged the old bed near the window so you can let the moonlight trail across you the way you did whenever we went across the lake to your grandfather's.

I'm sorry for what I wrote earlier. I don't blame you, not in the least. It's your father I blame, and of course I blame myself. There's not a sane person in the world who doesn't watch even the cruelest turn of fate and not think he had some part in it.

What I wanted this letter to accomplish, what so far it hasn't, was to get at my own explanation of all that's happened. As young as you are, I feel like you're old enough to at least try to balance the scales. It's a terrible thing, I know, to have to weigh and measure your own parents so, and I understand that because I am not the woman who gave you birth, I'm like feather against lead. But a pound of this and a pound of that is the same, even if I look and feel less substantial. Well, I'm not.

My father used to call me the Pittsboro burro. He said I was stubborn as a mule, and in some ways I still am, no matter what my leaving New Orleans for here may seem to you, if you even know that's what I've done.

That's the first thing you should know. I haven't quit on you. The second thing is exactly what happened to make your father think he needed to leave, and that will take a while. I'll sleep first before I get started. My own father is sitting outside out back waiting for the very same explanation. I can see the smoke from his cigarette drifting up to this window, curling itself into circles that float out toward the fields and disappear. He's let me go three days with little more than a few broken sentences as to why I'm here. I'll kiss him goodnight and tell him we'll talk tomorrow. Even from so far away, I'll do the same for you. You're a dear child, and I'm eager for dreams of you.

So we didn't go home. My father, shocked and silent, looking over at us from time to time, took us through the city instead, down West End Boulevard and Robert E. Lee, across Carrolton Avenue, and then up St. Charles. I stared out the window, and everything seemed to peel away before my eyes, the streetcars shambling forward on the neutral ground, rocking from side to side on their rusted rails, men standing idly on street corners and whole families sitting on their porches drinking coffee and reading the *Times-Picayune*, everything just like a normal Sunday morning, nobody with reason to know of the causeway's collapse.

For a while I thought my father might be taking us to Mass, to the Jesuit High School Chapel of the North American Martyrs, where we sometimes went on special Sundays, parking on the high school lot's blacktop. The boys lined up in the pews reserved for them, all of them dressed alike, either in their khaki pants and blue blazers or in their military uniforms, soldiers of God. All those boys were just a few years older than Lowell and me, but they seemed miles and miles ahead of us, their faces so sober and serious, as though the message God had delivered to them had taken a special courage to hear. The truth is, those boys — the older ones, at least — were probably worried most about the draft, about getting called not by God but by country.

My father didn't stop for Mass. Instead, he drove straight past the school and the chapel's high stained glass window, which depicted Saint Ignatius standing next to a horse, his body as lean as an El Greco figure. In his right hand Saint Ignatius held the horse's reins, and in his left what was supposed to be a Bible. Lowell liked to say that it looked more like a box of popcorn, which was true. It did.

My father kept driving and driving, returning to side streets we'd been down before, slowing down and then speeding up again. I couldn't imagine what he was doing, whether he was looking for someone or whether he wasn't looking at all, the Checker moving through the streets like a blind lizard wriggling through tall grass. When I looked over at my father, at his red face and squinting eyes, I wondered if someday he might go blind. His eyes were already so bad he couldn't take a single step without putting on his glasses. I imagined those eyes getting worse and worse until he would need to put his hands on Lowell and me to decide who was who.

Eventually, we ended up on Magazine Street, and my father stopped in front of his office, that dirty green Victorian house with its twenty rundown rooms and all the smells that were as familiar to him as they were strange to Lowell and me: the mixture of dust and rubbing alcohol, dirt and soap, the things you wouldn't think smelled at all but did, the ace bandages and white cloth tape, the x-ray machine, the shiny instruments lined up on metal trays, the waiting room out front with its chairs and sofas stained with circles of sweat.

I found myself thinking not so much of Catherine but of my grandfather's house in Mandeville. If we weren't going home, if we really couldn't return there, my grandfather's house was where I wanted to be. I tried to imagine what our life in Mandeville would be like, trying to make my peace with what had happened by drawing beautiful pictures in my head.

I'd already made up my mind which room I wanted, which

was the one I slept in whenever we visited. That room looked out over the back yard, so there wasn't as much of a breeze as in the two upstairs bedrooms at the front of the house, which both looked out over the lake. But from my room I'd be able to look down at my grandfather's garden, which had a giant half-circle of azalea bushes around a statue of the Virgin Mary. At the back of the yard, near the shed where my grandfather had kept his equipment — all those molds and buckets and burlap mix-sacks and chisels — was a pond lined with old charcoal-colored bricks. In the middle of the pond, which was always green with algae, were more bricks. On top of those was the statue of Saint Francis, the hem of his robe permanently green from hanging down into the water.

My grandfather had let Lowell and me toss colored plastic rings at the statue, trying to get them to go over Saint Francis's arm. Whoever got the most rings on the arm would watch while the other took off his shoes and walked through the slimy water to get the rings. Usually, I lost. But the truth was, I didn't mind stepping through that water. It was always cold, and the algae wrapped around my toes like friendly little fish. The only trick was to keep from slipping, and I was pretty good at that. I also liked to grab Saint Francis's shoulder and pull myself up next to him. I had to put my wet foot on one of the folds in his robe to slip the rings over the two fingers of his hand that were pointing up.

Once, when I'd just grabbed hold of the rings, my foot came loose and I was left hanging on Saint Francis's arm. Lowell laughed and laughed until my grandfather ordered him to rescue me. Lowell took off his tennis shoes and started walking across the pond, but he wasn't as used to it as I was and he slipped, too. Even I laughed when I heard him fall, but I kept hanging on until my grandfather got in the water with his shoes still on and helped me down.

Even though he was old, my grandfather was a strong man. He could put his arms around the waists of all but the biggest statues and carry them wherever he pleased. Compared to that, I must have been light as a pillow, and he took me all the way back in the house. While he was walking, I looked up at the upstairs window and saw my father standing there. He waved to me as if he were a little embarrassed, and I waved back. We'd left Lowell still sliding around in the water, trying to stand up.

"Good for you," my grandfather whispered. "Good for you." I didn't know what I'd done to please him, but I was glad I had.

I figured that once we were settled in Mandeville, and once Lowell and I had grown up a little, we could start making statues again. In the meantime, I'd do my best to get the back-yard garden in line, cutting the azaleas back into the square shape they'd once had and pulling out most of the banana trees, which never got much higher than my waist and always had brown leaves that peeled away at the slightest touch. I'd plant daisies at the Virgin Mary's feet and an ivy border for the pond. I liked the idea of having ivy climb across the bricks like on the old houses in the French Quarter.

My father hadn't talked about where we'd eventually go to school. Until Christmas, he'd said, I'd still go to Sacred Heart and Lowell would still go to Christian Brothers; he'd just drop us off every morning on his way to the office. But now that the causeway was down and probably wouldn't be open for a while, I didn't know what we would do. We couldn't drive around the lake every day, I knew, and I wondered if my father would just keep us out of school until the bridge was fixed and open again, which would be fine with Lowell and me.

I knew it wasn't worry over our going to school that had stopped my father from just driving around the lake and getting us situated there before deciding what to do next. It was something else, as if the causeway's collapse had worked on him like a boomerang, sending him back not exactly to where he'd come from but to somewhere close, somewhere where he could stick himself into a world he knew, as ugly as that world might be.

❧ ❦

When we pulled up in front of the office, I wasn't surprised to see a man sitting on the porch. There was usually someone there, day or night, afraid to go inside when the office was open, refusing to leave when it was not. Like most of my father's patients, these people didn't have any money. They didn't even pretend they did. They wanted my father, when he arrived for work or stepped out once he was done, to take just a quick look at them, let them know what kind of shape they were in, as if they couldn't judge their own injuries by the amount of pain they felt. But pain, my father liked to tell us, was for doctors a disagreeable but completely trustworthy guide. *Just follow it and you'll get where you want to go,* he'd say.

Usually, the front-porch patients had minor complaints, but more often than you'd think they did not. They had arms and legs that dangled near-lifeless from their joints. They had bruises as big and swollen as plums and cuts that ran from one bony spot to the next.

Lowell and I had spent our whole lives looking at such things. Sometimes I'd wake up in the morning and find my father in the living room, the curtains drawn and the lights off, the slide projector casting gruesome pictures onto the wall, hips and shoulders and knees stretched open with steel clamps to reveal what looked less like open bodies than aerial photographs of strange landscapes, with rivers and hills and plains that were actually blood vessels, muscles, skin.

"That's disgusting," I'd tell my father, and he'd turn the projector off to say good morning.

"It is," he'd say. "You're right." Then he'd go on to tell me about whatever it was the slides depicted — a particular kind of fracture, a peculiar and complicated dislocation, a tendon that had been wrenched away from the bone.

"I can't believe that's what you see when you do an operation," I said once.

"Sometimes I can't believe it either," my father said, and I imagined him in the operating room, his clothes covered in blood, a body opened up before him. I wondered how it was any person gained such trust that a patient would lie down and allow his body to be treated so. I had also wondered when I was a little girl about these patients' souls. My grandfather had told me that our souls were encased in our bodies like a dove imprisoned in a dungeon, and I imagined my father in the middle of an operation having to reach out with a bloody hand to snatch a soul that had suddenly escaped and gently place it back inside, behind the bars of ribs, near the patient's heart. Sometimes at night I looked closely at my father when he returned home from the hospital, watching how he kissed Catherine's cheek, one hand on her shoulder, and then reached down to touch Lowell's head and then mine. I looked at him for some sign of the soul-catching miracle he might just have performed.

I never saw anything, though, that suggested such miracles. What I saw instead was my father's exhaustion, the tired smile he wore in the evenings whenever Cathy made a request that he take her here or there, out to dinner or to some movie. Instead, my father would make himself a drink, put on his music, and sit still while the three of us hovered around him, Lowell and I climbing up into his lap when we were still small enough to do it, Cathy fixing dinner and darting into the living room from time to time with stories she'd managed to find in her own day.

Some mornings my father would be using the projector to look not at medical slides but at the slides of photographs he'd taken himself. When my grandfather died, my father had taken his camera back to New Orleans, and for a few months he took hundreds of photographs of Lowell and me, as if trying to make up for how few he'd taken in the years before that. Lowell and I would stand frozen and awkward side by side in front of our house, or we'd sit next to each other in the living room, our hands fidgeting and our elbows bumping while we waited for my father to snap the picture. He had to look down at the window on top of the camera, which showed him whatever the lens was seeing, and it always seemed to take him forever to get the camera focused.

They were unremarkable pictures, shaded yellow or red and, despite my father's efforts, usually out of focus. After a while, he gave up and put the camera away. But I remember waking up to find my father moving through whatever recent slides he'd taken. I would sit in his lap and we'd laugh at the ones that were really terrible, Lowell's eyes or mine closed, the photograph snapped when we were blinking, or Lowell caught in some fierce expression of impatience, his jaw set tight, his mouth pinched closed, his eyes glaring. It was an expression I recognized from my father's face.

The only truly good photographs I remember my father taking were the ones he took of his patients. These were simple portraits, just like those of Lowell and me, but they also seemed to tell the story of these people's lives in ways that the pictures of us did not. The morning I discovered my father looking at them, I stood behind him, in the doorway to the living room, and did not let him know I was there. I watched as he moved from one slide to the next: a white-haired old man with his arm in a sling, the man's head thrown back in laughter as though my father had just told him a joke; a stone-faced woman gripping the child in her lap, both of the child's legs encased in casts; a young girl, her hair covered by a scarf, next to an ancient woman, her grandmother perhaps, the woman's arm across the young girl's shoulder.

I was struck not just by how good these photographs were but by the fact that my father had thought to take them. When he moved past the last one and the wall went white from the projector's light, I stepped up and said good morning. "I like those," I said. "They're good."

"Are they?" my father said, kissing me. He thought for a moment and then said, "Well, thank you."

"What are they for?" I asked.

"They're not for anything," he said. "I just thought it would be nice to make prints and put them up at the office."

But my father did not, as far as I know, ever put them up. Maybe he gave them to the patients when they came back to see him. Maybe he put them away, let them accumulate in a shoebox the way my grandfather had done with the photographs of his statues.

I know now that my father was a good doctor. He was conscientious and compassionate and sure. He studied those medical slides and read his medical journals and, when he could afford it, attended orthopedic conferences. I came to realize that he was without reputation only because of these patients he chose to see, not because of how he treated them.

In his work my father had a surgeon's confidence and strength. Maybe this is not to the point, but I remember what had amazed me as a child: when Lowell or I began to be bothered by a loose tooth, my father would simply reach into our mouth with his forefinger and thumb and effortlessly pull the tooth out. "There," he'd say, laughing, holding up the tiny hollow tooth for our inspection.

How is it that my father transformed what might have been a brutal act into something magnificent and kind? It occurs to me that perhaps this is exactly what he hoped to accomplish with our leaving Catherine — taking an act that could not be anything but cruel and casting it in his own mind as an act of redemption, as a means of sparing himself and his children some otherwise inevitable suffering and pain.

I will admit here that I'm no different. It has occurred to me over and over to consider what my father might have been thinking in the moments before his stroke, sitting there and looking out over my grandfather's garden. No matter what the truth may be, this is what I tell myself: that some pleasant memory had taken hold of him — something recent, like the last time he had held one of Lowell's children in his arms and watched the child laugh, or the time I arrived for the weekend bearing five pounds of fresh strawberries I'd bought on the way at a roadside stand and my father and I had sat on the porch for nearly an hour slicing off the stems, laughing at the juice running down our arms, with bees hovering around us so that we constantly had to fan them away. The sweet scent filled us both with an unexpected happiness, which somehow consumed, for a while at least, the wary regard that usually marked our conversations.

When I'd filled one bowl and had to move on to another, I looked up to find my father staring at me. For a few seconds he didn't say anything.

"What, Daddy?" I said. "Are you okay?"

"It's just you're a beautiful woman," he said. "I hope you know that."

"Thank you," I said, and though there were other things I wanted to say, I did not. I let the moment rest with that small, simple beauty. I felt grateful.

But I was speaking here of my father's life as a physician. When he left his office and Lowell and I happened to be with him, he would tell us to go sit in the car while he saw to whoever was waiting for him on the porch. We'd walk out to the street, jump into the car, and roll down the windows, then we'd listen and watch as my father made friendly conversation and gently touched these people's injuries.

"You come back tomorrow, and we'll get an x-ray," he would say to each one. "You've got to come inside for me to do that, you understand." Then he would shake these people's hands if they could be shaken, and he'd see them off the porch and out to the street, to wherever it was they were headed.

Sometimes, though, we'd see them stumble around to the side of the house to pick up paper bags they'd set down, large department store bags with old clothes spilling out of them or small brown paper bags squeezed around glass bottles, and they'd get only halfway down the block before their feet gave way beneath them. My father, so kind a moment before, would tighten his jaw and drive off with them lying there. When we asked if they were okay, my father said they'd be up walking again soon enough.

I would look back at these people as we turned the corner, and I would actually pray for an angel to come down and scoop them up, give them a good place to sleep and some food to eat, take their pain away by wrapping them in holy robes. I wanted to believe that my wish was simply a Christian one, but I knew that it was not. I was afraid of their torn, dirty clothes and their smelly bodies and their awful black-toothed grins. I was afraid because when they spoke to me, I could never understand their mumbling, the slurred and somehow foreign speech. And I was afraid of the jerking motions they made at me when I walked past them, motions that were probably just an effort to wave hello but felt to me like secret threats. I prayed for them to be better in every way because I just wanted them to disappear.

I did not give my father enough credit for his acts of charity, caring for these people who were afraid or unable to go anywhere else. His specialty, his years of training, entitled him to large fees and a comfortable life. Like many other orthopedists, the doctors with whom my father had gone through his residency, those who discreetly directed certain patients to his door, my father could have ministered to people whose injuries were painful but temporary, brief misfortunes in what were or promised to be long and happy lives: teenagers hurt in backyard football games, old women who had fallen and broken their hips, men and women and children whose bodies would eventually heal.

I still do not know how my father understood his obligation, whether his charity was truly a Christian one or, like my summoning of angels, the result of some unacknowledged fear. Did he worry that if he turned away these patients, there would be no others? Or did he feel, as I had been taught to feel in my catechism class, that God's eyes were constantly trained on him, that a giant, invisible hand was raised in the air above his head, forever poised to strike him down and render a verdict on his life?

As with so much else about my father, I am left to make my own guesses about this matter but feel, nevertheless, incapable of guessing. Despite all these words, despite the story I am desperate to tell, I am uncomfortable holding and turning my father's life in my hands for inspection as though it were so much wet clay there for my shaping.

I'll go on, though, because I don't know what else to do, because there is, in the end, nothing else to be done.

⚜

When we pulled up in front of the office that morning and saw the man there, my father turned off the car's engine and sat for a moment, then he looked again at the porch and shook his head. Lowell and I, our hands in our laps, just waited.

Once you have given in to silence, it's sometimes nearly impossible to get yourself to break it, and the three of us had hardly said a word since leaving the causeway. At one point, when we passed Audubon Park, Lowell had pointed to a jazz band performing under the shade of a giant willow, and though the music was just a brief blast through the window as we passed, Lowell had leaned forward and said, "Potato Head Blues," clearly proud of himself for grabbing hold of the tune so quickly. But my father just nodded and didn't say anything, as if what we'd already seen that morning had taken the life and breath out of him as much as it had out of the man in the blue station wagon — Murphy, if that's who it really had been.

"Listen," my father finally said. "I'm going to have to see to this man. He'll need some attention. I want you to bring in a change of clothes and whatever you want from the trunk. You go upstairs and I'll be there as soon as I can." He paused and looked at us. "Maybe you won't like it here. Maybe I won't either. But for now it's the best we can manage."

"It's fine," I said, and for some reason I now felt afraid of my father. It was the first time I'd truly felt that way except for maybe once when I was nine years old and I'd ended up too high in one of the tar-patched oaks in Audubon Park. My father, Catherine, and Lowell had been feeding bread to the ducks over by the edge of the lagoon, and I'd just climbed and climbed until I felt the ground was miles away.

When my father looked back and noticed where I was, he called my name and hurried over. I could see him off in the distance heading toward me, swinging his bad leg out and around the way he had to do to get anywhere fast. Once he was standing at the bottom of the tree, all I could see was his hands gone to fists and his good leg shaking beneath him. He called my name again and ordered me down, and for a second I thought he might put his arms around the trunk and shake me off like an overripe apple.

He didn't, of course. He waited for me to come down and then put his hands on my shoulders. I was expecting a long speech, something about how he'd seen enough kids fall from trees and break their bones to make a person sick to his stomach, but that's not what he did. He squinted his eyes and just looked at me, as if he were feeling the worst pain, and that was when I felt my fear begin.

"Careful," my father finally said, in almost a whisper, and he squeezed and then let go of my shoulders. He had turned around and was walking back to Lowell before I started crying. I didn't know why I was or why I'd been so afraid.

That was the same feeling I had sitting in the car, as if I knew that once I was away from him, once I had a moment alone, I would cry and cry.

Lowell and I slid out of the car and leaned over in the back seat to get some clothes. Lowell grabbed a pile and quickly turned toward the house. When I caught up with him, he looked as if he might be about to cry, too.

On the porch, my father was already sitting down in one of the torn wicker chairs listening to the old man's story, nodding his head over and over while the man spoke and waved one hand in the air as if he were brushing away flies. The other hand was up against his chest and swollen to nearly twice its proper size. He told my father that he'd fallen.

"Where did you fall?" my father asked.

"Here," the man said. "These," he said, and he pointed to the porch steps.

"These steps?" my father asked.

"No, like them, but more," the man said.

Lowell and I were standing in the doorway and listening, but my father gave us a stern look and waved his hand. He had opened the front door, and Lowell and I went in and headed up the stairs. Lowell walked from room to room, lifting up his pile of clothes and using his elbows to switch on the lights. It was cleaner than I'd thought it would be, the floors all swept and the two beds made. For a moment I wondered if my father had meant to bring us here all along. That couldn't be, I knew, but I didn't understand why the rooms had been prepared the way they were.

I went to the living room and put my clothes on the sofa and sat down next to them. Lowell left his clothes in one of the bedrooms and then sat sideways in one of the easy chairs, throwing his feet over one arm and tilting his head back on the other.

"What if I call Catherine?" I said.

Lowell sat up and looked at me. I didn't know why I'd said that. I hadn't been thinking about Catherine except in the way you keep something you're supposed to remember in one side of your mind, waiting until you've made room for it up front by clearing out whatever else it was you've been thinking. Maybe getting the clothes in had done that, but whatever it was, I said it, and I'm sure my own face looked as surprised as Lowell's.

"What for?" Lowell asked, looking around for the phone, which was sitting on the floor in the corner behind him.

I pointed to it and said I didn't know. "Maybe I'll tell her we're here. Maybe she'll take a cab over and try to get him to change his mind."

"About what?" Lowell said, turning sideways again and throwing his head back.

"About everything," I said. "About leaving."

"Right," Lowell said, and he made one of his exaggerated groans. That groan, I knew, was meant for me, for what I'd said, and not for my father, for what he'd done. And it was only then that I wondered if Lowell knew more about why we'd left than I did. Of course, he was always acting as if he knew more than I did, but I wondered if he might know something anyway.

"Lowell?" I said, and he turned his head toward me but didn't sit up. "Should I call Catherine or not?"

"Don't," he said. "You'd make it worse."

"Why?" I asked him.

"You just would," he said.

"Tell me why," I said, but he wouldn't. He just lay there as if he were more exhausted than he'd ever been his whole life, which in truth was how I felt too. It was almost noon and we hadn't even had breakfast, but as soon as I thought about eating, my stomach felt as though it were already full, as though I'd eaten so much I would not be able to eat again for days and days.

"Tell me why," I said again, and I started crying. But after a few quick gasps of air, I stopped myself, which wasn't something I could usually do. "You tell me why, or else I'm calling," I said.

Then Lowell did sit up and look at me. We could hear, from the window, my father talking, using the calm voice he always used with his patients. "Come back tomorrow morning," we heard him say, and Lowell and I both kept quiet. "You get some ice, and get yourself cleaned up," my father said. Then his voice changed, as if something had suddenly made him angry. "I don't want that. Get yourself cleaned up, you hear. When you walk through that door tomorrow morning, we'll do an x-ray. You'll be fine, but get some ice on it. Go on."

Then we heard my father step inside the house. He yelled our names, and I motioned for Lowell to go on downstairs. "I'm calling," I said.

"Don't," Lowell said, and he walked over and sat down next to me and put his hand on my leg. It was the only time I ever remember him doing that sort of thing, and it just made me cry once again. "Don't," he said. "Just don't. It was the right thing, to leave."

"How do you know?" I said, pleading. "Tell me how you know."

"I just do," Lowell said, and his look back at me was one of pleading, too. He did not want to answer my questions, the look said. He could not.

Then he grabbed my hand and lifted me up. I know that most people think twins are always feeling that they're part of a pair, but the truth is, that wasn't something I usually felt. Usually, Lowell just seemed like my brother, as separate from me as one body is from any other. But standing there with his hand still in mine, I did feel whatever it is that must be different for twins. It felt like looking into a mirror and seeing a face that is your own but isn't quite what you expected. I felt as though I knew exactly what Lowell knew but hadn't ever been able to see it.

"Maybe she tried to kill him," I said, and when Lowell just looked at me, I said, "Maybe she did." I let go of his hand and saw his face go gray.

"That's crazy," he said, but his lips were trembling. "That's crazy, Meredith."

I stayed calm and looked straight at him. "She did," I said. "I know she did."

I left Lowell standing there and headed down the stairs. My father was in the front hall flipping through some mail he'd found on the floor, and I shot past him and out to the car, my father pronouncing my name so slowly that I was past the porch, out in the sunlight, before he finished.

I stepped into the street and pushed the button on the Checker's trunk. The hood bounced up, blocking the sun. I stared into the dark trunk, touching nothing. I just knew I was right, and I was trying to sort through the million things in my head that made me know it: the quiet discussions I'd overheard at night, my father's voice going from a smooth whisper to something else, something still quiet but somehow different, a voice where he hissed and spit his words.

What had I heard? That he felt beaten and betrayed? That he could not forgive her? That the four red lines running from beneath his chin to his collarbone, which Catherine, in some silent rage, had left there with her fingernails, had caused such shock in Lowell and me that we could barely look at him until, two weeks later, the lines had receded into his neck like footprints disguised by the gradual accumulation of earth and leaves?

The truth was, I knew, that I hadn't heard anything to make me think what I was thinking. No matter my father's tone, no matter the hiss and spit of his words, the rise and fall of Catherine's responses, or the pale cuts on my father's neck, their voices were always as garbled as the grim voices on the radio reciting the rosary. It seemed a dark mystery that when my father moved through our house singing, his voice was as clear in every room as if he were a grand tenor singing an aria at the Metropolitan Opera, but when he and Catherine argued, our house blanketed their words, covering whatever threats and pleading passed between them with the sudden whoosh and roar of the hot water heater or the hum of the window unit in the house next door or with nothing at all except my own cloudy breathing as I drifted back into sleep.

I reached into the trunk past my father's x-ray lamp and a stack of medical journals and pulled out the orange crate that Lowell and I had filled with the few possessions we'd decided to bring with us. Lowell had brought his stack of forty-fives, even though he didn't bring the record player, and he'd brought the black notebook where he drew all his pictures of buildings. He'd already decided, he said, that he wanted to be an architect when he grew up, but his buildings really weren't very accomplished; the walls of his houses usually tilted, the windows were uneven, everything looked as if it might tumble down any minute.

Lowell was good at drawing faces, though, and he'd packed the ones on heavy paper that had hung on his bedroom wall, sketches of Benny Goodman and Louis Armstrong and some other musicians I didn't recognize, their mouths up to whatever horn it was they played. He had also done a charcoal drawing of my father that was smudged but still looked just like him, all of the lines and creases in exactly the right place, my father frowning the way he did when you said something he had to think about before answering.

All I'd brought was a gold embroidered bag containing the jewelry that Catherine had given me for the last few birthdays — a barrette I couldn't wear because my hair was just too disordered, some earrings and a necklace with an opal in it, a cameo of a woman who Catherine said had a face that looked just like mine. I also brought the shoebox of my grandfather's photographs, which I'd never gotten around to making an album for.

I tried to lift the crate out of the trunk but couldn't, even though I was the one who'd carried it out. I kept thinking of my father and Catherine's conversations. If I hadn't heard anything, how was I certain of what Catherine had done, of the crime for which my father had left her? I was certain, though, and I figured if I kept thinking about it long enough, I'd remember whatever the words were that made me feel the way I did. I figured that if I went through this first long night without sleeping, I'd somehow hear them again.

There had been a night, hadn't there, when I had sat up in bed, startled from sleep by Catherine's voice. "You're the one, Thomas," she had said, I had heard her say, but I'd lain back down and let my father's answer, if he answered, become part of my sleep.

When I stepped back from the car and turned toward the house, I saw my father and Lowell standing on the porch. They were just watching me, Lowell with his hands in his pockets, my father with his feet turned out to the side the way he had to do to keep himself balanced. They looked as though they'd been watching me for a while, studying me, and I felt embarrassed, as if I'd been caught doing something I knew I wasn't supposed to be doing.

As I walked toward the porch, my father said, "I made some calls." I didn't know what he was talking about. I meant to go inside, to walk past them and head upstairs. I didn't want to be distracted from thinking what I was thinking for fear I'd lose the thread of my thoughts and everything would come unraveled. But my father caught me by reaching out his arm and pulling me to him, my head banging against his wet white shirt, my knee bumping his shin.

"It was him," Lowell said. "It was Murphy."

I looked up at my father, and he nodded his head. "He's in the hospital, at Hotel Dieu. I'll go see him tomorrow. They said he's fine."

The image of Murphy smiling at us from the blue station wagon flashed in my head, his wide-brimmed hat, his hand raised to wave hello, his black tie blowing across his shoulder. Then I saw the car going down into the water, Murphy shooting out of his seat and through the window, taking in water with every breath until he was swollen like a whale.

Although what they'd told me was the answer to a different

question, it felt like the answer to what I'd been thinking. What Catherine had tried to do to my father, I thought, must have had something to do with Murphy — with his disappearance two years before, with his coming back to us in that fleeting vision on the bridge, with his car ending up in the water.

I imagined that Murphy was not really alive, had not been alive even when shooting past us in the blue station wagon. I imagined that he was some sort of angel or ghost, returning to us with some awful message. I felt terrified. On the porch I clung to my father as much as he clung to me, afraid that I was closer to the truth than I wanted to be, afraid that God was giving me one of his revelations long before I was old enough to know what to do with it.

But I wanted to know. I clung to my father and looked up at him. "Can we go see Murphy, too?" I asked. "I want to."

"Let's see," my father said. "Let's wait and see."

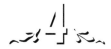

DEAR MEREDITH,

It's not as easy getting back to this as I'd imagined. Three days have passed since I wrote that first letter, and though I dragged myself over to this desk both of the last two nights, aiming to get started again, I didn't get a word written.

What I'd figured was that life would stand still long enough for me to tell my story, but it hasn't, and maybe that's a blessing, a gift of distraction to allow for some sorting and sifting before I try to make sense of what's passed. Maybe so, but I do feel I've been exhausted with my efforts.

The morning after I wrote you, my father stepped downstairs and told me with no more than a yawn and a shrug that he had a doctor's appointment in Durham, at the Duke University hospital. He was perfectly capable of driving himself there and back, he said, and I should spend the day however I pleased.

Of course, I told him I'd take him. Nobody should have to go to the doctor's alone, not when there's the chance he'll hear bad news after the doctor has finished his prodding and poking. My father's the age now, fifty-seven, when bad news about his body feels as certain as a hurricane once you've seen the gray eye swimming on the horizon. You can brace yourself, but you know that's about it.

And just the mention of hurricanes makes me think of your father with about as much fondness as I could be expected to feel at this moment. It always made me laugh the way he jumped into action whenever we heard reports that a hurricane was moving up through the Gulf of Mexico, headed for Louisiana. Quick as a flash he'd start running through the checklist he kept in his head, turning on his shortwave radio and ordering you and Lowell outside to put those X's of tape on the windows and pick up the fallen branches scattered across the lawn. Then he'd line the kitchen counter with batteries and flashlights and bottled water, and you'd think we were under attack from the Russians the way he acted like there wasn't a moment to spare.

As it turned out, we'd always spend a day or two cooling our heels while the hurricane drifted one way and then the other, as if it couldn't make up its mind whose life it wanted to ruin and whose it just wanted to interrupt for a few terrifying moments. Truly, with every one except Betsy, when we had to deal with the aftermath of actual destruction, your father had a great time with all his preparations. He always liked the image of himself as protector of his wife and children, although underneath the surface he held more than a little doubt that he was up to the task.

Your father's the type of man, and maybe most are, who will feel a sickness coming over him, a bad cold or some kind of bug, and for a day or two he'll act all brave and mighty, continuing on with his work like a true martyr, saying he won't let a cold or a flu bug stop him, no ma'am. Of course, those two days he's reminding you over and over how bad he feels, how much it is he's managing to endure. And then the third day or so, it knocks him flat and he crawls into bed like the smallest child, unable to stand to so much as fetch himself a drink of water.

You know what women do, Meredith? If you don't know already, you'll learn. What women do is find the time for being sick in the blank spaces of their lives, in between caring for their husband and children, in between all their other worries and concerns. And they don't talk about it like men do, either. I can't tell you how many of those who'd known my mother said to me at the funeral, "Cathy, we never knew until the last few weeks. Why didn't she say?"

She didn't say, Meredith, for the same reason most women don't say. We've got a notion of our life's fortune, both good and bad, as something private, as something belonging only to ourselves and our family. It's the hardest thing in the world to step outside that circle and confess to the troubles swarming there like one million angry wasps.

They say it's men who can't talk of matters concerning the heart, and that's true. That's your father for sure. But women have that power and so can decide when it's time to open their mouths and when it's not.

I know I'm making the split between men and women seem too simple, but my best guess is that your life, like mine, will prove out most of what I've already concluded. I hope that's not the case, but you ought to be prepared.

What I wanted to let you know but got away from is that there are two sides to your father. There's the side you know, Meredith, which makes Dr. Thomas Eagen both solid as stone and quiet as a sphinx. That's the side, of course, that drives him like an army general through each one of his routines, including all his Catholic ministrations. Did you know that every night, when he turns out the bedside lamp, he first lets his hand run across the Saint Joseph tag he keeps wrapped around the base before reaching up for the switch? He never once explained that act to me, and I think he even tried to deny he did it, but it was as much a part of his regimen as his morning cup of French Market coffee. There's also another side to your father, though — one where he sees himself living outside both God's and the world's good graces, like those jazz musicians he admires so, taking life's punches and jabs with an easy grin and a soul so mysterious and weightless it could just float away in the soft curls of smoke from his cigarette.

It would amaze me sometimes to see the calm he'd manage

in the face of something awful. When your grandfather died and we went to Mandeville in preparation for the funeral, your father lay down next to me that night, and I expected he'd be in need of real comfort. He wasn't. He was fine. Now I don't mean he was callous or unfeeling about his own father's death, because that's not what I'm saying. But it was as if he'd let that strange easygoing side of him take over for the moment. He lay there and wanted to tell me a story of his father, which was not anything he'd normally do. Under the circumstances, though, it seemed well and good. I thought it was a fine way of letting his father's life wash over him.

The story your father told, though — well, that's what surprised me, along with what he did after telling me. Your father said there was a stretch of time, when he was seven years old or so, when in the middle of the night your grandfather would rise from bed and step out behind the house to the garden.

Your father said he learned of this only because he'd sat up in bed one night when some noise out back had startled him awake. He went to the window to take a look, thinking he'd see some stray dog sniffing around and howling. Instead, the light on the back porch was switched on and he could see the shape of your grandfather, who was dressed in his pajamas and robe and seated on the bricks beside the pond. Your grandfather was weeping.

Your father said he watched until sleep overtook him, lying down again in his bed, not knowing the cause of your grandfather's sadness but thinking it must be something your grandfather didn't want him to know.

The next night, the same thing happened. Your father woke up, went to the window, and saw your grandfather out back. Instead of asking him what might be wrong, your father slept the following nights with a mind to wake up and go over to the window. Each time, your grandfather was there.

Finally, after a week, your father managed the courage to go on downstairs, or else he'd gotten himself so scared by what he'd seen that he needed to do it. When he stepped outside, your grandfather heard him and looked up. He didn't move, though. He let your father come to him. And I'll tell you in your father's own words what happened. Lying in bed, waiting for your grandfather's burial the next morning, your father looked up at the ceiling and told me. "God had given him a message in prayer, Cathy," your father said. "He told me God had said he should spend seven nights under the stars asking for forgiveness. 'And then what?' I asked him, and he said that after that he would be forgiven and the rest of his life would be happy. He said God had made him a promise that no further harm would touch that happiness."

Then your father laughed, Meredith, and stretched his hands out over his head, up toward the ceiling. "I never saw him cry again," he said. "Maybe he made it true himself. Maybe it had nothing to do with God's promise. But I don't think my father was unhappy in that way again the rest of his life. I don't think he was even capable any longer of understanding an unhappiness like that."

"Sure he was," I said. I felt like your father was headed toward some wrong conclusion. "Think of all that happened to you," I said, putting my hand on your father's chest just to feel his breathing. "Think of how he must have worried on your account."

"Worry's a different thing, Cathy," your father said. "It wasn't worry that sent my father out there those seven nights. It was the feeling that he'd done something himself to ruin his life. It was the feeling that he bore some responsibility."

"What had he done?" I asked.

"I don't know," your father said. "But he found a way to put everything into God's hands. He found a way to let joy overtake him."

"That's nice," I said. Your father didn't answer.

"Isn't it nice?" I said.

"Well, who wouldn't give up seven nights of sleep for a promise such as that?" your father told me. "I know I would."

I was lying there wondering if I would, too, if I could honestly say I'd like to give up the concerns of the world, the pain everyone knows is in store for them, in exchange for some heavenly promise of happiness. Wouldn't you lose everything of what it means to be human? I wondered. Wouldn't you be left with no feelings at all?

I'd just decided that I couldn't do it, that I couldn't make myself believe in such a bargain and wouldn't want to, when I heard your father swing himself out of bed and stand up. I didn't ask him what he was doing because I already knew. I just lay there and waited to hear the back door swing open. When it did, when I could see even from the bed that the porch light was casting its glow across the garden, I stood up and went to the window.

There was your father, Meredith, standing where your grandfather had stood those seven nights so many years before. Instead of weeping, though, your father just stood there and looked around, as if he half expected your grandfather's spirit to greet him. Then that quick he turned and came back inside and a minute later was next to me in bed.

"Thomas?" I said when he'd settled in. I sounded frightened, I knew.

"I'm okay, Cathy," he said. "I was just wondering how it would feel."

"How did it?" I said.

"Cold," your father said, and he laughed. "It felt cold." Then, just like that, he fell asleep and didn't wake again until morning. I figured he'd found his own way of saying goodbye, and though it had scared me because it was so strange, I decided I'd let it be.

Believe it or not, it was that side of your father, the mysterious side that could do such things as march outside in the middle of the night, that drew me to him. It wasn't the notion of him as a responsible husband and father. For one thing, you have to think of how young I was when I met him, only nineteen, living in a city like New Orleans for the first time in my life, thinking I'd found the greatest of all possible adventures. As soon as I met him and heard his whole story one night over raw oysters and okra gumbo at Mandina's, I knew here was a man life had tried to wreck by killing his wife and leaving him with two children, but he'd kept his own spirit alive somehow, no matter his bad fortune, and he felt as soft and precious to the touch as a newborn pup.

Maybe it's not proper to talk of such things with his only daughter, but what I'm trying to see for this single moment is not you, my dear girl, and not your father, but the man who was until a week ago my husband. Not even that man now, as he is today, but how he was then. Would you believe I could hardly keep up with him? I always felt like I had to reach out my arm just to keep hold of a scrap of his shoulder. He was always here and there, hiring Negro nannies you probably don't remember so he could meet friends in those dark-alley bars for this or that musician, dreaming of standing up and singing some sweet ballad, a white man cast among black folks as easily as a white stone cast into a dark sea, shining up from the bottom like a precious jewel.

Your father felt comfortable swimming in those depths, and I couldn't venture to say whether or not it had anything to do with his own mother's color, though I've seen a photograph of her and you would never have known, not in a million years, unless there was someone keeping track of those things, which in a small town like Mandeville there always is. So while I don't know why he prefers taking care of his no-money, know-nothing patients, as if their lives are worth more to him because they do not have a penny to their name and cannot keep themselves sober, my guess is that it's a debt he believes he owes for his father's decision that his son would be a white man, as pure and white as the statues he made — a decision that would have caught in his mother's throat and would have been reason enough, if she hadn't already left, for the woman to pack her bags and disappear exactly as your father has done.

There's a difference, of course. Your father took his children with him. His own mother left him behind. Maybe he was destined to repeat his mother's act, the way an old smudged line of dirt can reappear on a window each time the sun sets, but he'd learned through his own pain at least half of a lesson. Why he didn't learn the other half — that leaving is a terrible solution for all concerned — I don't understand.

But I'm getting ahead of myself, explaining what the dog

wants before he wags his tail. I was talking about my own father, about what has happened these last two days.

The reason my father had made his appointment with the doctor, I found out, was because of pains in his chest that have been waking him up at night. My father is not one to find a fancy turn of phrase, but he told me those pains enter into his dreams like a flaming meteor across the night sky, and he feels the burning trail down into his fingers and toes. Then he wakes up and finds his hands clenched into fists on his chest like he's been trying to pound the awful pain out from inside him.

How is it, I wonder, that suffering does all it can to make poets of every one of us, stirring up a kind of speech we never thought we'd utter, like we're all Shakespeare's King Lear standing in the middle of the storm or, for that matter, a man like your grandfather weeping in a statue garden? That may not be how my words read, but it's certainly how I feel, like the sky is falling all around me and all I can do is send out to you this faint message, which in the end is no louder than the beating of my own heart.

Of course, on our way to the hospital, my father acted like he was telling a story about some childhood friend whose name he only half remembered, like it was something that happened to someone else years ago rather than something that was happening to him. I was nervous enough as it was driving his rusted-out Chevrolet, maybe the only car in the world uglier than your father's Checker. It was the first time I'd sat behind the wheel of that car in years and years, and it reminded me of the last time — when I'd just finished Chatham County High and was meeting all my girlfriends in Chapel Hill the night before I set out for New Orleans.

My friends were holding a party for me at the Carolina Coffee Shop, one of those places with dark wood booths you'd go to late at night for a secret conversation with some boy you thought was heaven itself but your parents never liked. Well, for me that boy was Billy Reed, called Skinny by everyone who knew him, including me. Skinny wasn't invited to the party, which was just a chance for all my girlfriends to shower me with wide-eyed best wishes as I set off all alone for a city where I knew not a single soul, something that just about killed my father and maybe did do its share on my mother.

When the party was over, Skinny was waiting outside for me, leaning up against my father's car and smoking a cigarette. I said hello and tried to move past him. I'd made my goodbyes the night before out on our porch, promising I'd write, promising other things I don't remember, and I'd thought that would be it. But he reached his hand out as I opened the car door and said, "I'm going with you, Cathy."

For a moment I thought he meant to New Orleans. The look of shock and surprise I gave him must have tipped him off to my mistake, because he put out his cigarette with his shoe and quickly said, "Tonight, I mean. Right now."

Well, I hadn't realized until that moment that the reason I was leaving was not only because I wanted to be in New Orleans, which seemed like the best city in the whole world, it was also because I wanted to get as far away as I could from boys like Skinny, who for a while I thought I loved but didn't. I knew I didn't because whenever I was with him I felt like there would never be anything extraordinary about the world. The dirt roads and tobacco fields and houses and even the moon and stars only looked like what they were and not like part of some grand design for my life, if that makes sense.

What I wanted as much as a different world to see was a different way of seeing it. I wanted the world and everything in it to lean toward me and take me in. That's the feeling most people get from their hometowns, like there's a welcome embrace offered by this or that familiar place, a restaurant or barber shop or whole neighborhood where they've learned every inch of the terrain, where they don't ever have to look at themselves because they're part of things as much as any hundred-year-old tree.

But I didn't feel that way. I felt like I needed a whole different landscape, a different quality of light, other questions to ask myself in the dark at night when I tried to fall asleep. I think that fact goes a long way in explaining how easy it was for me, so young, to fall in love not just with a man ten years older who had twice my education, but also with his two children, little more than babies. It was something I wouldn't have dreamed of in a million years, which is exactly the point.

And I will tell you, Meredith, because it is something you are one day going to feel, I had a womb that burned for my own children, for feeling a new life growing inside me. I wanted to know, as much as any woman could want to know, the kick inside, the rush of blood in another body inside my own. It's a feeling you don't lose, I guess, until you've had a child, and I've heard women say that you don't lose it even then — that the oldest of matrons, whose blood stopped running longer ago than she can remember, still feels it sometimes, as sharp and undeniable as if she were flowering again in her first spring as a woman.

I'm just twenty-seven years old, Meredith. That's still so young, younger than you can imagine. I see my own reflection in the window by this desk, and I am still amazed by what I see. My face had begun to change in approximation of your father's, and I can imagine what I might have looked like twenty years from now if things had been different, if all of this hadn't happened.

Well, it did, and I suspect my face will eventually find its own shape again or maybe someone else's. It's true, I can imagine that, even with all this pain. You have no idea how these things are.

I've got a million loose ends now and will try to get back to them. First, I should finish with that last night before I left for New Orleans, which seems like so many years ago now I can hardly believe it was only eight.

I had to practically shove Skinny Reed away from my father's car, which was parked in the alley behind Franklin Street. Although there was no light except from the back window of Sewell's hardware store, I got a good look at Skinny's face just after I put my hand on his chest to keep him from me.

"Cathy?" he said, his shoulders slumping and his hands out with the palms turned up. His eyes were already wet.

"I've got to go, Skinny," I told him, and it was then he started crying, his whole body shaking so he had to lean forward.

That was the one time in my life I left a man, though in truth he and I were just children. But maybe it should be enough for me to understand why your father didn't want to face me, why he left me sleeping in bed rather than have to remember whatever final look I gave him.

I don't know what look that might have been. I honestly don't. But as I was driving back home that night I looked in the rearview mirror over and over, trying to grab hold of a face that I just knew would soon be gone, replaced by some other.

It was when I looked back out to the road that I saw what struck me as the most amazing thing. It was well past midnight, and I was heading south on Highway 15, which back then was lined with farms and not the imitation wood homes they're building there now. Well, as I looked down from the rearview mirror my eyes caught a light shining in an old tobacco-curing shed. The boards were all rotten and curled up in spots. The light was coming from a mercury lamp on the farmhouse up the hill. Inside the shed I saw a woman and a man locked in an embrace, their arms stretched out as if they were dancing. I could tell, just from the slope of their shoulders, that they weren't young but old.

Maybe that sight wouldn't have seemed like anything to anyone else, but I swear it felt to me like a vision, like I was seeing myself fifty years into the future. I felt at that moment like I knew my life would be a long and happy one, like God had offered me just a flash to put my mind at ease before I set off for the city of New Orleans.

Usually, of course, something like that disappears from your mind just as quickly as it happens, like a dream you only remember for the few seconds you're not yet fully awake. But that moment somehow stuck with me, and I must admit that no matter what's happened, I still believe it. I don't carry it with me all the time, of course, and I've got to dig deep sometimes just to find where I've put it. But if I've got any strength at all right now, that moment's a large part of it. I probably sound right now as crazy as you've ever heard me sound, but that's okay. I'm fine.

Well, it was when I was driving my father's car, taking him back down Highway 15 toward the hospital in Durham, that I realized I'd never told anyone, not even your father, about what I'd seen. It was a moment I'd kept to myself out of superstition, like the wish that telling prevents from coming true.

I looked at my father, who was resting his head on the window, and I told him I had something to say. He slid himself up in the seat. He was thinking, I'm sure, that I'd finally mustered the strength to tell him why I'd come home. Instead, I told him the story of what I saw that night eight years ago, and I told him what I believed seeing it meant, the same as I've just told you.

For a few moments after I'd finished, he didn't say anything. He ran his hands up and down the worn thighs of his pants and shook his head.

For a frightful second I found myself getting angry, wanting to scream out loud for having given up that secret. But then he reached a hand over to me and started talking. "I don't know what's gone wrong in your life, Cathy," he said, "but whatever it is, I'm not here to blame you. I hope you know that."

No matter how old anyone is, Meredith, it never gets easy to accept even the slightest amount of tenderness from your own father. It will give you more comfort than you can imagine, but it will never, not in a million years, be easy, not for you and not for him. I don't know exactly why that is. Nobody does, I imagine. But no matter what's said, there's something like a line of gold thread running through a man's words when he talks to his daughter, and gradually over the years it gets to be long enough for you to pick up in your hands and weave into a cloth that feels like love itself. It's another thing, though, to hold up that cloth for inspection, and the best I could manage at that moment was to nod and keep looking at the road.

"As for what you've just told me," he said, "it may not sound like much, but I can tell it is. Every person has feelings like that, feelings they carry with them through the years. I've got my own. They're a good thing, usually."

I nodded my head again but still didn't look over. "What have you got?" I asked, hoping to keep him talking so I wouldn't have to say a word.

"Cathy," my father said, sighing as if I'd asked him how to take a combine apart and put it back together. But I really wanted to know, so I asked again.

"Your mother," he said. "Every one's about your mother."

"Go on," I told him. He'd taken his hand away from mine and was rubbing his thighs again. You ask a man to speak of love, and it's like his tongue has been cut off.

My father did try, though, I will say that. He told me that one afternoon, years ago, when my mother had gone off into town, he took a can of gasoline and poured the gas over a bunch of anthills that had sprung up on the edge of the field nearest the house. Weeks before, my mother had worried that the ants might make their way into her kitchen, and she'd asked my father to do something about it. But she must have forgotten all about it, because the next morning when she walked outside, she saw the burned-out circles of grass and went back in to tell my father.

"She didn't know what they were," my father said, "so I told her there'd been a full moon the night before and the moon had left those circles behind. Moon burns, I called them, and I said it was a rare thing but sometimes happened. Just for the briefest blink she believed me. Her eyes were shining like the child who learns something wonderful about the world he never knew before." My father laughed and raised a hand to his chest.

"Then what?" I asked him.

"Then she saw I'd pulled the wool on her," he said. "She made a fist and gave me a good punch in the shoulder. 'Henry Reynolds, you've gone and spoiled my one moment of happiness,' she said, like she wouldn't have been bothered that I'd made the whole thing up if I'd left it at that."

My father shifted in his seat and put an arm up in the car

window. "That's one thing I remember," he said, then he looked over at me. "You'll get through this, Cathy. You will."

I nodded my head, and we drove the rest of the way without talking. I spent that time thinking about you and your father, not grabbing hold of anything in particular but imagining the two of you having just this sort of conversation someday, one where he cannot begin to set your world straight but can at least lead you to believe you can do it on your own.

It seems a sad thing right now that your father has got so much explaining to do, telling you more and more with each passing year about the two mothers you've lost. I'm not proud of it, but I can't help hoping you find more of yourself in his stories of me than of the woman who birthed you.

No matter how you might end up feeling, don't let him keep his silence on either score. That's the sad fact about your father, and it's true of just about every man I've known — they don't feel the need to answer unless asked, as if their hearts are powered by an electric switch someone else has got to turn on and off.

A man's heart. That brings me back to my own father as sure as a slap in the face. Why is it that women so often meet their deaths by way of the very parts of them they spend their whole lives attending to and putting to good use, their breasts and wombs, while men die from that one organ they do all they can to ignore? Maybe someday all those doctors will discover that it does a heart good to have it break. Women's suffering, they'll decide, is therapeutic. It gives them a long life.

All that's ridiculous, I know. It's just my mind circling in the clouds so it doesn't have to land somewhere it knows won't be pleasant.

I was talking about my father. After he'd seen the doctor, after they'd performed every test they could think of, he acted like the news he'd heard was not the worst thing in the world, but I knew it was. He'd already been told what the problem most likely was, and this visit just confirmed it. He'll need open heart surgery, a bypass operation, because two of his arteries have stopped letting blood through and a third one is threatening to go. They want to do the operation soon, as early as next week, though my father has refused to tell his doctor yes or no.

"I'll think about it," he told me.

"There's no thinking here," I said. "You've got to let them do it."

"Leave me alone on this, Cathy," he told me, and I did. There's no room for persuasion when someone is considering his own life and death. You stand by and wait, and that's about it. Maybe you show them, in any way you can, what they've got to live for, but there's not much more you can do.

For now, then, I'm putting off thoughts of whatever plans my mind might have led me to. I want to see you, I know that. I wish there was a way to make you know that, too.

I'll go ahead and mail this letter along with the first, not that they've gotten even close to what it is I feel like I have to say. Don't think I'm putting you off, Meredith. I'm not. I've promised to tell you all that's happened, and I will. I swear that even with my own father facing this terrible time, I feel torn. It's all I can do to stop myself from getting in his car and making the drive back to Louisiana, walking up to your grandfather's house and knocking on the door and taking you up in my arms.

All I've got to offer right now are these words, as little as that might be. Understand that we'll have our chance. I'm determined. Kiss your brother for me. Kiss your father. I'll write more.

YOU MIGHT THINK a mind shuts down when the body goes through the kind of misfortune my body did, a worse force, the doctor tells me, than felt by an astronaut launched in his rocket to space. At least he's got the sense to wear a helmet, the doctor says, and I do laugh.

Least he's got himself an oxygen pack and not a million tons of water, I say right back, and the doctor laughs with me, shaking his head.

My mind did not shut down, not for a moment, but it wasn't like I reached any grand conclusions or saw my life run before my eyes in a flash the way they say it does. I'm doing that now, all right, but I wasn't then.

My first thought was, *Well, this is no way to get the holy baptism you never had, conducting one of your own in the Pontchartrain. You've done the worst of it getting yourself all dressed up in some other man's clothes, and here you go making folks think again what they've been thinking for years, that Murphy Warrington is not one to be trusted, probably drunk on some corner of Delachaise or South Rampart like he's been going on these last two years.*

What do they know? I'm drinking water. I'm using every ounce of strength I've got remaining to hold my breath, but I'm taking in one mouthful after another, and the water is seeping in through my eyes like they're two bathtub drains and under my fingernails until I can feel them peeling right off, which is what they did.

I can't see, not without my glasses and not with all that water pouring in my eyes, so I shut them tight, only to see in all that blackness the two Eagen children staring at me from Mr. Thomas's car like both of them know what's about to happen, and they're waving their tiny hands goodbye. Why didn't I stay behind them, keep my distance, watch them instead of me head on down into the water?

Those children smiled, didn't they? Goddamn them.

No, they're good children, a good man's progeny. Three quarters good, one quarter misery. Though my arms and legs are as cold and heavy as stone, I'm turning my head from side to side, trying to shake myself free of all that water, and I expect to see Mr. Thomas and the two children swimming around next to me, which even at that moment I think would be an awful sight, the end of a long, sad story.

Then there's that quick flash of Mollie Moore, the same as has been haunting me for all these years. Every other time it's been all horror and shame, thoughts of touching her between her legs to damn myself and the fine curve of her back so I can count with my climbing fingers her spine's ridges like the finest string of shining black pearls, pulling myself into her just like that. But this time, in all my pain, it's a wonder that nothing, not even such a moment as this, can rip that woman from my mind, and if that's not changed, if I'm still dragged forward by the bull's fifth leg, then nothing else has changed either and I decide for that reason and no other that I'm going to be fine.

It wasn't until I felt the back of my neck touch the air and then my body flip of its own accord so that the bright light struck my shut and swollen eyes that I stopped thinking of that woman and fell unconscious. I woke up only after they'd pumped me dry and hooked me up to wires and tubes in this hospital bed, just one more hard-luck old nigger knocking on heaven's door.

I was beginning to think I'd dreamed it, that I was suffering from the delirium tremors after a bad bottle I didn't so much as half remember, when the white woman nurse with pink lipstick walks into the room and says there's a Dr. Thomas Eagen requesting my attention. I'd have thought he was the last man I'd want to see, but I watched that blur of a pink lipstick mouth say the name again and despite myself I felt taken care of, like I was standing next to his father in the days before Mr. Thomas was so much as born, before I caused all the trouble for Mrs. Mollie Moore Eagen. I said go ahead, send him in.

"He's on the telephone," the woman said. "He said he'll see you tomorrow, with your permission."

My permission? I thought. I laughed, though it hurt from my chest to my knees to do so. I laughed and laughed.

"He'd like an answer," the nurse said, and I nodded my head up and down or at least thought I did. The nurse just stood there like her shoes had been nailed to the floor.

"I'll see him," I managed to say. "Go on and tell him I will."

"You sleep now, Mr. Warrington," the nurse said. For a second she didn't leave, though. She looked at me with what I took to be three doses of fear and one of admiration, like I was a famous criminal she'd stumbled upon in some alley. Sure enough, she said, "You were on the news tonight. Channel six. They said that car was stolen."

"It was," I said.

"Well, the police will want to see you. I thought you'd want to know."

"That's fine," I told her. "Send them in, too."

"In the morning," she said, sweet as pie now. "I told them you were too sick." She turned for the door but stopped. "You're not, but that's between you and me, you hear?"

"Yes ma'am," I said, not laughing this time but acting as serious as could be. Most people don't understand how little the law means when you've just heard Gabriel's trumpet, but I knew the woman meant well and deserved my thanks. "I'm grateful," I said, and she slipped out and closed the door behind her like she was sneaking her way out of someplace she didn't belong, as quiet and small as a scared white mouse.

Well, I figured I had a long night of waiting for Mr. Thomas, who would finally get his chance to say whatever it was he'd been meaning to say these last two years, looking for me all that time without the least bit of success even though I was right there practically under his nose, living on Prytania Street, just one block across and three down from his place of employment. I'd caught sight of his car probably a hundred times in those two years, but he never saw me. His own eyes are nearly as bad as mine, the both of us two blind mice.

The difference being I'd put my own eyes out. While Mr. Thomas was no doubt on the lookout for me, I had no intentions whatsoever of having commerce with the man. I wish to God Miss Catherine hadn't found me, either, but that's just my luck.

And you'd think such shame as mine wouldn't carry forward one generation to the next, but it does. I couldn't look at that man without thinking I'd ruined his life, giving him the wrong start from age five on by making his mother pack her bags as the price for lying down with me in my bed.

I don't know why it was different with old Mr. Eagen. I stood next to him and looked in his face and shook his hand a million times after doing what I did. We built those statues working side by side and strolled into Saint Alphonse's Catholic Church every Sunday, and I raised my eyes to God, the one and only nigger in a sea of white. I will tell you, the shame was nothing I couldn't handle.

It was the man's wife, after all. There were times I thought to get down on my knees and ask forgiveness like a slave begging up to his master, but the truth was I wouldn't have meant it. The few and only times I've let myself think of the foolishness of there being such a thing as love in this world, I also told myself I'd already known it in the human form of Mollie Moore and would not likely know it again. What chance has shame got in the face of that? Love's not a carthorse pulling some nigger's cloth scraps. It's wild, like those spotted ponies they say Mr. Christopher Columbus brought over to the islands and set free.

That's what I told myself time and again. Only after that, I'd see Mr. Thomas come stumbling along, crying tears he didn't even know what for, and I'd want to put a stake through my own heart and twist it.

Maybe the difference was Lowell Henry Eagen was a full-grown man and Thomas Eagen was nothing more than a child. Man to man I felt fine. I felt better than fine most of the time, to tell the truth. No matter her holy matrimony, Mollie was as earthbound as old Murphy, and there was something right to that, and we both knew it, touching each other like we'd never so much as gone near another's body before. That was Lowell Henry Eagen's misfortune, not mine. None of the white folks in Mandeville would have taken a single step forward to string me up if they'd known I'd been with Mollie. They'd have stood on our doorstep and told Lowell Henry Eagen he'd gotten what he'd asked for. They belong with their own kind, they'd have told him.

Maybe that's the shame of it, not the way her body curved into mine, as eager as I ever was, but the fact of my doing what I did, Mollie and I doing what we both did together, for that's the truth, would have made them think they were right all along, that some off-the-boat Irishman's maybe not so good as other white folks but he's got a pocket of loose change compared to any penniless no-account nigger. That just proves it. I hear them saying it again and again. That just proves it. It makes me sick to my stomach even to this day.

No one did know, though, and for that I'm grateful. If I'd kept my mouth shut, if all my gnashing of teeth and loathing had bored its way deep inside my belly instead of squirming out my mouth, there'd still be no one with so much as a clue. I wouldn't be waiting for Mr. Thomas to stand by my bed in the morning the way Mollie stood next to mine and say he's sorry I didn't take in twice as much water and sink like a goddamn stone.

If I had to say it, and if I was a man with as much courage to spare as bad sense, I'd have told Mr. Thomas straight out. I'd have said I was the man who did that to your mother, only to watch her pack her bags; ready to go with her if that's what her heart desired or put a knife to her throat if she'd thought to leave her husband a letter confessing her crime — not for my sake, but for Lowell Henry Eagen's sake. If your wife's bent on leaving in any case, you don't need to know what for, not if that would only go and make it worse, which this one surely would have done.

She didn't write any such letter of confession, and she made it clear she didn't want me near her. I did drive her to the train station that morning while Mr. Eagen was making a delivery in New Orleans, but that was nothing. She said she was only going off to see her aunt, and I pretended I knew no better and told Mr. Eagen so.

Of course I knew. I'd seen the careful attention Mollie Moore had given Mr. Thomas before I took him off to early school. I saw her put aside the distraction of mind and body to put a shaken hand on the child's head and kiss him and straighten his clothes, tugging this way and that on his shirt, brushing her hands across his pants legs. "You know how Mama loves you?" she asked the boy, and he nodded his head and squirmed to get free the way children do. I saw the tears starting up in Mollie Moore's eyes, how she wanted to say something to make this child understand the choice she'd made, knowing he'd never understand. I knew it that moment. I did.

It put me in mind of Lowell Henry Eagen, whether she'd thought to give her husband a secret word of parting, some bit of tenderness only she'd know was the last they'd share. That I don't know.

What she did with me was swing open the door when we'd pulled up to the station as if she'd step out without a single word. Then she thought better of it and said, "I'll be back soon. You tell Lowell I will."

"Yes, ma'am," I said, and maybe I made something of a face at that remark because Mollie Moore shot back at me in usual fashion, "Don't you go thinking I don't love that man, Murphy Warrington, on account of what I've done with you."

"I don't," I said, holding on to the steering wheel as if I wanted nothing but to get myself on home, the real truth being I wanted this woman again that very moment, anywhere she chose.

"I do love him," she said. "You don't know how much."

I didn't have an answer for that, so I sat in silence and let Mollie Moore slam the door shut. Maybe I could have said something about how respect and love are two different animals. One is the sort you stand back from and admire. The other you pull close and cling to for your own dear life. Mollie Moore Eagen had no end of respect for her husband, for how he trained his eyes so on his heavenly statues and never let any of the world's dirt touch him. But was that the same as love? Was it?

Mollie had a bag stuffed with what little clothes she'd brought, and she held that tight against her while she waited for me to drive off.

This is the one and only chance, I told myself, but I couldn't think of what to say that would make for a fit and proper sendoff. How does a nigger tell a white man's wife, no matter her own color, that she'd be better off clinging to him instead, especially when what she'd be clinging to was no safer than the edge of a rocky cliff?

So I let her go, and my mind turned away from that final moment to find some other, and not our lying down together in my bed but a time before that, before Mollie had said a single thing to suggest her intentions concerning me. The time I considered was when some customer of old Mr. Eagen's, a man named Rigaud who sold the statues we made at some garden shop outside of Triumph, Louisiana, for twice the price he paid, had brought his sailboat up to the sea wall and said how he'd like the Eagen family to join him on a lake excursion. Mr. Eagen said no. He said he had work to attend to, though I think the simple truth was he didn't like or trust this man, who didn't treat the statues the way Mr. Eagen felt they should be treated.

Mollie Moore, though, said she'd like to go. She said she'd

spent a couple years now watching all those white-light-flashing boats on the water but not once had she set foot off the shore, not only on the Pontchartrain but anywhere. "Come on, Lowell," Mollie said. "We'll have some fun."

Old Mr. Eagen shook his head no but said it would be fine enough for her to go ahead and won't Murphy come along. I understood his meaning, which was he didn't want his wife alone sailing on the Pontchartrain with a man he didn't trust, so I said yes, I'd be happy for a bright and shiny summer afternoon's sail, and so the three of us crossed over to the water and made our way into the boat, Lowell Henry Eagen standing on the sea wall steps and waving his wife a happy goodbye.

The moment I stopped to consider upon Mollie's leaving was when Rigaud pulled out a bottle of the orange wine they make in Triumph, the bottle with his own name spelled out across the label. When Mollie saw that name there on the bottle, she asked Rigaud if he grew his own oranges and he said he did, tipping up the white sailor's cap he'd put on and showing off his patchy red forehead like he was a king crowned in the blazing sun.

"I've got a two-hundred-tree orchard," the man said, "and I'm planning for two hundred more."

Well, I could see the look on Mollie Moore's face, and I knew she was imagining seeing those two hundred trees all lined up in rows and spilling oranges across the ground like a million golden sunsets one after the next.

"Oh, I'd like to see an orchard like that someday," she said, gazing out across the water like she'd been blinded by her own imagining.

"I'd be honored to show you about," Rigaud said. He was standing at the boat's silver wheel, with Mollie and me sitting down below him, and he let his hand fall to rest on Mollie's shoulder.

Mollie stood up as quick as if she'd had an electric shock. "I bet Lowell would like to see it, too," she said, and there was no hiding her intent of letting the man know she wasn't playing the same game as him.

"That would be fine," Rigaud said, like it was an apology, and Mollie sat back down. But then she leaned to me and put her hand on my back.

"If this was your boat, Murphy, where would you take me?"

I didn't at the time understand her meaning, and my first thought was to say, *I'd take you home, Miss Mollie, that's where.* But we'd begun drinking the orange wine, which was fine-tasting even with the man's name staring straight at us, and I let my thoughts lead me to sailing Mollie Moore over to all those orange trees and be the one to show her what she so longed to see. I couldn't say such a thing as that, though, so I just said, "I don't know where, Miss Mollie. Wherever you'd like to go."

She slapped my back then, not hard but playful. "You don't know the first thing about a waking dream, Murphy Warrington," she said, and she laughed. "I think you and Lowell both have spent too much time at working. You forget what it's like not to."

Then Mollie Moore looked at me and smiled to show she meant no offense, but there was something else to that smile, I could tell, and it was that single look that I thought of at the train station the last time I saw her, her face there in the sun with the shining water behind it like she was one of those mermaids who'd just rised up to save some nearly drowned sailor. I wouldn't have dared to consider that years later I might be offered the opportunity to see that face closer to mine than I did that moment, and not just her face but her whole body and shape opening up to me, taking me in in such a welcoming manner, there not just for my eyes but also for my hands and all else.

Sitting at the train station and watching Mollie Moore disappear up the steps, I said my own silent goodbye by changing what happened that day on the boat to my taking the woman's face in my hands and saying, *I'll take you there now,* throwing Rigaud out into the water like a too-small-to-eat red snapper, and sailing on down to the man's orchard. There we were, Mollie Moore and Murphy Warrington, not some full-fledged nigger and a white man's wife but just one man and one woman strolling among the orange trees like they were placed there only for our benefit, the branches twining each together the way Mollie Moore and I would twine ourselves beneath them.

It was only the train's whistle that interrupted my thinking, and I found myself crying like a child and thinking I knew finally what I wanted to tell the woman, what final words I should have said: *Murphy Warrington knows about waking dreams, Mollie Moore. He knows because you showed him.*

It was not until some years later that I heard Mollie Moore had gone ahead and had that child but gave it away like a spoiled rabbit's foot promising bad luck instead of good. I didn't know if that was true or the other story I'd heard, that both were dead in two years' time and buried up in Natchitoches. Do I think of that child? Yes I do. I've had half a mind on one million occasions to find myself a car and drive up to Natchitoches to see for myself what is and isn't there.

I had the mind to do so this morning, didn't I, thinking I'd be better off spying on my own past life than on Mr. Thomas and his children. And no one would look as far as Natchitoches for a stolen car, would they? So maybe that's what I was thinking when I stepped on that gasoline pedal and passed Mr. Thomas.

That's not true. I thought about it, I did, but I figured I'd just get to the house before them and step inside for a look around before I made myself scarce. I wanted to see the inside of that house for no more reason than any other man wants to see where he once lived.

I could have told my whole history to Mr. Thomas, couldn't I? But instead I chose his wife, not the mother of his children, who was dead practically before anyone's hand had cooled from shaking hers hello. I told Catherine Reynolds, don't ask me why.

No. I know why, of course I do. It's like the criminal who's too much of a chicken-ass coward to return to the scene of his crime but is too proud to let it go at that. He wants someone to know how he's forever changed the shape of the whole goddamn universe by the force of his own will, by letting it be known that he's got the power to drop one small stone in a mighty sea and alter the push and pull of the tides.

Poor Miss Catherine, nothing more than a wisp of a white girl, too young to be mother to those Eagen children or to cope with a man like Mr. Thomas, a man who was longing to know the taste of his own blood but never could, smarter than any child I've ever known but just as slow as a hunchbacked turtle. Miss Catherine couldn't know the hundred black devils swarming through her husband's body like it was a barn full of bats because he didn't know they were there himself. He's as poor a man as myself in his own way.

It was a Monday in May when Miss Catherine surprised me in Mandeville with two old rocking chairs tied with about a mile of twine to the top of Mr. Thomas's car. She'd picked them up in New Orleans and driven them across the lake herself, wanting me to stitch the torn seats so they'd be ready for the porch by that weekend.

I was standing out front with my hands in my pockets, just watching the sailboats bob in the water like so many children's toys, when the woman drove up. I took my hands out and crouched down near the ground like I was looking at some creature who'd happened to catch my attention and was giving me some concern. I did see something — a black beetle climbing up a grass blade only to bend it with its weight and end up back on the earth. I thought it would probably take two lifetimes for that beetle just to make it across the lawn.

When the car door opened, I stood up. Miss Catherine, God bless her, had the notion of me as a handyman, a regular do-good Mr. Fix-it. While she was as wrong as wrong could be, I told myself there was no ill will in that way of thinking. I figured she'd searched in her head for some way to explain what it is I did living all these years in the house of her husband's father, and that was the best she could come up with and still keep her distance from what she figured was a wrong way of seeing me, as the Eagen family's old black domestic or as the sullen-faced, slope-shouldered nigger who just wouldn't quit the farm no matter Abe Lincoln's four-score announcement that every black man and woman had the unalienable right to just get up and leave and make the best of it come what may.

I knew Miss Catherine thought I belonged back in New Orleans, working alongside her husband to care for the worst of my own kind. I suspect Mr. Thomas never told her what I told him, that the city of New Orleans was no place for me, that in two months I'd wrecked myself more than I had in all the rest of my sixty-odd years. *Send me home,* I requested, and Mr. Thomas offered me my old room and the care of his father's house. "Yes, sir, Mr. Thomas," I said. "That would be fine."

Well, soon as she drove up, I helped Miss Catherine unwrap all that twine from around those chairs, and I carried them up to the porch. She came trailing up right behind me, scraping her heels on the walk, like she was afraid my arms might just give way and drop one of those chairs. I set them down on the porch gentle as setting down a baby and looked them over with my head cocked to the side. I did know how to play that woman. I told her they sure looked ratty but I would do my best to get them stitched in a week's time.

In truth I wasn't about to try that stitching myself. What I meant to do was take some of the money Mr. Thomas always left in his father's dresser drawer and drag the chairs over to the repair shop. I'd tell Lavelle Gaitreaux, "Now, this is a surprise for Miss Catherine Reynolds Eagen, so don't you ever go telling her you've done this work, you understand." Then I'd tell Mr. Thomas what I'd done and he'd say I'd made a fine and proper decision. "Lord knows what they'd look like had I done it myself, Mr. Thomas," I'd say, and we'd both laugh.

But Miss Catherine lingered for a while, saying she was exhausted from the drive, and I just knew she wanted to see me get started on those chairs before she headed back, taking with her a picture of me hard at work so she had reason to believe the job would be done by the weekend.

While she waited, I tried my best to find other things to do. I pulled out the mop and made my way through the kitchen, trying to let her see that maybe she was in the way and ought to think of leaving. She didn't budge, though, but instead just lifted her feet and put them up on another chair while I swung the mop beneath her.

I figured out she just wanted company because she seemed clam-happy to sit there and sip her ice tea while I set to work on dusting the living room, but then she called me back to the kitchen and asked me to sit down with her.

"Pour yourself something to drink, Murphy," she said, so I got myself an ice tea, too. I didn't think she meant a real drink, and I wasn't in a mood to test her patience.

"Yes, ma'am?" I asked, sitting down across from her.

She put her hands on the table and lifted them only to push her hair back behind her ears when it slipped forward. Then she says, out of the blue, that she wants to know about Mr. Thomas's first wife. "You knew Barbara," she said. It was clear she was feeling more than a little discomfort, stammering that Mr. Thomas didn't talk much about the woman on his own, in fact hardly at all, and didn't like it much when she asked.

I was not so absent of mind as to miss the sadness and gloom behind Miss Catherine's question. Here was a woman, I thought, who'd been married to a man for five whole years and she was still haunted by the ghost of the dead woman who'd been married to that man for less than two.

"I don't know much of anything, Miss Catherine," I told her. "She was a nice enough woman, and it's a terrible shame what happened, but there's not much I can tell you."

"What did she look like?" Miss Catherine asked, and I had to catch my own breath.

I was thinking that it couldn't be that through all those years she'd never seen so much as a picture of the woman. And never mind that, it's no piddling thing for a black man to set about describing a white woman, especially not when that white woman is young and pretty, which Miss Barbara certainly was.

I guess Miss Catherine caught hold of my discomfort because she waved her hand in front of her face to let me know I could forget the question.

"Somewhere here there's got to be some pictures," I said, getting up, stumbling a little on the back of my chair.

"I've seen photographs of her, Murphy," Miss Catherine said, and she motioned for me to sit back down. "That's not what I mean."

"Forgive me, Miss Catherine," I said, "but I don't know what you're asking."

"Let's have a drink," the woman then says. "What's here?"

"What would you like?" I ask, trying to find the right tone, like I wasn't about to think, not for one second, what she meant was both of us and not just her might think it fine to have a drink when the sun was not yet halfway across the sky.

"Anything," she says, and she holds out her glass. "Just pour it in here."

I got out Mr. Thomas's Scotch whisky, which otherwise I never touched despite myself, and poured her a little. When I went to put the bottle back, Miss Catherine said I should pour myself a glass, too. So I did.

By the time I sat back down, Miss Catherine already looked out-and-out distracted. "Tell me this, Murphy," she said. "Tell me about the accident."

"Mr. Thomas, you mean," I said. "His leg?"

"Yes," she said. "Tell me that."

The woman started sobbing then, so I said, "It's fine, Miss Catherine. It's fine." But I wondered how this bright day had turned so dark all of a sudden for this woman, driving clear across the lake on the pretense of delivering two rocking chairs when in fact she wanted to ask an old nigger questions she should have rightly put to her own husband.

"It's fine," I kept saying until Miss Catherine let up and said she was sorry.

"No need," I told her. I've always been one to believe that pain is pain no matter where it comes from, and all this woman required was some comfort before returning to her rightful spirits.

There wasn't much to remember about Mr. Thomas's accident, but I told Miss Catherine what I could. I said he'd been riding his bicycle early one morning, delivering papers through Mandeville like he'd done every morning for going on a year. He must have been ten years old, or maybe eleven. The fifth grade, whatever that age was. It was a Sunday, when the *Times-Picayune* was twice the size of any other day, and the basket out front of the handlebars must have tipped him off balance. He ended up swerving into a car that was going maybe five miles an hour, no more, but the fall he took broke his hip.

It wasn't the fall that ruined his leg, I told Miss Catherine. It was the infection that got into the bone. When all was said and done, including three kinds of surgery, the doctors told him he'd be in a wheelchair, but he wouldn't have it. So they told him he'd need crutches, and he wouldn't have that, either. After nearly an entire year in the hospital and three months in bed at home, he just refused to go out the house until he was walking on his own. It was that kind of story, one to make every single human being proud of Mr. Thomas.

I told Miss Catherine what I honestly believed, that the whole episode had been worse in a way for old Mr. Eagen. "You don't understand how something like that can be until you see it, Miss Catherine," I said. "He used to say that he'd prefer to lay his own life down than watch his son go through that suffering. That's a mighty large claim, Miss Catherine, but I believed it. I knew it was true. There was such pain in that man's face for his child that it made you want to lay down your own life, too."

Miss Catherine just nodded. But then she looked at me and said, "Did you ever want your own child, Murphy?"

"Not me, ma'am," I said right back.

"Not ever?" she said, and I was growing uncomfortable. I found myself rubbing my feet on the floor enough to make sparks to start a fire.

"Maybe I once did," I said, "though it's no use to think of it."

"It's no use for me, either," Miss Catherine said, and she shook her head side to side and looked down at her hands.

"That's Mr. Thomas's feelings, not yours, I take it."

"Yes, it is," the woman said, and she looked up at me.

I knew I was swimming deeper than I'd intended, but I

couldn't help it. I will say this for myself, no matter how it sounds. I felt sorry for the woman, and it was that feeling as much as any other that made me go on the way I did. I may not have been smart enough to know the trouble I'd cause myself, but I have always been one to see the connection between things, how you can draw a line through a life and watch it take on its shape the same way a child can draw with even the shakenest hand from one dot to the next.

So I didn't need any complicated explanation to understand why Mr. Thomas didn't want more children. His first wife had bore him two only to leave this world. Somewhere inside he had to be thinking the same would happen to Miss Catherine. Even a doctor of medicine who knew better would feel that way deep inside.

I didn't tell Miss Catherine all of that, though. I figured what she needed was hope and not the feeling that Mr. Thomas wasn't likely to change, that he'd seen enough in his life to dig a hole deep enough for him to be stuck there for good.

No, I didn't do that, though maybe I should have. Instead, I got up and poured us both another drink and said I had my own sad story to tell. I swear I could feel that story rising up to my throat from down in my intestines, where it had been growing and growing all those years.

"You're the first person to hear this, Miss Catherine," I started, "and I've got to believe that this stops at your ears and goes no further."

"Of course," she said, and she looked at me like she might find after all what she'd come here looking for.

"This isn't about Mr. Thomas," I told her, "though God knows it's played its part in his life all these years. You take from it what you will."

Miss Catherine went to say something, but I stopped her. "You just listen," I said, and I sounded angry, which after all that time I guess I still was. I waited until I could smooth my voice over and Miss Catherine no longer looked afraid, then I started talking.

"What I believe, Miss Catherine," I said, "is that I am a good man inside, but I've paid a price going on nearly two thirds of my life for what I've done. I'm going to say it right out, and if you don't want to hear any more, I understand. I don't like to hear it myself."

Miss Catherine nodded and smoothed her hair.

"It was something I did that made Mr. Thomas's mother quit this family," I said. "It wasn't Mr. Eagen or any sickness inside the woman except the one I put there, though it's only fair to say she had her part in it."

Miss Catherine was sitting as still as a stone, and it did cross my mind that maybe I was wrong to be getting started on this. I tried to think then of a lie I could tell, but nothing would come. That's the thing about talking the truth, I think, the thing that makes George Washingtons out of the simplest-minded of men: it grabs hold of you by the collar and gives you no mind for lies any longer, like you've been scrubbed clean.

Before I even said another word, I was beginning to feel strengthened, as if Mollie Moore had been a heavy tumor I'd carried all those years in my chest and was now finally coughing up.

"I lay down with the woman," I said. "I gave her a child. She didn't have any choice about leaving."

The look Miss Catherine gave me at that moment was a sorrowful one, not angry, though I could see the fear starting in the outside corners of her lips and eyes, something every respectable half-minded nigger gentleman has learned to see in the face of a million white women, just the slightest stretching of skin that says you ought to look the other way or find some kind of pleasantness in your manner awfully quick before someone shoots you dead.

"I've said enough," I told the woman. "You don't need to hear it."

"Go on," she said.

Well, I couldn't imagine what she wanted me to go on about. I'd told her how I'd lay down with Mollie and given her a child, how it was that fact and no other that made the woman quit her husband and son. Wasn't that enough to send her on her way?

Miss Catherine saw me fumbling for words and said, "How did it happen, Murphy?"

"I can't really say, ma'am," I told her, but I knew I wasn't being honest. All I had to do was shut my eyes to see Mollie as I first saw her, nothing more than a child bride Mr. Eagen had brought down from somewhere up North, though he didn't say where. He brought her up to the doorstep without so much as a single piece of luggage and only a tiny black purse strung across her chest. She had a white dress on, a simple thing, and once Mr. Eagen told me his news, I wondered if that was the dress she'd been married in, because the woman had no other.

I was twenty-seven years old at the time. Lowell Eagen was five years older. Mollie Moore couldn't have been more than twenty. I'd been working beside this man for nearly two years, practically since the day he just up and moved into that Mandeville house, which had sat empty since the prior owner, Judge William Lancaster, had stopped spending his summers there. My own father had worked for the judge, keeping the house and garden in good repair, and when Mr. Eagen moved in and set up shop out back, I'd wandered around the side of the house to offer my services.

"Judge Lancaster said I should stop by," I told him by way of introduction. It was a lie, of course, but I figured he wouldn't know any better.

"Lowell Eagen," he said, extending his hand. "Your name's Warrington? From Sharp Street."

"Yes, sir," I said, surprised. "How'd you come to know that?"

I was more than a little worried the judge had in fact mentioned my name. He wouldn't have used it kindly, though. He would have told Mr. Eagen to watch out because I was without gainful employment and had once stolen a watch from off the mantel and tried to sell it. My father found that out and made me march up to the judge and return it. That was years before, when I was still a boy, and while I hadn't thought the judge was the type of man to keep his own ledger book of injustice, maybe he was.

But Lowell Eagen shook my hand and said, "There's only about twenty families in this town, half of them colored."

"I guess that's nearly the case," I said, though it wasn't. There were a hundred nigger families, at least.

"As far as I can tell, not one of those families, black or white, is Irish," he said. Then he stood back and squinted his eyes and said, "You're not Irish, are you?"

"No, sir," I said. "You can see I'm not."

"Well, that leaves me," he said, laughing. "If everyone's going to know who I am, I figured I ought to know who everyone else is, too. Nice to meet you."

He shook my hand again. I was on the verge of thinking the man was crazy, wandering around town asking what everybody's name was and where they lived. But then he looked back over his shoulder and said, "I've got to get to work. You wouldn't know anyone who needs a job, would you?"

"Yes, sir," I said. "I do."

"Who would that be?" he asked.

"I mean me," I said.

"Well, that's fine," he told me. "Roll up those sleeves."

It was not my habit, I admit, to trust a white man as far as I'd like to throw him, and it took me until the end of that first week when Mr. Eagen handed over two five-dollar bills and said he'd see me on Monday for me to believe my life had taken a turn that wasn't for the worse.

A month later, Mr. Eagen asked if I'd move in downstairs. I'd been living with my mother, who for reasons I no longer remember had shown me the door two days before. She'd probably decided that no matter how old she'd gotten, she was still taking care of me more than I was taking care of her, which was no doubt true. I'd asked around, but I didn't have the type of friends who'd offer me so much as a dirty floor to lay down on, and I'd spent those nights sleeping near the train station, in a warehouse as full of rats as the rendering plant outside of town. But Mr. Eagen acted like he didn't know that. He just said his house was too damn big for him to live there on his own, and he left it at that.

"That would be fine," I said.

"I'm glad," he told me, and he shook my hand like we'd just

done each other equal favors. I don't know why, but Mr. Eagen was one to shake your hand at the dropping of a hat. It's something to think that in my lifetime I touched that white man's hand more than all other white men's combined. There's nothing to that except when you think of how you can live alongside someone for years and years and not so much as brush your shoulder against theirs. That's how my own father was, like at some point he'd been sealed inside a glass jar you'd bump your face against if you tried to get too close. I was the same way, I guess, though Mr. Eagen made me feel like I wasn't. He just reached past whatever it was surrounding me and grabbed my hand and shook. I liked the man. I did.

Well, when Mr. Eagen brought home his bride, I figured that was the end. I figured he'd want me out the door as soon as he could whistle, but he said no. "I may need you here, I suspect," he said, although I didn't have the first idea what he meant.

Seeing her on that doorstep for the first time, I wouldn't have guessed in a million years that this woman was a nigger, with her black hair fine and pulled back behind her head, her shoulders long and straight enough to balance books on. I could search deep in my mind and say it was true the light didn't seem to catch her quite right for a white woman, as if she was forever standing in some shadow, but I wouldn't have thought anything of it if she hadn't told me so herself.

Time and again she'd find me alone in my room downstairs or out back in the shop, and she'd set about talking to me, as familiar as could be. I'd act polite for as long as I could, saying yes and no or whatever else the conversation required until I could find a reason to excuse myself. The woman made me uncomfortable. Her bony limbs would flail about while she talked and talked, like a child who can't decide what is and isn't important so she goes ahead and tells you everything in a rush of words equal in force to the falling walls of Jericho, so you had to put your hands over your ears just to protect yourself.

It was a while before I realized that this wasn't the only thing making me so uncomfortable in the woman's presence.

Most white people figure a black man's forever looking at a white woman and thinking of her in the wrong way, hungry as a starved dog, but the truth is that's not the case. A black man does all he can to see that woman as someone of no particular interest, no matter the pleasures of her shape.

That's what I was doing with Mollie Moore, I realized soon enough. If I'd wanted to drink her in, I would have done so from the very first sight, when she was standing on that doorstep with her two feet together and her shoulders thrown back like she'd gone to a school that taught you this and no other was the way for a woman to stand.

I had to turn away sometimes when I came upon her in the kitchen, leaning over the sink scrubbing vegetables or washing dishes. I didn't want to consider for the slightest second her thighs running smooth against the cabinets, the long thin muscles of those arms, her legs and breasts as perfect as any man would have them. I'd catch her out back looking over Mr. Eagen's work, and she'd look like a holy statue herself. I'd hide like a child, though I couldn't stop myself from looking.

Even after we made that boat trip together, I went back to keeping my distance, maybe even more so after that.

Well, she finally got herself wound up and wholly exasperated by my manner. She must have been thinking of all she would say because she marched downstairs one night and stood above the chair where I was reading and said, "Let me ask you something, Murphy."

"Yes, ma'am?" I said, looking up from the book like I only meant to be disturbed for a moment. In truth, I was trying at Mr. Eagen's request to be serious about reading. He had a supply of books upstairs that was probably better than the local library, though I hadn't ever gone inside that building long enough to make a proper comparison. When I was at the colored school I'd been a good student, though I figured out it was only because the teachers looked at my thick glasses and decided one after the other that they meant I was smart instead of just near-blind, and I was left with no choice but to be what those teachers expected.

Mr. Eagen had told me to take as many books as I wanted downstairs, so I did. The nights when I was just too tired to stroll over into town, nights when Mr. Eagen said I must have run out of money to spend and crazy stories to tell, I spent reading while he and Mollie listened to their music upstairs. I'd hear them dancing to the music like they were having the biggest party, though it was always just the two of them.

This particular night, the music was going on as usual, and I was just enjoying my solitude, paging through but not actually reading some man's story of life during the time of Christ, the Romans with their swords and helmets, the Jews with their sad-ass sackcloth. This book was intended for children, with pictures nearly every page. Mr. Eagen had more books on religion than you'd expect from the pope, and I spent more time trying to figure out why that was than pulling them down from the shelves. It was the same with making all those statues. He never explained himself. It was just something he did, something he said he'd learned from his own father, going on back to when the family was in Ireland and not America.

I hadn't heard Mollie Moore come down the stairs. All of a sudden she stepped just beyond my reading light and said she wanted to ask me a question.

"Why is it you don't like me?" she said. Her hand tapped at her waist like she was preparing to strike no matter the answer I gave.

"I like you just fine, Miss Mollie," I said, which was the truth when you subtracted my discomfort.

When I look back now at my life, I see that women, black and white, are always telling me things, like there's something about my homely looks that makes them think it's just fine to talk — like Miss Catherine so many years later and her wanting to bear a child with Mr. Thomas.

Well, Mollie starts in on a rush of words, and I sit there like she's a tornado whipping at my sleeves. "You don't like me just fine, Murphy Warrington," she says. "You don't like me the least little bit, and I know why you don't. You think it's wrong for a Negro woman to be married to a white man, and so you've got to act all the time like it doesn't bother you, like it's the most natural thing in the world."

I was struck dumb, though that was no matter because she went on and on. "I've gotten by most of my life without it even being an issue," she said, "and I'm not ashamed of failing to mention it to every Sam and Joe on the street who'd like to know. I don't care, you understand. I'm happy to pass for a white woman. If that's my reward for my great-grandmother being forced to lie down as a young girl with a white man she didn't want, then that's fine. If my life's easier that way, that's only right. But you listen to this. I'm happy to be known as a Negro, too. That's fine with me. So I don't want you treating me like I'm one or the other. I don't know how you think of Lowell, but he's not your master, and I'm not your master's wife."

She caught her breath, and before I could say anything, before I could even think of what it was I had to say, she started up again. "I'll tell you how I think of you. I think of you as Lowell's friend. I'd like to consider you my friend, too. But if you keep up with that hangdog nigger routine with me, I'll see that Lowell shows you the door. You understand?"

"Yes, ma'am," I said, and I practically bit my tongue. Maybe I did. But as soon as she said she was a nigger, it was like I already knew, like something had been staring me in the face but so close I hadn't managed to get my eyes focused to stare right back.

Then I couldn't help myself. I laughed and laughed. I'd been thinking all along that Lowell Henry Eagen was a little on the wrong side of what's considered normal, shaking my hand over and over and treating me as if he'd found some long-lost childhood friend, but I had no idea how deep that feeling ran, enough to make him marry a black woman and bring her down to Louisiana. At least he had the sense to marry himself a nigger who didn't look like one, I told myself. At least he was smart enough for that.

I laughed enough to get Mollie laughing too, though it was clear she didn't know why I was doing it.

"You learned your lessons right," I told her. "You sure did."

"Yes, I did," she said.

"Well, it's a secret I'll keep, I swear it."

She stopped laughing and waited until I came to a stop myself. "It's not a secret," she said. "It's just not an issue."

"It's an issue for some, I'd guarantee."

"It shouldn't be."

"'Course not," I said, but I had to shake my head. This woman was not only a nigger, she was proving herself a half-minded one. She thought that by telling herself it wasn't an issue, it just wouldn't be. I could have told her then that she had a terrible sadness ahead of her. I didn't know, of course, what that sadness would be, and I sure didn't think I'd be its bearer, but it was clear from that moment on that she was headed for trouble.

After that night, I had a different reason to keep my distance from Mollie. She seemed to me like a woman bent on hanging from a cliff, and if I so much as felt kind-hearted enough to let her grab my hand, she'd send me tumbling down with her. So I stood by and watched while she did her best to prove her claim that being a nigger wasn't an issue. By proving it, she made it an issue, of course, but there was nothing I could tell her. So she let her secret slip out like it was no matter at all, talking about herself to the folks who strolled in and out of the house making deliveries of this or that or going out back to look at the statues and the garden Mollie kept so nice.

She wouldn't come right out and say she was a nigger, of course, but she said just enough about the mother and father who'd raised her and the lightning-smart brother living in Chicago that word got out. The blindest, dumbest rabbit's still got giant ears, my mother liked to say, and of course it's true.

At first the word about Mollie being a nigger was just a trickle as from a rusted pipe. But once it was clear to all concerned that the woman was pregnant, a black woman carrying a white man's child, the pipe burst and near everybody made it their business. The local folks stopped coming to buy Mr. Eagen's statues, and they stopped talking to him at Saint

Alphonse's. For a while, that was the extent of it, but around the time Mr. Thomas was set to be born, we got the full treatment — a cross burning just this side of the sea wall, directly out front of the house, along with letters slipped through the mail slot saying they'd do the same to all three of us.

I told Mr. Eagen he'd do well to take Mollie away for a while. I told him I'd see to the house until things died down. Mr. Eagen, though, wouldn't budge. He said you only get used to something when you live with it day in and day out.

"Some things people would rather do away with than get used to," I told him. "Cockroaches and niggers, for example." Mr. Eagen laughed, so I said, "And even cockroaches know enough to head for cover when someone switches on the light."

Like with everything else, Mr. Eagen laughed and laughed, as if he was having the grandest time. Instead of letting the matter quiet down, he made a phone call to New Orleans. He called some man he knew who worked for some Catholic newspaper called the *Clarion Herald*. They sent a boy over to do what he kept calling an intimate profile, complete with pictures of Mr. Eagen's statues and one of the charred earth where the cross had been burned, Mr. Eagen and Mollie standing over it with their backs to the lake. By then Mr. Thomas had been born, and Mollie held him in her arms wrapped in a blanket. They wanted me to stand there with them for that photograph, but I declined. Who wants their picture in the paper like that?

I told Mr. Eagen he was crazy for making news of his personal business. I said we soon wouldn't have two pennies to scrape together if we even had our own lives.

As is usually the case in my too-long life, however, I was wrong. All of a sudden a different kind of white person started flocking to the house, ones who wanted to sit and talk with Mr. Eagen and Mollie to all hours about equality and civil rights before looking over the statues, acting the whole while like they were precious works of art simply because Lowell Henry Eagen had himself a black wife and a black man in his basement he called his friend. We couldn't make enough statues to keep these folks satisfied.

Those days were something, and I confess to taking my own pleasure in so angering the seersucker-and-straw-hat Mandeville whites, while all the black folks on Sharp Street laughed and shook their heads. I knew they were thinking I was a man doing something peculiar with my life, living side by side with a white man and his Negro wife, stirring up the kind of trouble most black folks only dreamed about.

So how did I get from there to taking Mollie to bed? It's a question I've asked myself going on a million times. The years passed, and Mr. Thomas went from being a squirming baby to a holy terror, running through the house playing like he was an Indian, always on the lookout for a head to scalp. I put away near all my secret thoughts and glances concerning Mollie Moore, though I admit there were times at night when she still entered my dreams, each of those occasions scaring me so that I'd set about avoiding her company for a full twenty-four hours, thinking I could make the next night a peaceful one if I just kept her out of my sight.

We were all full happy, I thought, and the white folks grew comfortable ignoring us, holding their hate in check just long enough to say good morning when we all strolled in and out of Saint Alphonse's Church. When they decided on buying a new Virgin to replace the cracked one before the rectory door, they asked Mr. Eagen if he would do it. I guess they figured they didn't have a choice.

I say that we were all happy, and I mean to include Mollie in that list, for she had blossomed like all those harsh white stares were nothing but pure sunlight. She was most cheerful about having herself a child she could talk away the day to, her husband ten steps out the back door. One way or the other, though, being a nigger, light or dark, has its price, and Mollie seemed always on the verge of suffering, a half-step ahead of some shadow she didn't see so much as feel.

There were times when I thought the problem was just Mollie transplanting herself from North to South, like one of those plants that thrives in the wind and cold but can't stand the heat. I wish now I'd looked at the woman more closely in the little time I had. I wish I'd asked myself what there was in her being married to Lowell Henry Eagen that wasn't enough.

Maybe it was as simple as the few words that passed between us once, Mollie's head on my chest, the both of us listening for him. "He's a good man," I heard her say with such sadness. "Too good," I said back, and all was silence, the both of us feeling as if those statues out back had ears to hear even our quietest breaths.

But forget me. Forget Lowell Henry Eagen and all his goodness. How does a woman such as Mollie Moore decide to do what she did? I still don't know. Sometimes I think it's the not knowing that gave the woman such power over me, so much that I spent the rest of my life never wanting another woman in the same way I wanted her.

When Mr. Eagen went off for his walk every morning at dawn, Mollie brought me down a cup of coffee and set it by my bed, intent on talking me awake. Did I think it unusual for the woman, another man's wife, to come downstairs while I was still lying in my bed? I don't know. I don't think I thought much of anything except that Mollie was her own woman, filled with all these stories she liked to tell, glad to have my attention even while I shook the cobwebs out my head.

I don't know why Mollie chose me and not her rightful husband for the story of her life. Maybe she felt he wouldn't understand. When all that hatred bore down on them time and again, Lowell Henry Eagen lifted his eyes to heaven as if he was damn near thankful for the suffering. There was no cross too heavy for Lowell Henry Eagen to bear. But where was Mollie Moore supposed to lay down her cares? The good Lord wasn't whispering sweet comfort in her ears, as with her husband. She'd already listened for those words, I knew, and she wouldn't have missed them if they'd ever been there to hear. But all she'd heard was a cold wind and the sound of her own heart. That's not enough comfort. She needed more.

So Mollie said the same of me as she'd say of her husband,

though she meant it different. "You're a good man, Murphy Warrington," she'd tell me when she was finished telling one of her stories, like how her father had started a bank for Negroes in New York City but her mother kept her job as a domestic, the two of them taking the same bus from Harlem every morning then going their separate ways, her father in a suit and her mother in nurse's white.

"She'd come home at night crying tears over this white family's misfortunes or full of joy over their triumphs," Mollie told me. "Her own family was doing fine. We were Negroes with our own house and weekend money. My parents had a happy marriage. Still, she'd taken to the Evers family as if they belonged to her. Even my father didn't understand it. She dragged my brother and me to their funerals and weddings, and we sat in the back row like we were only there by chance, like we weren't truly invited. My father wouldn't go. He said she acted like a nigger servant, which of course she was. I felt the same as he did. We didn't need the money."

I only nodded and drank my coffee. She didn't want a word from me about her stories. She just wanted me to hear.

When she'd tell me I was a good man, I'd shake my head.

"No, I'm not," I'd tell her. "I only act good."

"Underneath?" she said.

"Cold as the devil," I told her.

I was only joking, but the woman believed me. Maybe that's why on the morning I reached out my hand and pulled her toward me, she let me do it. Maybe she felt like I was the devil after all and she had no choice. Sometimes I think she grew tired of all the airs she had to put on, constantly making sure everyone understood she was no worse a woman than any other, wearing the proper clothes, making proper conversation, holding her knife and fork and shoulders and feet in the proper manner, the whole time proper just another word for white.

I'm an old man now, sure enough, but I was a young man when I made her body bend into mine, a body that knew itself to be rightfully belonging to this earth as much as my own, shaking and terrified but no less certain than the moon passing through the night sky.

"This isn't right," she said over and over, and I told her I knew.

"You come here," I said. I didn't care.

It wasn't one time I pulled Mollie to me like that. It was one morning after the other for nearly two months, the whole time Mr. Eagen gone on his walk, Mr. Thomas still asleep in his bed. Again and again she walked down those stairs, only now I was lying there awake, waiting, full of thoughts as would send the world spinning in a new direction.

It's true the both of us held each other like we were always one moment from jumping away. All Mollie's conversation stopped. We both had the terrible fear that Mr. Eagen might return any moment, his feet scraping on the welcome mat three times before the screen door opened. All that listening kept me feeling as if I was standing just outside my own body and Mollie's. Even to this day I feel sometimes like I watched it all happen as much as I was the one taking that woman to bed, noticing from a distance the way my hands grabbed her back and shoulders, the way she fell into me like a stone into water.

I asked her once when we were lying there together why she'd chosen me.

"You chose me," she said, loosening her grip so that it was only my hands on her and not hers on me. I wondered then if she'd known all along of the secret attention I'd paid her, if she'd seen me watching her and knew by some fit of magic how she'd entered my dreams over and over. Maybe it was as simple as the woman holding in her head the knowledge of my secret devotion, that knowledge working on her the way my secret worked on me, getting the better of a clearer line of thinking, taking us down into the deep together.

꧁ ꧂

It was past thirty years later when I told Miss Catherine that story, when I sent her back to New Orleans with a promise I knew she wouldn't keep.

"Mr. Thomas has no need to know this," I said, and Miss Catherine just nodded her head. The poor woman.

I already knew, before I was even finished talking, that when Miss Catherine and her family came back to this house five days later, those rocking chairs would still be on the porch, untouched, and I'd be gone. I already knew this story I was telling the woman was one way of saying goodbye. I didn't know for certain when Miss Catherine would get around to telling Mr. Thomas. I just knew she would, and I knew I'd no longer be welcome. I hadn't deserved any welcome for thirty years but had stolen it as much as I'd stolen that watch from Judge Lancaster when I was a boy.

It was just this morning when I stole again, only the third time in a long life. But the thing that matters is what you steal, not how much. I knew I'd stolen something of Lowell Henry Eagen's and Mr. Thomas's own life, and there wasn't any way of paying that back.

Now I can do nothing but wait for the man to step inside the door and stand by my bed. This time, I figure, he's going to want to hear it straight from my mouth into his own ears. I swear, if I'd known this was how things would end up, I wouldn't have waited for God to get me like he did, making that goddamn bridge fall away beneath me like it was only air. I'd have done the job myself instead.

It's a worse price to pay to lie here waiting like this, so maybe that's the answer to why I didn't go ahead and drown.

Now I'm sick and tired of everything, and mostly myself. The clock on this wall ticks and ticks, but the arms don't move. It feels as though there will never be enough light scraped together to make it morning. Maybe I'll be lucky. Maybe there won't be.

MONDAY AFTERNOON, my father took us to see Murphy. He picked up Lowell and then me from school and drove over to Tulane Avenue, past the red-brick Fontainebleau Hotel with its neon sign that changed from light green to olive to blue, then past the Dixie Brewery with its gold domed roof. Perched on top of the roof was a giant beer can that Lowell claimed was really a water tower. "River water," Lowell said, leaning toward the windshield to see. "They have pipes running underground all the way to the Mississippi."

"Not really," my father said, looking over at me as though I actually might have believed it.

The three of us were riding in the front seat as we had on the causeway, since the back seat was still cluttered with clothes. It would be a week before my father told us to take everything inside, as if it took him that long to finally admit that we weren't going anywhere, that Mandeville might as well be on the other side of the globe. Even so, Lowell and I didn't take the clothes in. We just pulled things out as we needed them, as if the Checker's back seat were just one big closet.

Hotel Dieu — the House of God — was the hospital where Lowell and I had been born. That name made me feel as though my mother had died in God's presence, and as hard as it is for me to imagine now, I actually took some comfort from that fact. Wouldn't God, like anyone else, always pay attention to whoever was staying in his home? I asked myself. Wouldn't he see that they were comfortable and had everything they needed?

When I found out the truth from my grandfather about when and how my mother had died, he also told me that she'd had the chance to hold both Lowell and me before she took her last breath. I tried to imagine how that had felt, whether I'd so much as looked up at her face or had just cried and cried. It's hard to imagine being a tiny baby, so small that someone could hold you in one arm and pull you up against her, the other arm holding another tiny baby, my brother Lowell.

In the front hall of Hotel Dieu was a pink marble statue of Saint Vincent de Paul, more majestic and sober than the ones my grandfather made, with more of a pointed nose and angular jaw. I liked my grandfather's better because it was friendlier, less stern. That was true, in fact, of just about all of my grandfather's statues. They all looked as if were they suddenly to come to life, they'd want to laugh or shake your hand before going about their saintly business. They looked like the sort of saints who'd choose to spend their time among little children or providing comfort to the sick.

Behind the hospital's statue of Saint Vincent de Paul, there was a photograph on the wall of the Order of Charity nuns who ran Hotel Dieu, all of them lined up in rows in their habits as if they were a baseball team posing for a group picture. There was also a painted portrait of the pope, his cheeks done in a powdery bright red and his holy vestments a shiny, unbelievable pink. It almost made me laugh because the portrait was so overdone, as if the artist had been thinking that of course the pope would have rosier cheeks and brighter robes than anyone else on this earth.

I pointed to the portrait and Lowell laughed. He held his hand out to me and said, "You may kiss my ring."

That was too much for me, though, and I refused to do it.

My father gave Lowell and me both a stern look and led us along.

I was grateful to Lowell for the way he could turn anything into a joke, how he could make me feel, if only for a minute, that the circumstances we were in weren't all that unusual or difficult. I have wondered sometimes if it's Lowell and not me, despite all my affections, who has more of my grandfather's character, being able to find some measure of faith and belief in the goodness of life, its pleasures and rewards, no matter its pain and disappointments. Anyone could have looked at Lowell, at his easy confidence and grace, and said, *Here is a boy who will lead a good, happy life.*

At the hospital we took the elevator up to the second floor, and once we'd found the right room, my father left us standing in the hall while he went inside. I felt uncomfortable just standing there with all the nurses and doctors shooting past us, pushing metal carts this way and that and talking to each other in loud voices. I looked at Lowell, and he was staring down at his feet, lining them up along the edges of the gray tiles covering the floor.

"What are you thinking?" I asked him.

"Nothing," he said, without looking up.

"You must be thinking something," I told him.

"What about you?" Lowell asked, still lining up his feet on the tiles, putting the heel of one foot in front of the other.

"I'm thinking I don't want to go in there," I said. "What are we supposed to do? Act like we missed him?"

"I don't know," Lowell said.

I thought about leaving, going back down and waiting in the car, but then my father opened the door to Murphy's room and waved us in. Lowell and I walked in but stood back by the wall. I felt afraid, and instead of looking straight at Murphy, I looked past his bed to the window, which had curtains pulled all the way closed. There wasn't enough light in the room, only a single lamp on the wall above Murphy's head, shining down on him.

"Come on, children," Murphy said, and I saw him raise a

hand to wave us toward him. His fingers and palms were pale, gauze taped to the fingertips, and there was a needle and tube running into his wrist. I saw the clear liquid inside it moving one way, then the other, as he lifted, then lowered his arm.

"Miss Meredith. Mr. Lowell," Murphy said. He nodded twice, his voice little more than a whisper but as light and happy as it always had been, as if he were forever on the verge of remembering a joke someone had told him.

Murphy's body wasn't all swollen the way I'd expected it to be but instead looked thinner than ever, just a ripple under the white blanket, a blue hospital gown hanging off one of his bony shoulders.

"Hi, Murphy," Lowell said, taking a step toward the bed. "We thought you were dead."

Murphy laughed. "I thought so myself," he said, and he reached out to touch Lowell's arm, his long fingers wrapping around Lowell's elbow. Lowell let himself be pulled up against Murphy's bed, and he leaned down when Murphy lifted his other arm to put it behind his back. Murphy held Lowell against his chest and said, "I want you to know, young man, how good it is to touch another warm body. I did think I was dead, but I decided to settle for a brief swim. Don't let anyone tell you the Pontchartrain's not ice cold. It is."

Murphy let Lowell go, and Lowell looked over at my father and smiled. I figured Lowell had meant that he'd thought Murphy was dead these last two years and not from what happened on the bridge, but he didn't say anything. I kept my place by the wall, wondering where Murphy could have been all that time, disappearing from our life and then coming back as if it were nothing, as if we'd all just closed our eyes for a second and opened them to find ourselves staring at each other once again.

I thought of the day, a few weeks before we left, that Catherine and I, without telling my father, had gone to my mother's grave. I'd asked her if we could go. I'd gotten my first period that week, and I wanted to let Catherine know.

If there is irony in the fact that I wanted to visit my mother, dead from childbirth, the week my own body readied itself for bearing children, I don't make much of it. Visiting my mother's grave had simply seemed a serious enough excursion to warrant the sort of discussion I longed to have.

Once I'd told Catherine my news, she was as sweet to me as she possibly could be. After we left the cemetery, she took me out to buy a new dress and a pocketbook. She acted as though what I'd told her was cause for celebration rather than concern, and I am grateful today for her kindness.

Catherine told me I should think of my body as a grand and glorious mystery that I'd get to know better year by year. "There'll be pains," she told me, "and it won't be pleasant. Sometimes you'll think you've been singled out for the worst sort of misery." She held my hand the whole time she spoke, touching my fingertips one by one with her own.

"It's a misery not one man in the whole world will understand, though they think they do," she said. "That's a lonely feeling but a blessing, too, you'll find out."

"What's the blessing?" I asked her.

She laughed and said, "Well, that's a good question. You learn forgiveness, I guess."

At the cemetery, when we decided to take a walk after standing for a while by my mother's grave, I asked Catherine about her own mother, what she had been like.

"When I was born," Catherine said, "it was five years after the youngest of my brothers. With five children now, my mother knew I was the last, and I think she treated me with a special kindness because of that. I know she did. She liked to tell me that when I was a baby and woke up crying in the middle of the night, she'd scoop me up out of my crib and nurse me and then just hold me in her arms the rest of the night. I asked how she managed to get enough sleep, and she answered by saying, 'Sleep is for the weary, and a child sweeps all your weariness aside.' I admired her so for knowing to say such things as that."

Catherine waited a few seconds and then said, "I'm sorry. You know, it was a terrible shame you were asked to live your first five years without a mother."

I told her I'd been too little to remember much at all. I knew that we'd had maids who lived in our house and cared for us. I remembered different things about each one: Nancy's braided hair, the spicy food Corriene prepared that my father said wasn't fit for children, Delrita's loud laugh.

"Still, you didn't really know what a mother was," Catherine said, as if she were talking to herself and not to me, as if she were the one who thought there was a difference between the mother who gives birth to you and whoever raises you.

"I did," I said, and I thought of all the picture books I'd read as a little girl, how I had always paused to study the mothers who bent at the waist to listen to their children or to lift them into their arms. I thought of the mothers on our block who brought their babies outside on warm days and let them lie on blankets laid out in the shade on their lawns.

I also thought then of the way stepmothers were presented in so many stories, as pale and thin women with stringy hair, a secret cruelness revealed by the corners of their mouths when they smiled. Catherine was not like that, not ever. There was never a moment of cruelty in her manner. I wanted to tell her, although I couldn't find the right words, that the time she had been with us seemed somehow to stretch back through the years, casting her kindness over them as well.

But standing in Murphy's hospital room, I felt as though Catherine had simply disappeared. And here, in her place, was Murphy. I didn't understand why we were here visiting him instead of finding out how Catherine was doing. It was as if for no good reason my father had shifted the feeling in his heart from his wife to this old, nearly drowned black man.

"Miss Meredith," Murphy said. I looked at him. He shook his head, closing and opening his eyes as if he were trying to wake himself from a dream. "Well, I sure was right," he whispered. "I always knew you were going to be a tall one."

"I'm not," I told him. I was already two inches shorter than Lowell.

"Well, a young lady doesn't want to be too tall, in any case," he said, and he closed his eyes again.

My father was standing at the foot of Murphy's bed. He had his arms folded across his chest, and I wondered if that's where he stood when he talked to his hospital patients, telling them good news or bad — that their injuries would never get completely better or that they'd soon be as good as new.

My father leaned down and put a hand on Murphy's bed, touching Murphy's foot through the blanket and holding it. I felt at that moment like I needed to scream, like that was the only thing I could possibly do. I can't think of any other time in my life except for one when I thought of my father, looked at him, and felt something like hate rising up in me.

That other time, so many years later, was when my father stood up in my grandfather's garden after pronouncing my name, refusing to talk about the causeway's collapse and all that had followed for us. I didn't say anything to him when he stepped away from the table. I didn't know what to say. So I let him go inside the house and shut the door before I called after him, before I stood up myself and cried out.

"Please," I said again, yelled, pounding my fists on the table. I don't know if my father even heard me, although I imagine he must have. And hearing me, what did he do? Did he consider how it had come to be that he had no way to offer the least bit of comfort to his daughter, to hold me in his arms, to tell me that he had meant well, that he was sorry?

Over and over I have wondered if my father ever wished that he had said something to me, that he had been able finally to talk about all that had happened. I don't mean to say that I hope he died with this regret on his mind. I don't need to wish such punishment on him. He'd had enough of that. But I would like to think that my father had at least spun the story through his head enough times to reach a single conclusion — that he owed his children something for standing beside him, for choosing to stay with him as we had.

I realize now that what I needed from my father was not so much an apology as some expression of gratitude, even if that gratitude was offered, years later, over something as apparently inconsequential as the weekend visits Lowell and I separately made during those final months — when he was living alone in Mandeville, when he'd finally made his way to the house he'd tried to get to twenty-five years before. Without those visits, all that would have been left for him were hours and hours he would have to fill as best as he could, listening to jazz records, sitting alone in the garden, considering the ways in which loss had overtaken him time and again throughout his life.

Standing in that dark hospital room, looking at my father, at Murphy, at Lowell, I didn't say anything. No one said anything. Then Murphy turned his head to look at us one by one, and he shut his eyes.

"We're going to leave now," my father said. "Murphy needs some rest." He let go of Murphy's foot.

Murphy closed his eyes and tried to push himself up in his bed, the hospital gown pulling further off his shoulder. My father walked over to Lowell and me.

"In a few days," he said, "when Murphy is discharged, he's going to come stay with us."

"That would be fine, Mr. Thomas," Murphy said.

"We'll go from there," my father said, still looking at Lowell and me.

"I thank you," Murphy said. "I'm grateful."

My father walked around the bed and put a hand on Murphy's bare shoulder. "We'll see you tomorrow," he said.

"I'm not getting up, believe me," Murphy said. "You'll find me right here." He laughed for just a moment and then stopped.

"Good," my father said, and we walked out of the room. Lowell closed the wide door behind him.

"He looks old," Lowell said as soon as we stepped away from the door.

"He's fine," my father said. "He just needs to rest."

We started down the hall, but a doctor who knew my father was heading toward us, and we stopped to say hello. Lowell and I had never met this man before, so my father introduced us, putting his hands on our backs, the signal that we should shake hands. We did.

"Twins," the doctor said, laughing, which was the way most people acted when they met Lowell and me, as if we'd dropped down from another planet, as if we were testament to some mysterious force in the universe.

The doctor nodded at Murphy's door and said, "A patient?"

"No," my father said. "We're just visiting."

"Family?"

"No," my father said, acting as if he were ready to go. The doctor stood there, though, with his hands in his white coat.

"How's Cathy?" he asked.

My father waited for a second and then said, "She's fine. We're doing fine. We should go."

Lowell shook himself free of my father's hand, which was still resting on his back, and marched off toward the elevator.

I left my father behind and ran to catch up. "Lowell?" I said.

"I'm okay," he told me.

"No, you're not," I said.

"Yes, I am," he said. "It's just he's a liar. He's the one."

"I know," I said.

My father walked up, and Lowell pushed the button for the elevator. My father grabbed Lowell's arm and pulled him around. "Listen," he said. "This is no one else's business. You understand. You don't just tell people these things."

"It will get pretty obvious, don't you think?" Lowell said, shaking himself free again.

My father looked as though he was about to slap Lowell — something he'd never done — but he didn't. "Yes, it will," he said. Then he looked over at me, but I felt frozen and couldn't move. The elevator door opened, and Lowell stepped in.

My father stayed where he was, and the elevator door closed. "Let's give him a few minutes," my father said.

We waited, my father looking at me as if he expected me to say something, then he pushed the button on the wall and we heard the elevator cables creaking.

Standing in the elevator, the floor shaking beneath our feet, I thought of the time Lowell and I had gone with my grandfather to deliver a statue to a church in Belle Chase, Louisiana, a few miles down the Mississippi River from New Orleans. It was a Saturday morning, and my grandfather and Murphy had stopped at our house on the way. When Lowell and I said we wanted to go along, Catherine said we could. Lowell asked my grandfather if he could ride in the back of the truck along with the bundled statue we were going to deliver, but my grandfather said Murphy would.

"Please," Lowell said. "I really want to. I do."

My grandfather said no again, that it wasn't safe, and he swung open the door and motioned for Lowell and me to climb in.

Lowell sulked the whole way to Belle Chase, ignoring my grandfather's questions about school, his head turned to look out the side window.

The church in Belle Chase was named Sainte Jeanne d'Arc. When wc arrived the monsignor was standing in front of the rectory, waiting for us. I watched my grandfather and Murphy lift the heavy statue out of the truck. I hadn't asked my grandfather who the statue depicted, and before they unwrapped it I wondered if it would be Saint Joan. I'd seen one before that my grandfather had done, her long hair splayed across her armored shoulders, her head tilted up toward heaven, the blank gaze on her face somehow suggesting both defiance and resignation.

The statue my grandfather had brought, though, wasn't Joan but Saint Fiacre the Venerable, his hands held together in prayer, his head bowed so that his beard touched his chest, the knotted ends of the rope tied at his waist hanging down to his knees. My grandfather and Murphy placed the statue among a group of others in the rectory garden. There was no statue of Joan there, and I wondered why not until I looked up at the top of the church's tower, where usually there would just be a cross, and there she was, covered in gold paint, a great gold shield across her chest.

Once the statue was in place and the monsignor had handed my grandfather an envelope and thanked him, we looked for Lowell but didn't see him. We all called for him, Murphy heading over to the cemetery out back, my grandfather and I going into the church. When we didn't see him there, we went back outside. The monsignor raised his hand, smiled, and pointed to two Japanese plum trees at the far end of the garden. Lowell was standing between them, his hands held together and his head bowed exactly like the statue we had just delivered.

I looked at my grandfather, who looked down at me with a stern expression. He took my hand and we walked over to Lowell together. The monsignor followed us. We stood before Lowell, directly in front of him, but he still didn't move. "So this is the old block of stone, Monsignor, I'm expected to drag back with me."

The monsignor laughed, and Lowell did, too, though he kept his head down. My grandfather continued frowning. "I'd like to meet the man who thought to form this pathetic creature," he said.

Murphy had stepped up, and my grandfather turned to him. "Throw this bit into the back of the truck, would you, Murphy?" my grandfather said. "We'll make rubble of it later."

And Murphy stepped up to Lowell and took him in his arms, Lowell keeping his body stiff as long as he could manage. Murphy gently threw him on top of the mattress in the back of the truck and slammed the truck's gate.

"Let's be off," my grandfather said, and I climbed in between him and Murphy. Once we were out on the highway and moving fast, I turned to look back at Lowell through the tiny window behind me. He was clinging to the mattress, afraid that a bump would send him tumbling out. But he was smiling, his hair blowing across his face, his eyes nearly shut from the force of the wind.

"He's okay," I said to my grandfather. "He's fine."

"He's soon to be rubble," my grandfather said. "That's for sure." But he was smiling, too.

"That's the Lord's sweet grace upon you children," my grandfather said then, putting his arm around me. "He mends your hearts even more swiftly than they're broken."

Going down in the hospital's elevator, I wondered how long what my grandfather had said of us would remain true, how long we could expect our hearts to keep healing.

We found Lowell waiting in front of the hospital, sitting on a bench, his eyes red.

"I'm sorry, son," my father said to him, sitting down.

"I know," Lowell answered. He stood up, and my father reached for his arm, but Lowell stepped away.

"I can't do more than apologize right now," my father said. "I know you want to hear more, but an apology is all I've got."

"I know," Lowell said again, and he headed off for the car.

We rode home with Lowell sitting in the back seat, all the clothes pushed over to the side and spilling in his lap. He kept his face up near the window. When my father tried to get him to talk, he wouldn't.

That's the way things went the whole week, with Lowell or me or my father feeling fine one moment and then the next moment not wanting to say a word. It was as if we were all just rusted wheels inside a clock, our edges so worn we were never quite grabbing hold of one another long enough to have things work the way they were supposed to.

My father didn't talk about Catherine, at least not to me. He didn't say when we might go to Mandeville, or even if we were still planning to go. I went to school and didn't say a word to anyone about what had happened. I wondered and wondered so much I couldn't keep track of my own thinking.

You'd think it would have been an easy thing just to pick up the phone and call Catherine, but it wasn't. After we'd been gone only a few days, I already felt afraid that if I did call, she wouldn't recognize my voice. Or when she said hello, I might not be sure it was her. I needed to see her face again, not just talk to her on the phone.

What I remember most about that first week on Magazine Street, though, was how full the house was of silence. We didn't have music the way we always had before, and my father didn't walk the floors singing his favorite songs.

Though he didn't say so, I knew Lowell missed listening to music most of all. At home he'd spent hours and hours curled up on the living room couch, nodding his head while he played one record after the other and read the back of the album covers. My father would sit down with him, and they'd talk about music as if it were the most important thing in the world. Maybe Lowell was drawing his pictures of houses and faces when he disappeared into his bedroom every night after dinner, but I didn't know for sure because he locked the door and wouldn't let me in.

I tried to do my homework but couldn't. One night I felt so cooped up I asked my father for some money to go down to the Woolworth's. I didn't think he would let me go, but he did. He said yes, just as if we were living in the middle of a normal neighborhood with front lawns and playing children, instead of being stuck amid a row of dusty secondhand shops, every object in those stores something that at least one person had decided wasn't worth owning.

Once, someone had called my father the Secondhand Surgeon because of his office's being set among all those stores and probably also because all his patients seemed as used up as the furniture and books and clothes lined up behind those dirty windows. I'd thought he would take offense at that name, but instead he seemed proud of it. A friend of my father's who made signs for a living — that was the sort of person my father liked and admired, much more than other doctors — carved the name into a piece of wood, and my father put it on the door of his private study, which was overflowing with medical books and old x-rays and his few framed photographs of Lowell and me, most of them taken when we were still babies, our heads bald, both of us smiling at who knows what.

The sign had a hand carved into it, the five fingers as thin and crooked as a dead tree's limbs, and beneath that was written THOMAS EAGEN, M.D., THE SECONDHAND SURGEON. The whole sign was painted a shiny gold, which was probably meant to make it look expensive but had the opposite effect instead, as if it had been molded from cheap plastic instead of carved from an old oak tree the way my father said it was.

The night I walked down to the Woolworth's, I asked Lowell to go with me, but he said no. "I'm busy," he said, and he closed his bedroom door practically before it was even open. So I walked the five blocks down Magazine alone. It must have been before eight o'clock, because that was when the Woolworth's closed, but it was already dark outside and a little cold.

There is nothing so much as walking through the night to make a child feel grown up, like she's been cast out on her own and has to make the best of it. Although I was a little scared, I also felt happy to be out like that. I felt as if I could do whatever I wanted. I could use the money my father had given me to take a cab to go see Catherine, if that's what I chose, or buy a pack of cigarettes to try again what it felt like to smoke, something I'd done before, stealing a pack of my father's Chesterfields but throwing them away after I took in one breath only to cough and cough.

So I was almost feeling happy walking along Magazine, the first time I'd felt that way since my father had told us we'd be leaving. At Woolworth's I went ahead and bought a black notebook with blank white pages, which I was going to use to make an album with my grandfather's photographs, and I walked back outside and was heading home when a man started walking right next to me.

At first the man didn't say anything, so I just looked up and said hello and tried to walk a little faster.

This man had a nice face, really, with black hair that he must have put oil in because it was shining from the streetlights, a circle of light reflecting off his head. He wasn't limping the way my father did when he walked, but there was something that wasn't right about the way he moved, as if his body couldn't get the motion quite right; one of his feet turned in at an odd angle. He kept up with me, though, even when I got scared and started going faster and faster.

"Excuse me," the man said.

"I can't talk," I told him. "I'm going home."

"Yes, you're going home," he said. "Where's home?"

"Right there," I said, pointing ahead even though I was still two blocks from my father's office.

"Who's home?" the man said. There were people standing on the street all around us, conversations we had to step through to get past. I looked for someone I could walk up to and pretend they were my family. *I'm home now,* I could have said if I'd found someone, but I didn't.

I don't know what it is about being afraid that makes you see and remember the smallest things, but I think back to that moment and feel as though I can still see today every detail I noticed — the precise cracks in the sidewalk, the strange angle of that man's feet and the shape of my own in their pointy black loafers, the warped green shutters on every window, one covered in dark green ivy that didn't seem to be growing up from anywhere.

"Who's home?" the man said again. His coat brushed against my shoulder, and his hand touched the back of my coat. I started running but tripped the way women always do in movies, allowing the murderer time to catch up.

"Is your mother home?" the man said, leaning down to help me up.

I don't know why I did, but I shook my arm free and answered, "My mother's dead."

The man stopped walking. "My mother's dead, too," he said. He began looking around, as if he'd suddenly realized he was lost.

I'm sorry, I thought. *I'm sorry for you.* And I ran home the rest of the way. I'm not sure today whether the man actually was dangerous or whether, believing that the neighborhood might be unsafe, he simply meant to help me home.

Once I reached my father's office, I ran inside and went straight up to my bedroom and shut the door. I sat on my bed and sorted through my grandfather's photographs, separating them into categories: saints and birdbaths and gravestones and all the cemetery decorations, the tiny creatures and little books and musical instruments and perfect flowers. I looked at every one of the photographs. There were hundreds and hundreds of them. I felt as if I were still running, still out of breath, and I kept hearing my own voice in my head until it sounded like someone else's. *I'm sorry for you,* the voice kept saying. *I'm sorry. I am.*

I thought of Catherine's mother and the one letter she'd sent me. "Even for an old woman like me, these are days of grace," she'd written, "with the evening din of locusts, the church bells ringing through the dry air of autumn, the fine smell of cracked mud." She'd said how she would always drag her husband back outside each evening to watch the way the setting sun caught the changing colors of the leaves.

What else? I didn't remember. Had she been a good mother to Catherine? Had she written letters like that to her own daughter, full of words that sounded like they came from poems?

When my father knocked on my door, I told him to come in.

"You okay?" he said.

I made room on the bed for him to sit down, but he didn't.

"I'm going off for a while. I'll be back soon," he said. "You should go to bed."

"I will," I said. "I'm tired."

When my father turned to go, I asked him to stop. "Will you at least tell me one thing?" I said. "Will you at least tell me if we're going to see Catherine again?"

"I don't know," he said, shaking his head.

"I want to," I told him.

"I know you do," he said.

"Then why can't we?"

"We just can't. Not right now." He walked over and touched the top of my head.

"This isn't fair," I said.

"I know it's not."

"Why can't you just tell me why we left?" I said.

"We didn't have a choice," my father said. "I didn't. It's complicated."

"We could have just stayed," I said. "That's a choice."

My father moved away from me again, toward the bedroom door. He put his hand out and leaned against the wall. "I have to go out for a little while," he said. "You need to go to bed."

"We could have stayed," I said, and I started crying. "We could have."

"We couldn't," my father said, and I could tell from his voice he was getting angry, though his face looked exactly the same.

"Why couldn't we?" I asked.

"Meredith," my father said, "if we had stayed, then Catherine would have ended up leaving." He stopped for a moment, looked down at his hands, then looked back to me. "Maybe I wouldn't have wanted her to leave, but she would have," he said. "If you look at it like that, we didn't have a choice." He stood in the doorway and stared down at the floor.

"That doesn't make sense," I said. "I don't understand."

"I know you don't," my father said. "I'm not sure I do, either. But right or wrong, I decided that we didn't love each other anymore. Do you understand that?"

"No," I said.

"You need to go to bed, Meredith."

"I still want to talk to her."

"Of course," he said. "I do, too. Believe me, I do. But that doesn't mean it's what I should do. Now go to bed. I'll check up on you when I come back."

My father closed my bedroom door, and I heard him go down the stairs.

I sat on my bed with all those photographs scattered around me, and I cried and cried, crying not for Catherine but for my grandfather, wanting him to be alive again so he could hold me in his arms and go through each one of those photographs and tell me every one of his stories. I wanted him to tell me about my father before I was born, the kind of boy he'd been, how all those Jesuit priests had sat by his hospital bed for hours and hours, teaching him history and math and English and Latin, my father getting smarter and smarter the whole time.

My grandfather had told me it was a good thing that my father was able to become a doctor rather than spending his whole life making garden statuary. He said there was nothing so grand as saving a life.

My grandfather also told me that once, when my father was away at Tulane Medical School, he'd had a dream that every statue he'd ever made had broken. He'd looked at the statues one by one and thought his whole life's work had been ruined. But then in the dream my father had appeared and reached out his hand to touch every statue, and they were all whole again.

"That's the miracle doctors perform," my grandfather told me. "I'd needed a reminder that was so. I needed to put aside my own hopes for him."

"What had you wanted him to do?" I asked.

"It doesn't matter," my grandfather told me. Then he lifted me and held me in his arms. "Remember this. You should love your father for his goodness, not his failings. That's what we're told. That's what Christ said we should do. It's what I've tried to do."

I asked my grandfather what my father's failings were, and he shook his head. "They change with each season and year to year," he told me. "That's true for everyone."

Looking through the photographs on my bed, I wondered what my father's failings were now. What would my grandfather say about his own son's leaving his wife, the way his wife had left him? It had always seemed to me that my grandfather had never been married, had never had a wife. I wondered if years later that's how my father would seem to me and to the children I might have. They'd think it perfectly natural that my father lived alone. They wouldn't be able to imagine his life any other way. What would I tell them? I didn't know. That was too far away even to consider.

My father left us for a few hours every night that week. He wouldn't say where he was going when I asked. "I'll be back soon," he said each time. "Go to sleep."

Once he'd left, though, I would get up and knock on Lowell's door. Each time, he'd say he was busy.

"Come on, Lowell. Let me in," I'd tell him, but he wouldn't. I felt desperate and tried to pray, but I didn't know what to ask for except for everything to go back to the way it had been before. I wondered where my father went at night, if maybe he went back to our house and tried to talk things out with Catherine. But wouldn't he have told me if that's what he was doing? I didn't know.

Those first nights on Magazine Street were as long as I've ever known. I tried to get used to the feeling of being in a different house, of having different walls around me, staring up at the swirling, cracked white plaster on the ceiling. As silent as everybody was, the house itself was full of noise. The floors creaked and stretched even when no one was walking on them. The water pipes gurgled and shook. The radiators beneath the windows rattled and spit.

I lay in bed and thought of the picture book my grandfather had once given me, about a family living in a two-hundred-year-old house where the peeling paint curled away from the walls in beautiful wrapping-paper strips and the rooms were lit by halo-circled candles and a soothing fireplace. This house wasn't like that.

That family in the picture book had moved into the house because they'd lost their city house in a fire, so they all moved to the country and worked together to make the house look like new, finding things as they cleaned up that told them all about what their great-great-grandparents' life had been like. They found old letters with wax seals and dried flowers pressed between the pages of a Bible, one that had a family tree inside the front cover, every branch with a name and other branches shooting out of it, reminding the grandfather of stories he would otherwise have forgotten, stories he told to his grand-children while they sat around the fire.

I was still awake when my father got home every night, though I pretended to be asleep when he opened my door and came in to look at me. Then I'd hear him sitting in the living room, turning the pages of a book or magazine, putting it down and picking up another, his cigarette lighter clicking open and closed.

Sometimes my father went downstairs to his office, and I'd hear him walking from room to room, his worn slippers scraping the floor. Catherine had said that because of his bad leg, his walk sounded like a waltz. Sometimes when I was sitting with Catherine but neither one of us was saying anything, I'd look at her and know she was listening to my father moving through our house, a waltz going through her head while she followed his steps.

Lowell once said my father sounded to him like a sea captain with a wooden leg, and Catherine had laughed. "That's what he thinks, too, I bet," she'd said.

At night, I missed Catherine more than I could ever have imagined. I thought of the million times she'd looked at me just as if I were her own daughter, her arms always out to take me in. I didn't believe my father when he said that she would have left if we hadn't. He was just lying. I knew he was. So I fell asleep every night thinking of Catherine with her arms empty but outstretched and waiting.

That week, after we visited Murphy in the afternoon, my father still had patients to see; the waiting room was filled by the time we got back. In the past my father had occasionally hired a nurse to help him out at the office, to send in the patients from the waiting room one by one. Even before he'd brought Murphy to New Orleans, though, he'd given up on hiring help. He couldn't afford it anymore, Catherine had told me. She'd say the wolf was not quite but almost at our door, and I didn't understand exactly what she meant but knew enough not to ask. Wolves were dangerous.

That first week, Lowell spent a lot of his time in the afternoons wandering along Magazine Street, going into all the different shops. Usually, I just went upstairs and tried to do my homework, but that Friday I went with him instead. He'd already made friends with the shop owners who sat reading or listening to music behind their dusty counters, which were really glass cases filled with odds and ends, old jewelry or ugly ceramic vases or yellowed linen. The dark pieces of furniture were arranged in the shops as if waiting for someone to use them, as if Lowell and I had mistakenly wandered into the house of someone who'd died years before and no one had come around to clean things up. There were faded silk flowers on the tables, old coats thrown across the backs of chairs, postcards stuffed into creaky desk drawers.

Lowell rifled through everything and no one seemed to care.

He sat down in the torn-cushioned chairs. He stuck his head into cabinets and rapped his knuckles against the wood as if he knew what he was doing. "Come on, Lowell," I said. "Let's go somewhere else."

"You can go if you want," he told me. "No one's keeping you here."

One of the shops had old records stacked in cardboard boxes, and that was where Lowell spent most of the afternoon. He flipped through the records and pulled them out, holding them up to the light to look for scratches. We didn't have any money, but Lowell pretended we did, saying that this Art Tatum record was a good deal and so was the Tommy Dorsey because Sinatra was singing, but the Billie Holiday was not. "You should hear her voice on this. It was already ruined," he said, and I thought of my father's voice, wondering if it could be ruined, too. Maybe one day he'd wake up and not be able to sing. Maybe that had already happened.

After Lowell was finished looking at records, I told him I had an idea, something I'd been thinking about all week. "Let's get some money from Dad," I told him. "Then we could take a cab and go see Catherine."

"What?" Lowell said, staring at me.

"We could go to the house," I said.

Lowell said goodbye to the shop owner and nearly pushed me out the door to the street.

"Well?" I said.

"She's not there," Lowell said, rolling his eyes as if he were talking to an idiot.

"How do you know?" I asked him.

"I just do," he said.

"Lowell," I said. "Can't you just talk like a normal person? How do you know she's not there? Did you call?"

"Dad said so."

"To who?" I asked.

"Who do you think?" he said. He waved to a black man walking past us.

The man waved back and said, "Hey, Lowell. What's the time?"

"No time at all," Lowell said, and they both laughed. The man stepped into the shop we'd just left.

"Who was that?" I asked.

"Jerome," Lowell said. "He works there."

"Jesus, Lowell," I said.

"What?"

"Nothing," I told him, but I felt exasperated. Why would my father tell Lowell things he didn't tell me?

I left Lowell and went back to my father's office, where I went straight upstairs and locked myself in my room. We'd gone out for dinner every night after my father finished seeing patients, before he left to go wherever it was he went, but I decided that I wouldn't go that night, that I'd skip dinner and not talk to Lowell or my father. They could call me, and I wouldn't answer.

When my father did knock on my door, though, he said we needed to go back to the hospital. "They're going to discharge Murphy," my father said. "We need to go get him."

"I don't want to go," I said. "I'll stay here."

My father waited for a second. "Are you sure that's what you want? I'd like you to go."

"I'd like to stay here," I said.

I heard my father let his breath out. "Okay," he said. "That's fine. Don't open the door, though, and don't go out."

"Where would I go?" I said.

My father acted as if he hadn't heard me. "We'll be back," he said. "Stay here."

I heard my father and Lowell go down the stairs and close the front door. I waited a minute and then walked out of my room. I dialed our number at home, but no one answered. I didn't know the number of Catherine's father in North Carolina, but I just dialed the operator, and she switched me over to one in North Carolina. That operator asked me what city I wanted, and I told her Pittsboro. "Henry Reynolds," I told her, and she gave me the number. It was that easy.

I dialed the phone, and after just one ring Catherine answered.

"Hello?" she said, and I tried to say hello back but couldn't.

"Who is it?" Catherine said. "Hello?" There was a moment of silence, then she hung up.

I don't know why I hadn't been able to talk. I hadn't believed Lowell, I guess, that Catherine had really left. I hadn't believed my father that we didn't have a choice about leaving. Now I did. I hung up the phone and started crying.

I picked it up and dialed the number again, wanting to curse and scream, but I hung up before the first ring.

At that moment I felt that no one in the world had a worse family than mine, that it kept getting divided into pieces until there was just about nothing left. I wished now I'd gone with Lowell and my father to get Murphy. I wished I'd never picked up the phone.

I walked to the living room and looked out the window. I decided I wouldn't do anything except stand there until they got back. I'd look at the streetlight until my father's car appeared beneath it. Then I'd go down the stairs with easy, graceful steps. I'd welcome Murphy inside as if he were my best friend, letting him pull me up against him the way he'd done with Lowell. "I'm glad you're okay," I'd tell him. "I'm glad you're here." Then I'd kiss my father and say *I love you.* I'd even tell Lowell I loved him, too.

I looked up from the street to my reflection in the window and saw that I'd stopped crying. I felt better. I heard my grandfather's voice in my head just like the time he'd carried me into the house after pulling me off Saint Francis's shoulder. "Good for you," my grandfather had said, and that's what I heard now in my head. "Good for you."

Just like that, I had decided I was going to be fine. I would have to be.

DEAR MEREDITH,

Well, tonight I don't feel you're as lost to me as I did this last week, but I can't say the same for your father, who is determined not just to break my heart and spirit but to trample both like they're just so much dust under his shoes.

He called here tonight, less than an hour ago. With the phone's first ring, I knew it was him.

I looked over at my father, his feet up on the coffee table and his shoes off. His dusty wool socks had slipped down and looked to me like an elf's feet in those jangly slippers.

"Go ahead, Cathy. You get it," he said. "It's probably some fool selling cemetery plots."

He laughed, but under his circumstances it struck me as a pitiful thing to say, and I thought even at that moment, with the phone ringing again, of what it would be like to lose him, having just lost my other family. You don't know how much worry I've had hanging over my head on his account as well as yours.

I let the phone ring one more time and picked it up. The first thing your father said, not even bothering to say hello, was that he was thinking of me and wanted to make sure I was okay. I could hardly believe it. He had the same tone of voice as the one he'd use when calling from the hospital to let me know he'd be there most of the night — apologetic, all right, but full of a secret excitement he couldn't quite disguise. Give your father a choice between chaos and contentment, and he'll choose chaos every time. Maybe that explains just about everything.

Almost the first thing I did was ask him to put you on the line, but he said you were already asleep. I believed that for half a second, but then it occurred to me you're an hour earlier so for you it wouldn't even be nine o'clock.

"Thomas Eagen, where are you?" I said, and he told me he'd left you both just for a few minutes and was calling from a public phone.

"Murphy's with them," he said, and I admit I gasped for air. That wasn't what I expected.

"You go back to your children," I told him, and he said he would as soon as we were done.

"I wanted to make sure you were okay," he said.

"Why wouldn't I be?" I answered. I was already mad.

"I also wanted to tell you what happened," he said.

"Well," I asked, "what did?"

Then he told all you've been through, the causeway falling like it did and Murphy ending up in the water and almost drowning.

I don't know what good it does to say it now, but I'm sorry. I'm sorry you had to live through such a thing as that. You don't know the fear that shot through me while your father spoke, even though I knew you and your brother were safe at home. It's been eight days since that morning, but I felt like the causeway was falling just then.

Of course, your father contributed to that feeling by telling the story the same as he tells all others, holding out on where he's going to end up until you're practically clawing at him to get the words out. I swear I clenched my jaw the whole time and didn't let up until he said, "We're all fine. We weren't hurt."

Why didn't your father call me before, Meredith, right after it happened? I asked him that, and I bet you could guess what he did. He just sighed and said "Cathy," like pronouncing my name was enough explanation. He's done that to you, I know, acting like his thoughts and feelings run so deep there's no way he can even get started on them. Lord knows he's an exasperating man.

I'll be the first to admit there are times when saying a name is actually enough to cover everything you feel. I've felt that way beginning these letters, as if all my love is contained in just spelling out your name at the top of the page and everything after that isn't really of consequence, as if these words are meant more for my own peace of mind than for yours, which is probably true.

You don't know this, but when I first married your father, I decided I'd write you letters you could read once you'd grown up yourself and married. I thought to fill them with all manner of thoughts you'd find useful, pointing out all the shapes love takes on when your life is tied forever to another's.

I was so young, Meredith. I found, when I sat down to write those letters, that I could hardly get down anything more than baby talk. The problem was I couldn't imagine you as being any older than you were. Even more than that, I couldn't imagine your father and I as how old we would be, a few years from being grandparents to the children you would bear. The very thought scared me into silence, and I tore up the few things I'd written.

So I feel some accomplishment in what I'm writing here. How is it that with so much uncertainty I now feel ready to write you everything, no matter what? Maybe it says more about you than me. Maybe it says that already, just that quick, you've grown up enough for me to see you as a woman and not a girl.

You don't know how close you are. You're lucky in that respect. Even through all this, though, I want you to know I still believe being a woman is a gift from God. Of course, it's one of those gifts that requires a momentous effort on your part, like a beautiful Oriental chest that arrives in the mail inside a giant cardboard box with the words ASSEMBLY RE-QUIRED printed on it in big red letters.

That's a funny thought, isn't it? Well, that's the way my mind is working right now, and I won't apologize for it, though I'm now as guilty as your father of putting off what you want to know for the sake of some stray-dog thoughts.

I'll get back to it now. When your father just sat on the phone in silence after pronouncing my name the way he had, I said, "What else is it that you have to say, Thomas?" I was implying that I was ready to hang up the phone, which I was.

"I don't know," your father said. "This isn't how I wanted it to be."

"How did you want it to be, Thomas?" I asked him. That's what you have to do with your father sometimes, Meredith — lead him from one sentence to the next like a dog unused to a leash. Otherwise, he'll try to take off in a different direction and just about strangle himself.

But what was his answer? It was "I'm sorry. I can't talk about this."

"Then don't," I said. "Go back to your children."

But he didn't want to get off the phone just yet, as if he could take his own dose of comfort from me just by staying on the line, feeling that we were somehow connected. So he went on to tell me whatever he could think to say, including how Murphy was released from the hospital Friday (it's Monday now) and is staying with you. I told your father that even so, he should take you all back to the house so you'd have a decent place to live, but he said he didn't think he was going back there.

"You weren't leaving that house, Thomas. You were leaving me," I told him, but all I got in return was your father's silence. "Well, you do what you want," I said.

I thought then about the way your father's mind works. He didn't want to go back to that house, I knew, because he was afraid he'd start longing for my presence, waking up confused in the middle of the night, believing I should be lying there next to him. He knew he'd get up and walk from room to room only to feel I was around the next corner. Your father does love me, Meredith. That's the shame of it. He's just afraid, and he thinks that fear is truer than all his other feelings combined.

What's he afraid of? That's what you're asking, isn't it? Well, that's the million-dollar question. As you know, your father's not one to speak of the past; most of the time he acts as if one moment is gone forever just as soon as another begins. Don't think that means he doesn't carry the past with him as much as any other person, though, because he does.

It makes me think sometimes what a good farmer your father would have been, because that's the way farmers are, going ahead and planting year after year without so much as a thought for the year before's bad crop and all the years before that when there's been too much rain or not enough or a cold snap or a heat wave or a plague of this insect or that. It just goes on and on, one year to the next, farmers like my father pushing their caps back to wipe their foreheads while staring up at the sun, forgetting a million and one misfortunes and thinking instead *What have I got to do next? What's next on my list?*

There was only one time I can remember when your father found occasion to admit that he'd spent a good long time taking a look at all that had gone on in his life. While I wish I could say I learned enough from his words on that occasion to put my finger on whatever it was turning inside him, the truth is I ended up feeling mostly confused. We'd only been married a year or so, and it may be he'd simply had too much to drink, although I'd like to think it was more than that which loosened his tongue.

It was a New Year's Eve, and we'd left you and your brother with your grandfather in Mandeville for a few days, and we'd gone to watch the bonfires they have out on the levee. We drove over to Bucktown and parked the car, then we wandered arm in arm like teenagers from one old bar to the next, singing songs along with each bar's jukebox until it was getting near midnight, with people gathering around your father because of his voice. I've never understood how it is that your father has trouble making two minutes of meaningful conversation with his family but can then turn around and let strangers watch him sing all those old songs about love.

One of the jukeboxes had Bing Crosby singing "Pennies from Heaven," and they made your father sing it three times straight, everybody joining in for the mournful whistling at the end like a choir of drunken angels. You should have heard all the applause when the song was done, just like your father was someone famous they'd happened to discover in their midst.

Anyway, I hadn't expected much from the evening despite your father's claim that the bonfires were really something to see, stretching out for miles along the levee. Well, once it was almost time, we walked outside and up the muddy slope, and at the stroke of midnight your father pulled me up against him and kissed me. I can't tell you how sweet and wonderful that is, Meredith, being held in such a manner by the man you love. You'll think I'd gone and watched too many of those old movies where the woman swoons at the touch of the man's lips, but I swear I did swoon. I closed my eyes and thought how there would never be a time I'd feel lost again. That's how young I was.

Well, when I opened my eyes, I saw the lake lit up like someone was truly making a movie and had brought in a thousand floodlamps to shine across the water and capture the hundreds of sailboats swinging up and down and the hundreds of bodies gathered along the sea wall.

That's not right. It was more than that. What it felt like was a happy end to the world, every inch of this earth going up in flames. Instead of lamenting the loss, every person was glad to have it done, all their cares being swept aside in the heat and glow.

I swear my face felt flushed and warm for two days after. What your father and I did that night, though, was wait until most everyone had left for whatever parties were waiting for their return, and we walked along the levee until we found an empty stretch of the sea wall. I helped your father sit down on top of the wall, which scared me because of his leg and the slippery steps leading down into the water, and we sat there in silence, our arms around each other. The fires had calmed down, though they were still bright enough to cast a red-and-orange glow over the water as with a glorious sunset. Your father took his arm off my shoulder and held my hand.

Then he laughed and said, "Tell me something, Cathy."

"I will," I said, and I laughed, too, thinking he was just being silly, wanting to fill the passing moments with meaningless chatter.

But then your father said, "Tell me what you see when you look at me, Cathy."

I knew already from the tone of his voice I'd been wrong. It wasn't some small talk your father was pursuing. But I didn't know what he wanted, so I said, "I see a good man, Thomas Eagen. I see my husband. I love him and his children both with all my heart."

Your father kept looking at me, Meredith, as if I'd not yet spoken a word.

"I see the man I love more than life itself," I said, but that didn't do it, either.

Your father's eyes were just about hidden by the reflection of the flickering fire in his glasses, but I saw enough to know he was feeling troubled. I saw it even in the way he held our hands together in front of him, like he was a child who'd just learned to clasp his fingers.

"That's not it, Thomas, I know, but I'm afraid I can't do better," I said.

"You can, Cathy," he said. "Look at me. Tell me what you see. Don't tell me about your feelings. Forget about your feelings."

He was angry now, I knew, with thoughts that had nothing to do with my reply. "Thomas," I said, "you tell me what you see."

"I see a girl who's mighty pleased with herself for having grown up so in such a short space of time," your father said. He reached out then and touched my hands. "I see a girl who wanted more of the world than she could properly handle and she thinks she found it in this old man and his two children."

Your father waited then, as if he were checking to see whether his words had injured me. I didn't show him anything, though. I just kept hold of his hand as if he was talking all manner of sweetness and light.

"I see a girl," he went on, "who despite herself and all her hopes is getting worried because she's afraid this man, her husband, doesn't know up from down or left from right and hasn't much chance of steering his life or her own on a proper course. I see a girl who's beginning to wonder what there is for her beyond worries of money and looking after a man who's got himself a physician's license and a whole bunch of poor folks reaching out to him like he was Jesus Christ."

"Thomas, that's not what I think," I said. Maybe that wasn't the whole truth. Maybe your father had gotten at some of my worries. But they weren't what mattered about my feelings.

"Cathy," your father said then, "what would you say if people told you you'd married a nigger?" I felt he was somehow being cruel to me now, even though he was talking about himself.

"Thomas Eagen," I said, "you're not a nigger. And in any case, I don't like that word."

Your father laughed then, like he was bent on having fun at the expense of my discomfort. "No, I'm not a nigger," he said, "though there are those who'd say I am. Actually, what they'd say, knowing only that my mother was a Negro, is that I'm mulatto, a mule. That would make my children quadroons. Theirs would be octoroons." He laughed some more. "It's mathematics, though the truth is it's more complicated than that, given my mother's color. Since somewhere along the line there was white blood in her, things do get a bit confusing. Still, it's mathematics."

"It's no such thing," I said. "It doesn't matter."

Your father looked out at the glow on the water. "A hundred years ago in this city," he said, just like he was presenting any other of his history speeches, "a quadroon girl, a girl like Meredith, let's say, was only good enough to be a white man's mistress. I don't mean that's just what people thought. There was an actual law to that effect. A white man couldn't marry her, but he could provide her with an apartment in the Vieux Carré. He could dress her in fancy clothes. He could even have children by her. He couldn't marry her, though."

I didn't understand what your father was getting at, unless it was to point out that things were better now, that people were turning away from such laws. At least that's what I hoped he meant.

"They even had quadroon balls, Cathy," your father said. "It was all very elegant and proper, the white men showing off their quadroon mistresses like they were fine china. There were even arrangements to be made with the mothers of these women. Arrangements, Cathy. These men paid money for the right to keep a quadroon mistress."

"Why didn't the women want men like themselves?" I asked your father.

"You mean men who were the same color, quadroon men?" He made it sound like I'd said something wrong.

Yes, I nodded. That was what I'd meant.

"Quadroon women wouldn't be seen with quadroon men," your father said. "They wouldn't have anything to do with them. Why? Because they could have white men instead. They couldn't have them completely, of course, but they could have them enough to make them feel privileged."

"Then what about Lowell?" I asked. It all seemed so terrible and confusing. "What would have happened to him?"

"He'd have been treated like a black man," your father said. "He'd have been seen as a nigger, pure and simple."

Never had I felt such unease with your father as I felt at that moment. I just didn't know where his thoughts were leading him. I felt like I was standing on the edge of a dark forest while your father set off into the trees.

Then your father started in on a story. "When I was a boy," he said, and I breathed a sigh of relief, thinking he'd put all that talk behind him. "When I was a boy," he said, "my father used to take out photographs of my mother and show them to me. 'Your mother was a Negro,' my father told me. I looked at the pictures and didn't say anything, so my father said, 'You don't know what that means, do you? You don't really know what Negro or nigger means?' I told him it meant she was dark-colored, though she didn't look like she was. 'What else?' he said, and I told him I didn't know. 'That's good,' he said. 'Don't ever let anyone tell you it means anything, because it doesn't.'

"Well, that seemed like good advice to me, but of course as I grew up and looked around, I started to think my father had lied to me. It did mean something. That was obvious. Why hadn't he told me it did?"

"I don't know, Thomas," I said. "It doesn't mean anything to me, either. Maybe he was just saying how he felt."

Your father looked at me then, Meredith, and said, "The point is, I didn't know then what to do with that information. My mother was a Negro, okay. What was I supposed to do? I still don't have an answer to that. What am I supposed to do?"

"You're not supposed to do anything," I said.

"Is it that simple?" he said.

"It is," I told him.

Your father nodded his head, not like he was agreeing with me but like he was following his own train of thought. "What do you think it meant to my father that he married my mother?" he asked me.

"It meant he loved her, no matter her color," I said. I believed that, Meredith. I knew it was true.

"Okay," he said, and he put an arm on my shoulder to let me know he wanted some help getting up. We stood there and your father looked down at his feet.

"I'll tell you what I think," he said. "I think my father didn't have so much as the first clue about what he was doing. I think he had a notion of what was right and proper in God's eyes, and that thinking blinded him to what was there."

Your father started walking and I stayed beside him. "Listen. I am the last man, Cathy, who would think that one's color means good or bad, that one deserves a certain fate because of the color of one's skin. I am the last man who would believe such a thing. You understand?"

"I do," I said.

"But that's not the same thing as saying it doesn't matter. It does matter. It matters just as much as anything else that has a say in how you're treated in this world. It matters the same way as it matters who your parents were, what ideas grabbed hold of them that they passed on to you. If my father thought this whole life on earth was nothing more than a dark veil to be lifted after his death, if he thought there was no explanation for what's good or bad on this earth beyond the confusing, mysterious work of the Lord, which no amount of inquiry will ever reveal, what has he given me? What am I left with?"

"I don't know, Thomas," I said. "I don't know that I understand you."

"You don't," he said, angry. But then he put his arm around me. "Of course you don't," he said.

"I'd like to," I said.

"Yes," your father said, and he pulled me to him. "I don't want you thinking I'm ashamed because my mother was a Negro," he said. "That's not the case, Cathy."

"I know it's not," I said. I was glad he'd said so, Meredith, and I believed him. I still do.

"I'm ashamed because I haven't found the place for that fact," he said. "I feel sometimes that my father did the worst thing in the world by not spending the rest of his life searching for my mother on the unlikely chance he'd find her and could put her in front of me and say, 'This is the woman responsible for making you. Know who she is. Love her.' "

"I'm sure he wanted to," I said.

"No," your father told me. "He made his peace with it."

"Then why don't you?" I said.

Your father looked at me and said, "I've tried, Cathy. I keep trying."

"That's enough," I said. "That's all you can do."

We set off walking then. Not for a second did I think I'd given your father any lasting comfort, but I felt glad for the conversation anyway. I felt like for the briefest moment your father's heart had opened up and spilled out a little of its pain, as mysterious as that pain still seemed to me. For my own part, I hoped I'd managed to replace at least a portion of that pain with an equal measure of light, though I have no idea if that was so.

Well, after that, we walked back along the levee, and I looked at your father the whole way, his face lighting up as we stepped past each of the dying fires. I thought then of what I'd thought before, of what a handsome man I'd married, and I felt more love for him at that moment than any other. There's no stronger feeling a woman has for her husband than the feeling he needs her protection, and that's how I felt at that moment. I didn't know what it was I had to protect your father from. The truth is, I couldn't think of a single thing. I just knew I did, though, and that was enough.

Well, it's something to think this letter started with such anger and is ending with feelings of love. You don't know how sorrowful it makes me to admit that once I'd found out something of what your father needed protection from, and that was himself and his own searching mind, I failed to give it. I didn't know how to offer that sort of protection. What could I do? And by then I had my own pain to deal with. Who was going to protect me? I didn't know that, either.

I'll get to all this in my next letter, Meredith, I swear I will.

I know now, from talking with your father, that you haven't gotten my first two letters, which I sent to your grandfather's house in Mandeville along with something I found here that I thought you might like to have. I won't spoil the surprise by telling you what it is in case you get this letter before you get the others. Your father said he'd send Murphy over to Mandeville in a few days to retrieve them, but I know how that is. All I can do is hope he will.

There's not much to those letters in any case. I promised to tell you what I know your father won't, at least not correctly, but I got sidetracked by all that's happening here and by my own thoughts, which set about wandering back through my life the very way I've done here.

In two days, my father is going into the Duke hospital for a heart operation. It took some doing to convince him he had no choice, but now he's resigned to it. He's already packed his bags for the three weeks the doctors have told him he'll have to be there recovering.

Just watching him pull that old brown canvas suitcase from out the hall closet was enough to bring tears to my eyes. It made me wish my mother was alive just so she could have saved him the trouble, by folding his underwear in neat squares the way she did, smoothing his pants cuffs and tucking a clean handkerchief in the left back pocket of each pair so he wouldn't forget.

I almost told my father what he really needed was not clothes but a few pairs of pajamas and a couple of bathrobes, but then I thought better of it. He'd scream if he thought that's all he'd be able to wear for three whole weeks. Instead, I'll sneak out tomorrow and go into Chapel Hill and buy that for him.

It will be so hard to stand by helpless while they get him ready for that operation. I'll manage, though. My brothers and sisters and their families will all be coming to the house tomorrow to give my father their best wishes. All I've got is tomorrow to write you another letter, though, so I'll make the time for it. I'll have to get through my story then because I'm afraid that letter will be the last until my father is through the worst part of his recovering.

I'll tell you, Meredith, it's been my only luxury to have these hours at night to write you and then fall asleep thinking of seeing you again. I will see you, my dear sweet girl. I know that. I just wish I knew when. Let's both of us pray it's soon. Pray for my father, too. He'd be glad to hear that you have. I miss you.

THAT SECOND WEEK on Magazine Street, a week Lowell and I spent more in the care of Murphy than of my father, I did manage a certain happiness. In Murphy's presence, with his gaunt body towering above me, I became as accustomed to life on Magazine Street as Lowell had managed that first week. I found comfort in the growing familiarity of the second-hand shops, where Lowell and I darted through the dim, uneven aisles without upsetting a single dish or lamp or vase squeezed onto the dusty shelves, Murphy trailing behind us, pleading, "Mr. Lowell and Miss Meredith, just slow yourselves right down."

Despite a nearly constant litany of complaints, Murphy's recovery was remarkable. Dressed in my father's clothes — his had been thrown away by the woman who ran the rooming house where he'd lived — and wearing a new pair of glasses the hospital had given him, wire-frame glasses that he claimed simply pushed the world up closer to his face instead of making it any clearer, Murphy seemed transformed, looking more like some eccentric Negro gentleman philosopher than a white family's poor servant.

That week I learned the names of the men and women who

worked in the shops — Marcus and Buddy D. and Evelyn and Jerome, Antoine and Gabrielle and Mathias and Ricky T. They treated Lowell and me like precious curiosities, welcoming us like two castaway orphans who had been afloat on a dark, stormy sea. I do not know how much they learned of our circumstances, although I am sure Murphy recounted what he knew and probably, as was his inclination, like my father's, embellished the facts to make our story, and thus his own, more compelling.

Whenever Lowell and I stepped into the shops after school, we were offered gifts pulled off the shelves or from behind the glass counters: an old phonograph that folded into a black leather box and some jazz records for Lowell, books and costume jewelry for me, a tiny ceramic picture frame I'd admired and figured I could use for one of the photographs of my grandfather's statues.

Lowell and I took home a glass-enclosed clock and an old tin coffee grinder for my father. When we presented him with these gifts, he received them like strange objects he'd never before encountered, turning them in his hands and staring down at them in blank amazement. "That's fine, thank you," he said, and he put them down without asking how we'd managed to acquire them.

When he turned away, Lowell and I looked at each other. We did not know what to make of his lack of interest, the lethargy and distraction that had overtaken him.

"What's wrong?" I asked Lowell once my father had gone.

He shrugged his shoulders and frowned. "You tell me," he said.

But even today, I can't say that I truly understand what happened to my father that week, although I eventually learned from Murphy how he spent much of his time. Lowell and I rode the streetcar home from school every afternoon, and my father was not there waiting for us. He returned for the dinner Murphy prepared, but the four of us sat at the kitchen table in virtual silence, my father occasionally looking up to ask Lowell and me if we were okay, if we had everything we needed.

We were fine, we told him, and he nodded, looking at Murphy for confirmation. "They're just fine, Mr. Thomas. They're good children," Murphy said.

"You let me know if there's anything they need," my father said, and he left money for us on the kitchen table before disappearing again. He did not return, I guessed, until nearly dawn, though I did not hear him come up the stairs.

After Lowell and I helped Murphy clean up after dinner, he took us back outside with him, where we roamed along Magazine Street, Murphy moving from one conversation to the next as though presiding over the neighborhood. The shops had all closed by then, but Murphy knocked on the windows and we were let in. While Lowell wandered through the aisles, I found a chair and sat down with a book I'd discovered, a leatherbound catalogue from a statuary company called Kenneth Lynch and Sons. The company was in Wilton, Connecticut, a city I'd never heard of, much less visited.

The statues in the catalogue were all marble and bronze, fancier than anything my grandfather had ever made. There were saints and Virgin Marys just like my grandfather's, but there were also Greek gods and young girls, sometimes naked, crouching to wash their hair and angels and cherubs and sundials and a young boy playing the mandolin.

I had never guessed there could be so many different statues, and I imagined one day going to Connecticut to visit Mr. Lynch, who must have been an old man like my grandfather, and asking him to show me the statues one by one. I wondered if they were spread out through a giant garden or simply stored in rows in a dark warehouse. I decided that surely Mr. Lynch, loving statues so, would have a giant garden, acres and acres, with hundreds of trees set along a rocky stream. I imagined visiting in autumn, a New England autumn, which I had never seen, the tree branches bare but the ground thick with fallen leaves the colors of sunset, the air so crisp and cold that my fingers, touching the statues, would stick for just a moment to the smooth stone surfaces.

I had found the book in Evelyn's shop, and when I'd shown

it to her, she'd paged through it and then said I could keep it. Evelyn, a giant woman with painted crescent-shaped eyebrows, called me "My Fair Princess." She liked to tie my hair up in colored scarfs. When Murphy wandered off with Lowell, she told me stories of her childhood, of growing up there on Magazine Street, on the second floor of her shop, which had been a fruit market owned by her father. I asked her what she thought of living right on top of her father's business, the way we were doing now. I asked her what her life had been like as a little girl.

"It wasn't just the colored who gave my daddy their business," she told me, standing behind me and gathering my hair up in her hands. "It was white folks who drove up in automobiles. I'd run back and forth fetching what they wanted, strawberry baskets or boxes of apples or string bags of oranges. They wanted two sacks of potatoes, I could carry it. I was a strong girl, like you."

She touched my shoulder and turned me around, a red scarf wrapped twice around my head and tied in a knot at the back of my neck. "You're a beautiful child," she told me.

"Thank you," I answered, and although I could not have said so at the time, I was grateful for the company of a woman, someone who could touch my face and hair without thinking what she was doing, just a friendly gesture to put us both at ease.

Evelyn told me that when she was a girl, Magazine Street was like a downtown for Negroes, who couldn't shop at the stores on Canal Street, who weren't welcome really even out on the street unless they were there to shine shoes or open car doors or deliver white people's messages.

"It didn't matter, because there was everything here," Evelyn said. "You just name it, and you'd find it somewhere on Magazine."

But when the law changed, Evelyn told me, and every store had to start taking Negro money, Magazine Street began its decline. "It used to make my daddy mad that his colored sisters and brothers would get on the damn streetcar to put their money in white folks' hands. All Jews and Catholics and high Creoles, he said. He was really something on that score. He screamed about it going on for five years. 'You wouldn't think the black man,' he'd say, 'the black man himself, would be so small-minded as to step outside his own garden to pick his fruit.' But that's exactly what the black man did. So there wasn't near the same amount of foot traffic on Magazine, and the white folks in their automobiles settled for what they could get at the supermarket, like it was the same damn thing.

"You should have heard my daddy. He'd split open a pear and say, 'Look at this, child. My pears is just popping with juice.' And I'd say, 'They sure are, Daddy,' though I don't know if I really could have noticed the difference the way he did. I once even made the mistake of telling my daddy what I was thinking, that I figured niggers had picked both the white man's and the colored man's fruit. My daddy nearly slapped me. He said it was something how white folks, no matter all that money, would settle for what comes easiest."

Sometimes, when Evelyn was talking, Gabrielle would cross the street from her shop to visit, storming through the door with some story she was desperate to tell — how two old white women from Virginia had just come looking for antique linen for a granddaughter's wedding present and had ended up shuffling out when they learned that the Gabrielle whose name was on the front door was this gangly black woman standing in front of them. "We thought you'd be French," one of the women had said, backing away toward the door.

"You mean I'm not?" Gabrielle told us she'd said, showing us how she'd held both of her arms up in front of her eyes.

Then the white women had fled, and Gabrielle had run out after them. "And here I was thinking you, being white and such, would have some intelligence alongside your money," she yelled. The women climbed into their car with Gabrielle standing next to them, laughing and cursing.

In her shop, Gabrielle spent most of her time repairing and ironing the linen she sold, fixing broken stitches and scrubbing out rust stains with white vinegar. She told me that while her hands would smell of vinegar the rest of her life, there was a special power in them. She said she could put her hands on a person's chest and decipher the hieroglyphics of the soul.

"What do you feel?" I asked when I let her put her hands on me.

"You're not prepared to hear it," she said, her fingers stretched up to my neck. "You've got to be prepared for the good news as well as the bad."

"It's good news?" I asked.

"Always both," she said, her eyes closed. "There's a dark side and a bright side to every soul, just as with the moon. In this case, reading the dark side's easy. The scribbling shines like specks of gold on a black baby's skin. It's what's on the bright side that takes some searching." She opened her eyes and said, "You remember that."

"I will," I said, though I thought she was talking nonsense. The next time she put her hands on me, I asked again what she felt. "I feel two breasts just getting started," she said, and she laughed. "Yes, I do."

I looked over at Murphy, who had been flipping through a stack of old *Life* magazines. He looked up at Gabrielle and frowned. "Watch yourself," he said. "This child isn't for your shaping."

But I was no longer afraid of the men and women in the shops or of those who in the evenings loitered on the street corners while passing a bottle around and laughing at the stories they traded between them. They threw their heads back, their faces glowed in the streetlights, and I found myself laughing as well, though I usually didn't know why.

Most of the stories they told were of misadventure — of carrying a borrowed television down the street, only to be questioned for an hour by the police, of trying to earn fifty dollars by scaring the pigeons off the top of Galatoire's, a French Quarter restaurant, but instead putting a three-foot hole in the roof so that rainwater trickled down into the soup pots in the kitchen. Everyone laughed and laughed at the thought of those fancy men and women eating gumbo or crawfish bisque mixed with rainwater.

No one, of course, could match Murphy's story of the causeway's collapse, and he told it night after night to whoever hadn't heard it already, pausing to complain about his sore back which he didn't expect would ever heal or the burning sensation in his feet that made him feel, he said, like his lower extremities had been inhabited by the devil. Murphy held his hands up to prove how his nearly drowning had cost him his fingernails, and he showed everyone the green-and-black bruises that were still on his wrists from the needles they'd put through his skin.

I learned from Murphy's stories that he'd stolen the blue station wagon from the woman at his rooming house and that my father had paid her money to keep her from demanding that the police bring Murphy in. That didn't stop her, though, from throwing away Murphy's clothes and his few other possessions.

"She was just being a good Christian," Murphy said, shaking his head and laughing. "She figured I'd left for the promise of another world."

Murphy wouldn't say why he'd stolen the car or where he was going that morning. When someone asked, he answered, "Sometimes a man wants to enjoy a Sunday drive, doesn't he?" and he laughed. Then he looked over at Lowell and me and said, "You children understand that, don't you?"

We did, we nodded.

"Yes, Mr. Thomas is known to his children for his Sunday drives," Murphy said, and everyone laughed again. I figured they laughed at that because when Lowell and I weren't there, Murphy had told them why we were on the causeway that morning. I could just hear how he must have told them: "The good Mr. Thomas, you see," he would have said, "had decided to leave Miss Catherine on account of some untold difficulties between them."

"Shame, shame," Murphy's audience would have said, shaking their heads from side to side but still smiling, carrying on as if such news were of no consequence, were part and parcel of the world's goings-on, which I guess it was.

All these people, the shop owners and workers and street

loiterers, knew my father, though. "The good doctor," they called him, with what struck me as genuine respect. I am sure that we were treated well primarily because we were his children. At one time or another, they told Lowell and me, my father had looked after each one of them or a family member, though I never did see any of them in the company of their families.

It honestly did not occur to me at the time, but when I think about that week I realize what an odd sight Lowell and I must have been, two white children in the care of an old black man, out most nights almost until midnight, the hour at which Murphy had decided we must be in bed, as though maintaining this single rule excused his every other lapse of discipline.

I hadn't realized that week that my father had stopped seeing patients, that he hadn't worked the whole week. I only found out on Thursday night, when Murphy led us home and a woman was waiting on the porch, her arm bound to her chest by a sheet that was wrapped around her and tied at her waist.

"The doctor's not in," Murphy told her.

"Tomorrow?" she asked in an accent that must have been Spanish.

"Not tomorrow," Murphy said. "The doctor's closed. Go to the Touro Infirmary." Murphy led the woman out to the street. Lowell and I stood on the porch and watched. "It's five blocks," Murphy said. "It's that way. No doctor here."

"No doctor?" the woman said.

"That's English," Murphy said. "No doctor."

The woman walked away, in the opposite direction from where Murphy had pointed. Murphy shook his head at her and said, "She'd do well to learn some English." Then he led Lowell and me inside and pointed up the stairs. "I'll be there directly," he said. "Go on."

Halfway up, though, I sat down.

"Miss Meredith?" Murphy asked, motioning for Lowell to continue up the stairs, which he did. Murphy sat down just below me but reached his hand up and put it on my shoulder.

"Where is he?" I asked. "What's he doing?"

"Mr. Thomas has got some things to take care of," Murphy said. "There's no cause for worry, Miss Meredith."

"Where is he?" I said again, and for a moment I wondered if maybe he was making plans to go to North Carolina to get Catherine, to leave us with Murphy while he did. But what would he do at night to make those plans?

I tried to picture my father wandering around on the street. I imagined the scraping of his shoe as he pulled his bad leg around, the bean-shaped metal taps on the sole, which kept the shoe's heel from wearing down, echoing in dark alleys while he tried to sort through all that had happened in the past two weeks.

Did he see himself as I had begun to see him, although I didn't realize that I had: diminished by his decision to leave his wife, whatever the reason? How could it be that he'd had, as he claimed, no choice? I wondered if, like me, my father woke up from seeing again in his dreams the image of the causeway collapsing, Murphy's car shooting down into the water, the white dust settling on the car the way the white dust had settled in my grandfather's workshop.

I kept thinking of those things, and Murphy rubbed his hand on my leg. "You're feeling lonely, Miss Meredith," he said. I nodded.

"Well, Mr. Thomas is feeling lonely, too. You understand?"

I nodded again, although I did not understand. Eventually, I would learn that what Murphy meant was that my father was seeing a woman, was taking care of his loneliness in that manner.

"You cheer up," Murphy said. "I've got a surprise for you."

I looked up, and Murphy nodded his head and laughed. "That's right, I've got a surprise," he said. "Your father wants me to go to Mandeville tomorrow to retrieve some letters Miss Catherine sent you."

I tried to ask how my father knew there were letters there, but Murphy told me to hush. "Don't try to sort things out when you're in need of sleep," he said. "I'll go tomorrow and come right back. It'll take most of the day driving around that lake, but I'll be back by evening. Two letters, I think Mr. Thomas said."

Murphy helped me up and walked me to my bed. I lay down without taking off my clothes, and Murphy pulled the covers over me. "You go to sleep," he said and turned out the light. He stepped out of the room and closed the door, but I called to him.

"Miss Meredith?" he said, just cracking open the door.

"Can I go with you?" I asked.

"I don't know," he said. "Let's ask Mr. Thomas. We'll ask in the morning."

I didn't go to sleep immediately but instead tried to imagine what Catherine had written to me. I thought again of her mother's letter, of the words that had sounded to me like poetry. "These are days of grace," she'd written. What else? All about the evening din of locusts, the church bells of autumn, the wind slipping through window screens and ruffling curtains until they seemed like beautiful dancers. It had all been beautiful, I remembered.

Then, as I was drifting off to sleep, or once I was asleep, I imagined going with Murphy to Mandeville, only to discover my grandfather there, alive, working in his shop, his sleeves rolled up above his elbows, white dust in the folds of his shirt and on his eyebrows and across his bottom lip, a thin line that, when I was a little girl, had made me laugh because it looked like milk.

"Meredith," I imagined my grandfather saying, "haven't you grown up?" And he would sweep me into his arms for only a second and then put me down and set back to work, crouching, his back arched to summon his strength as he smoothed the statue's surface or carved deep lines in the folds of a robe so that light would shine in and be captured there. I asked my grandfather to build me my own statue of Saint Francis, and he did, surrounding it with animals the way Saint Francis always was in pictures, deer and raccoons and squirrels gathered near for Saint Francis's protection, sparrows and robins and finches taking flight around him, suspended in the air with invisible wires. My grandfather made each of those statues, one animal after another. It took both forever and no time at all, and we gave them names as they were finished and then set them all out in a garden, not the garden that was there but another we had planted — a garden of roses, with hundreds of buds rising out of the dark green leaves, nobler than any other garden. Then my grandfather lay me down to sleep at Saint Francis's feet, and I breathed the rose scent and looked up at Saint Francis's kind face and knew that I was safe forever.

~✕~

In the morning, I woke up to hear my father and Murphy talking. I got up and straightened my clothes as best as I could. I now had a mirror in my room, an oval mirror with a chipped gold plaster frame that Gabrielle had given me. She had instructed me to brush my hair with one hundred strokes each night while I gazed into the mirror, claiming that by doing so I'd summon a secret energy from inside me and my hair would shine like fire in the moonlight.

I didn't believe her, of course, not that it mattered with my hair, which I could hardly run my fingers through since it had grown so long. I did look into the mirror that morning, though, thinking not about how I looked but about all that had dropped away from me the last two weeks — the books I liked to read at night before going to bed, the perfume bottles I'd lined up on my dresser that Catherine had given me when they were nearly empty, my few friends at school, Megan and Theresa and Lee, all of whom had decided that my smudged and wrinkled uniform and my constant exhaustion were signs that I had secretly found a boy to love who loved me, a belief that left them feeling betrayed because they had not.

I did not know what to tell them, not wanting to tell them the truth: that I was living above my father's office in a Negro neighborhood, that I spent my afternoons and evenings in the care of our Negro servant, with other Negro men and women, that my father disappeared each night and my stepmother had given up and gone to North Carolina, that I felt as if I had, the past two weeks, simply stood in the street and watched the moon trace a path across the sky, watching one day become the next so that the passage of time now confused me and I felt as though I had lived this way forever and my life would never be any different. I couldn't tell them that no matter all that had happened, I'd felt happy in that rush of time, happy to be in Murphy's care, happy to listen to Evelyn's stories and let her rough hands touch my hair, happy with the dangerous thrill of Gabrielle's hands on my chest or watching Lowell drink from the bottles that were passed around among the men.

I could hardly remember my life before we'd ended up on Magazine Street.

And Catherine: she had fallen away as well, so much that I could hardly bring her face to mind. I thought of how we would sometimes lie down next to each other and compare our features, so different, but the two of us looking for the similarities that sometimes prompted those who did not know we were stepmother and stepdaughter to remark how we looked so much alike. Did we? Perhaps such comments are a standard compliment, meant simply to please, but at the time I believed them and wondered why I could not see what others saw. Catherine insisted that she did see our resemblance, that she believed this similarity was a heaven-sent coincidence, a blessing to soften the sadness of my mother's death.

I once found, in the pages of one of my father's medical books, a childhood photograph of my mother, and I did not see any similarity between us, either. In the photograph my mother stood, looking awkward in her fancy white dress, in front of a giant cushioned chair, as though she'd leapt up just before the picture was taken, her dress floating around her knees, her body leaning to the side. On the back of the photograph, my mother had written to my father, "That's Me, Darling. 9 years old. Would you believe it?"

I'd taken the photograph and placed it in my drawer, hidden beneath my underwear. My father had other photographs of my mother, pasted in an album that I would sometimes pull down from the bookshelf, but I decided that he had purposely hidden this photograph in his book, and my keeping it therefore felt like a theft. I don't know why I'd picked up that medical book in the first place, but I remember paging through such books occasionally, out of simple curiosity perhaps, or maybe, the way children sometimes will, merely to shock myself.

When I stepped out of my room, I found my father and Murphy sitting in the kitchen.

"Did Murphy ask you?" I said, walking over to receive his kiss.

"He did," my father said. "I'm sorry, Lamb, but I don't think it's a good idea. You've got school."

"Please," I said. "I really want to go."

"Murphy has some other things to do. He's going to spend the night in Mandeville. You'll have the letters by tomorrow."

"How do you even know her letters are there?" I asked. "Did you talk to her?"

"I did," my father said.

"And you didn't tell me?"

"I spoke with Cathy earlier this week," he said, pulling the belt to his bathrobe tighter around his waist.

"When?" I asked.

I was angry, but I didn't want my father to see that I was. I thought there still might be a chance he'd let me go.

"I was going to tell you," he said. "I wanted Murphy to get the letters first."

"What do they say?" I asked.

"They're your letters," my father said. "You can tell me what they say if you like, but only if you like. They're letters to you, she said." He looked down at his lap and then back up at me.

"What have you been doing all week?" I asked him and felt myself starting to cry.

"Oh, Jesus, Meredith," my father said, and he pushed himself up and put his arms around me. "I'm sorry for all of this," he said.

"You keep saying that," I said.

"I know I do," he said. "I know I do."

"I want to go with Murphy," I said.

My father took his arms from around me and put his hands on my shoulders. I thought of the time he'd gotten so angry when I climbed that tree, when he'd just said "Careful" and I'd cried and cried over that single word.

"No," my father said this time, and I felt something slip from inside me, my own breath, anguish, a cold wind through a cracked window. I pulled myself away from him and went to my room.

"Meredith," he called after me, but I closed my door and sat down on my bed.

When Lowell knocked on the door and said he was ready for school, I told him to go ahead without me. "I'll take the next streetcar," I said.

I waited for Lowell to leave, then I opened my door. My father was standing there, still in his bathrobe. "Why don't you let Murphy drop you off at school? He's ready to go," he said.

"I want to take the streetcar," I said. "I'm fine."

I went down the stairs and out the door without saying good-bye. I looked up at the house, at the windows upstairs, and Murphy was standing there. I couldn't tell whether he was watching me, but I thought he probably was. I waited, but he didn't move. He acted as if he were looking up the street, but I was sure he was watching me.

I was worried that my father's car would be locked, but it wasn't. I looked up again at the window, and Murphy was still there. "Please don't tell," I whispered, hoping Murphy would know from my mouth's movement what I was saying. I raised my hands up in the air. "Please," I said again. Then I opened the back door, crouched down on the floor, and pulled a pile of clothes over me.

I waited there for Murphy, feeling my breath on my face, the warmth that spread over me until I felt as if I would suffocate. I tried to think of some story to tell myself, something about Catherine or my grandfather that would make me feel happy, but no story would come into my head.

I did feel, though, that I was leaving this happy week behind and setting off for something else. I felt so trapped that I thought of opening the door and rushing off to Evelyn's shop to ask her if she'd sweep me up in her arms the way I'd imagined my grandfather doing. I imagined my father and Murphy and even Lowell just disappearing, Evelyn keeping me as if I were her own child, even telling people I actually was. All day I could stand behind the glass counter and let her brush my hair, the two of us laughing at Gabrielle's stories. At night we could go upstairs and sleep in the same bed, and Evelyn would tell me more and more about her childhood as we both drifted off to sleep. She'd talk and talk night after night until I knew everything, until I could see everything that had ever happened to her just like a movie I'd watched over and over again.

Then, finally, I heard the car door open and felt the front seat push against my shoulder from Murphy's weight. Silence, then the rattle of the keys, a click.

"You're a dangerous child," I heard Murphy whisper. "I don't know you're there, so help me God."

Then he started the Checker's engine, and I felt the car moving beneath me, a loud constant rumble filling my ears as if the whole world were shifting to some different place and all I could do was take cover and wait.

DEAR MEREDITH,

Tomorrow my father goes to the hospital. It's nearly midnight now, but he's still outside smoking and staring up at the sky. My brothers and sisters have all gone home with their children, though they'll be back again early tomorrow. I can only hope my father is sitting outside thinking of his family and imagining the rest of his life once he's recovered from the operation, the pains gone from his chest, another ten years added to his life, which is how long they've told him the new arteries in his heart will last. They're not new arteries really. They'll be taken from one of his legs, which is something I don't understand. It seems to me those ones have been working as hard all these years of my father's working in the fields as the bad ones in his heart. Of course, he does sleep at night, which gives his legs a rest while his heart has to keep going, so maybe that's it.

The doctor has told him to lay off the cigarettes, but he just can't do it. Really, right now I'm worried more about him being out in the cold weather. He won't smoke inside because he knows I don't like it, which is thoughtful but not of much use if he's going to catch pneumonia in the process.

It really is cold. Every morning now, there's a layer of frost over the fields so that when the sun rises, the light glides right up to the house like it's being poured out of a pot onto a giant pane of glass.

With all that frost, the branches of the maple tree on the side of the house look so brittle, like you could just snap them off with your fingers. One of the farmers nearby has got a dog that thinks it's a wolf, though not a smart one. It howls at the rising sun instead of at the moon. It's that dog that has woken me each day the past week.

So I get up early to make my father his pot of coffee and straighten the house. Only then am I able to get the restlessness out of me and sit down with the morning paper. I hardly read it, though, thinking instead about you and your brother and your father. This morning, I ran through my list of things to tell you, knowing this was my final chance. You know how I felt? I felt like I imagine you must feel when you go into that dark room at the back of the church to talk to a priest you can't even see. You know he's there, but there's nothing to put your eyes on. I guess that's the idea, isn't it, figuring you'll let your soul glide right out into view so you can examine it.

Can he see you? That's a silly question, but I've always wondered about it. Sometimes I've had a mind to wander over there and step into that room, not to confess to anything terrible but just to see if I'd be heard. If I started out by admitting I wasn't Catholic, would I be shown the door? I don't know.

I better get started now, I guess, before I find myself too exhausted and too afraid of tomorrow's trip to the hospital.

The first thing you probably already know by now. I was the one who got Murphy on the bridge last Sunday morning. I guess in that sense I'm the one responsible for him ending up in the water, though he was supposed to be following you and not out in front.

I wouldn't be upset if Murphy has already gone and told your father all this. I meant well.

In any case, what happened is that nearly a month ago now I stumbled across Murphy one day after having lunch with your father at the Camellia Grill. You and your brother were in school, and I was taking a cab back home when I happened to look out the window and spot him sitting on the steps of a porch on Prytania Street, just around the corner from your father's office. This man I thought was Murphy was just like a flash in the corner of my eye as the cab headed over to St. Charles, and I figured I might have just imagined it. But I told the driver to go around the block so I could be certain. When I looked again and knew for sure it was Murphy, I asked the driver to pull over and let me out.

Murphy saw me walking toward him and nearly jumped out of his skin. He'd been drinking, and when he tried to stand up his legs gave way just like they were made of straw, and he sat back down. But soon enough he readied himself to speak, running his hands over his chest and coughing, and when he did speak he managed enough composure to make you think he was a fancy butler enjoying the fine weather on his day off. "Good day, Miss Catherine," he said. "Pretty, isn't it?"

"Yes, it is," I managed to say despite my concern. I'd never seen Murphy look so disorderly. His shirt and pants were so dirty you couldn't have begun to guess what color they'd started out as.

"Oh, Murphy Warrington, you're in need of some help," I told him.

"Yes, ma'am, I am," he said, "though you've gone and caught me just as I was asking for some heavenly intervention." Then he laughed and said, "Maybe we'd do well to wait a while and see if it comes my way."

"It won't," I said, and he nodded his head. I took that to mean he knew I was right, and while there have been few times in my life I've ever wanted to give someone a good scolding, this was one of them. I didn't, though, because it would have been the same as lashing out at a cat for jumping up on a table. Soon as you're out of sight and gone, he's back up there again.

"What can I do for you?" I asked instead, standing in such a way as to block the sun from Murphy's face so he'd have no reason not to look back at me.

"I'm fine," Murphy answered. "I'm more than fine."

"Thomas looked for you," I said. "He looked for weeks and weeks."

"Yes, ma'am."

"You knew," I said.

"Yes, ma'am," he answered. "There were folks who told me so."

"Why didn't they tell Thomas they'd seen you?" I asked.

"I asked them not to," Murphy said.

"You left on account of what you told me, didn't you?" I asked.

"That's been a long time," he said, "but yes, ma'am, I do believe I did."

Meredith, I'll get to what it was that Murphy told me before he left. I'd made him a promise that I wouldn't repeat what he'd said, and I kept it. Maybe I shouldn't have. Maybe I'd gotten my loyalties confused. But I was taught to keep my word, and I took the opportunity to tell Murphy so.

"It doesn't much matter, I guess," he said, running his hands along his chest again.

You're not following this well, I know, Meredith, so I'll tell you now. Telling you means that now I won't have kept my word to Murphy, but in light of all that's happened and considering my promise that I'd tell the complete story without omission, I've got a conflict here. So I'm only doing what I think is right.

For the life of me I don't know if this will mean nothing at all to you, like it's just a torn page from a history book you didn't want to read in the first place, or if this will make you see both your father and Murphy in a different light. The worst it could do, in my mind, is to alter in any way your fond memories of your grandfather, who I refuse to believe was anything but a loving husband when he still had the chance and a good father all the way to his last breath. The few years I knew your grandfather — and sometimes I think I knew him better than your father ever did, which is often how it is, I suspect, between father and son and whatever woman the son marries — the few years I knew your grandfather were enough to make me believe he was like a saint among the living, too good for this earth and so constantly disappointed when it did not return to him his generous good will.

Even considering these recent events, I'm not so angry as to fail to admit that your grandfather passed on a healthy dose of those qualities to your father, who for most of his life has been a man of kindness and charity and good humor. If that's all there was to his character, though, none of this would have happened. The only thing I can conclude, then, is that your father also acquired a certain restlessness, what I can only call a dissatisfaction of spirit, from your grandmother Mollie — qualities that must have been coursing through his veins the moment he was born.

As for Murphy, I don't know what to say. Maybe the greatest shame of the separation between the different races in this world, between white and black, is that we're left blind and groping as a direct result, unable to sort out the qualities of character that we use to make our judgments about those we meet.

That may not make any sense, but the conclusion I'm grasping for is that I don't know what allegiance I have to Murphy now, if any at all. He tried to help me out. I asked a favor of him, and he agreed. I don't know, though, that he had any sense of doing good, of doing what in his mind and not mine was the right thing to do. He might still have had the notion of being this white family's servant implanted so deep in his skin that he didn't think to say no.

But he could have said no, Meredith. He was free to do that — not just in what I asked of him, but in what your grandmother asked in her way so many years before. I'll explain all that, but I want you to see that it was his own fault in not understanding that he was free to do what he thought was right. He can't blame anyone else for that. I won't buy it.

You don't understand, I know. What Murphy told me just before he disappeared two years ago is that he'd slept with your grandmother and put a child into her. It was on that account that she left your grandfather, he said.

I wish I knew what it's like for you to read something like that right now. Is it just too long ago? Does it make you cry? I just don't know, but I felt I wanted to tell you in any case. I felt it was important for you to hear.

It's a sad story on all accounts, Meredith. Your grandmother decided it was better to leave than to stand up and face your grandfather or lie to him. You may wonder why she didn't just tell him the child she was carrying was his own child. I've thought about that myself. What if that child turned out to be as black as Murphy? Was it just worry over that fact, the color that baby's skin might be, that made her leave, or was it the fact that she'd gotten a child inside her by another man? That would at least be more noble, wouldn't it? Are shame and guilt somehow better than out-and-out worry? I don't know.

I will tell you now why I put such questions down on paper to you. I think of them not so much for what happened in the past but for what happened between your father and me. I sit at this desk right now and look out the window up to the dark night sky and swear to the heavens above that I was true to your father, that I have loved and touched no other man.

I'm pregnant, Meredith. It was your father who gave me this child. He left me, taking you and your brother with him, because he refused to admit that was so. Deep inside him, I'm convinced, he knew this child was his own. He knows it now. But he's hiding the truth behind his own failure to live up to this marriage and whatever other failures are buried inside him, though your guess would be as good as mine at sorting out what exactly those others might be.

It must be four years now since I first told your father how much I wanted a child. But only in this past year, for reasons that I can't explain except to say that I felt my time had come, did the notion truly grab hold of me. I was honest with your father about those feelings, Meredith. We talked and talked late into the night on one hundred occasions, but your father said no.

I say that we talked and talked, but I was the one, of course, who did most of the talking. Your father was his usual short and sharp self in reply. He didn't want another child, he said. As with so much else, he had trouble explaining himself, but he said he was as certain as he could be. I asked him what he was afraid of, hoping to draw out his feelings about your mother dying after having you and Lowell, but the question backfired. He said he wasn't interested in further discussion.

Well, I waited, but I felt I could only wait so long. "I want a child, Thomas," I finally told him again. "You have your ways and I've got mine for seeing life laid out before us in the years to come. I want a child. I just do."

As quick as that, those words put an end to our sleeping as if we were in the same bed together, though we still were. He didn't touch me after that, I mean.

Maybe I would have lived with the loss of his touch for a while and then decided, with a large measure of sadness, that I simply was not meant to have more children than those I'd been blessed with already, meaning your brother and you. Or maybe your father would have lived without my touch long enough to change his mind and see a child as the natural consequence of the love between us. But we never got the chance.

Shortly after your father stopped sleeping with me, I discovered with what I swear were equal amounts of horror and heavenly thanks that our discussions on the subject didn't matter. I was already pregnant.

I didn't know this until I was two weeks late with my period, which has always been irregular, and I worried over the matter for two more before getting the nerve to find out for sure from a doctor. The mistake I made then was I didn't just come out and tell your father what I'd learned. I should have, of course. If I'd been thinking clearly at all, I would have.

I've learned now how mistaken I was to go about it in the fashion I did, but I had your father's interests in mind. Instead of saying, "Well, Thomas, I'm already with child," I resumed my requests for him to make me pregnant, hoping to make him feel that it was his decision as well.

But I failed. Once again, your father said no. I told him how I felt again and again, one day stretching into the next. I said how wonderful it would be. I called up every ounce of sweetness left in me until I felt exhausted by the effort. Still your father didn't budge.

What could I do? I cried and cried. Then one night, I finally did what I should have done all along. I waited until you and your brother were in bed and I told your father the simple truth. I told him I hadn't set out to get pregnant but had, by him, two months ago, before he'd stopped sleeping with me.

And what do you think was his response? He looked at me and said, "What the hell have you gone and done, Cathy?"

I knew what he meant, of course. "It was you," I told him. "It was."

Your father stood his ground and said he didn't believe me. I cried again and swore to him that I'd been faithful, that I'd not thought to touch another man all the years we'd been married. I told him we could just go to the doctor, and he'd say how far along I was. Then your father would see. It was that simple.

But your father wouldn't have it. "I don't believe you, Cathy," he said, just like that. "It doesn't matter how far along you are. That doesn't prove anything."

"It does," I said, crying and crying. Then I stopped and looked at your father, Meredith. His eyes were fiery red and the muscles along his neck were like cords of rope pulled tight. I took as long and deep a look at him as I've taken my whole life, and I understood in that moment what was going on. I understood, like it was a hammer on top my head, that your father's refusing to believe me was the result of his looking into his own heart and not mine.

"You did," I said. "You've been unfaithful."

"Cathy," he answered, his eyes burning like the fires of hell, and that was one time my name was enough. I knew.

I said things to your father then that I know I should not have said. In my worst nightmares, I wouldn't imagine I had such things inside me to say. If my words had been knives, your father would have been nothing more than a body lying in a pool of blood. I'm sorry, but it was that bad.

I said I'd be honest with you, Meredith, and here I am. I called your father a cripple and a nigger. *No*, I said, *you're just half a nigger, which is worse than being a whole one. At least a whole nigger knows what to be proud of, and you sure don't. At least a whole nigger knows what he's seeing when he spies himself in a mirror.*

That wasn't all of it. I told your father he was the worst of husbands and fathers for taking such skills and training as he possessed and wasting them at his own family's expense just so he could time and again wake up in the middle of the night to put his hand on his own chest and feel what he believed was the soft spot in his heart. *Well, it's not a soft spot,* I told him, *it's not Christian love and it's not charity. It's not you living Jesus Christ's life and walking in Jesus Christ's shoes. It's where your heart is rotting away at your very touch,* I said. *It's the pain of your whole life. The worst of it,* I said, *is that you're bound and determined to spread that pain among your family like it's some infectious and killing disease. We'll all die from you,* I said. *We will.*

I cursed and cursed him and then reached out my hand and ran my fingers straight down his neck and left those scratches you remember. I hate to think what you and your brother thought of that.

I can't say how sorry I am, Meredith, how much I will never forgive myself for it. It was as if every ounce of goodness inside me, whatever small amount that is, slipped from my body in that single moment. You read in the newspapers of husbands and wives who turned on each other and put an end to their marriage by way of taking the other's life. I never understood that. Now I do. That's how hurt a person can be.

Well, there was all of that, and I still hadn't made my worst mistake, giving your father a way to tell himself that he'd been right all along, that he didn't have a true wife. I was so angry and hurt that once he'd pulled his hand down from his chin and we both knew that the scratch on his neck was nothing he'd die from, I went and told him that he was right, that this wasn't his child I was carrying. That's how mad I was. I wanted to burn something deep in your father's heart so he'd never forget it, and that was what came to mind.

So here I am, Meredith, without my husband and without the two children that I feel are mine as much as this child inside me.

I don't know what your father has told you, if anything, but if it's different from what I've said, it's not true. I've told you everything, not holding back a moment of my bad judgment or the terrible things I said.

And you should know the truth about your father, too. I found out, despite all your father's denials, that there was truth to what I'd seen in his refusal to believe me. It took some doing, of course, some sorting through his private papers and desk drawers, the sort of thing I wouldn't have done in a million years for any other reason except to save the very life inside me.

I found my answer in your father's study, in the bottom of an old Dutch Masters cigar box where your father stores all those flashlight batteries for God knows what good reason. It was a letter, just a short note really, asking for the two of them to meet at, of all places, the Negro cemetery in Covington, like she'd read of such things in a dime-store novel.

To the woman's credit, it seems she'd previously cut off her ties to your father, but here she was back again. "My love," the letter said. "I shouldn't have treated you so. Now I need to see you again one more time before I go. If you can forgive me, you'll come. Please. Your darling."

I swear that if the woman had signed her name I would have thought nothing of seeking her out and striking her dead between my hands like a fly buzzing near a picnic lunch. That's how hurt I was. You don't ever think you're going to feel that kind of rage in your life, but I did.

I put the letter back, but I told your father I'd found proof of what he'd done. "You're the one, you bastard," I said, and he just held his hands out toward me and said, "You don't know, Cathy. You don't know everything you think."

"I know enough," I told him, and that was that. I could see that in the time it took to step out of the room in different directions, we'd become like two bloody animals after the most horrible fight, going our separate ways to tend to our wounds.

You and your brother, as far as I know, slept through all of this, I don't know how. Or maybe you didn't and only pretended to. I looked in on you both, and as I stood in the door I knew, as much as I've known anything in my life, that I'd lost you, too, that this was the other price your father would make me pay.

You were curled on your bed, Meredith, with the covers slipped down to your knees, and you looked so sweet to me in that dim light, just like one of those tiny statues your grandfather made for decorations in the Negro cemetery, a little girl curled on top of a stone like it was the softest bed. It was you I cried over that night as much as for myself. I swear I did.

Well, do you even care now what happened between Murphy and me? Maybe you don't. You can ask him yourself. Maybe he'll tell a different story, too. Maybe he and your father will find a way to weave their two stories together so that mine seems like only so much imagining.

The truth is I tried to help Murphy. That was my thought. "What can I do for you?" I asked him, that simple. I wanted to do whatever I could.

"There's nothing," he told me. "I'm just fine."

"I'd guess that's not the case, Murphy," I said, and I asked him where it was he was living.

"Right here," he said, and I thought he meant out on the street, but then he pointed to an upstairs window. "These are fine accommodations," he said.

"Who's paying for them?" I asked.

"That's another issue I've been addressing," he said.

I walked up to Murphy then and put my hand on his arm and said, "We're going inside." There are times when it pays to be forceful, to suggest that you've made up your mind and no amount of resistance will alter your course.

Holding Murphy's arm, I could just feel the thought going through his head that he should shake himself free of me and be on his way. The thought of that frightened me, I admit, and I was a little concerned that his being drunk might lead him to strike out at me right there and then. But I pulled his body up, and he felt as light as an unstuffed scarecrow. We walked up the stairs side by side in silence.

I won't describe for you the squalor of Murphy's room, but

it wasn't a fit place for the dirtiest rat, much less a human being. He did have a coffeepot, though, so I made coffee, twice as strong as even your father likes it. I sat and watched Murphy drink three cups.

I surely never had the feelings for Murphy that your grandfather, in all his blindness to the truth, had for the man, but I did feel he was someone whose life had been mixed up with this family for so many years that I didn't think I could just leave him alone and pretend I hadn't seen him. I knew I wasn't going to tell your father, though, because your father would have wanted to see him too and find out why he'd disappeared two years before. So I decided just to give Murphy as much money as was in my pocketbook, saving enough for my cab fare home, and I left, saying I would call on him again to find out how he was doing.

I told him his best interests would be served by paying a visit to your father, prepared to tell a story your father would believe about where he'd been those two years and why he'd left.

"Yes, ma'am," Murphy said, but not in such a way as to make me believe he'd pay half a mind to my advice.

Of course he didn't. Well, I might have let Murphy drift off again into memory if it wasn't for the problem that arose between your father and me.

Once I became certain of your father's plan to leave me rather than resolve the difficulties between us, I went to see Murphy again. I found him nearly as drunk as he'd been the last time, so I made another pot of coffee and sat down with him.

"You once confided in me," I told him, "and now I'm returning the favor." He sat there in hangdog silence, looking down at his cup of coffee. "Before I start on this, I need to know if I can trust you," I said.

"Excuse me, ma'am," he said, "but I've got enough wits about me to know I'm in no shape to make such a promise."

"Well, I'm going to trust you, Murphy," I told him. "I'm going to trust you because I don't have one other soul in this world to trust. That's pathetic, I know, but that's how it is. I just don't have a choice."

"Yes, ma'am," he said.

"I only hope that trust is rewarded," I said, and I went about explaining my circumstances, telling him just about all I've just told you.

When I was done, Murphy sat there in silence. "I've got two hundred dollars here," I told him. This was money I'd managed to save from what your father gave me, Meredith. "I'm going to call you when they're set to leave, and I want you to follow them," I said. "You call me whenever they stop, wherever that may be. It's going to be Mandeville, I'm sure of it, but if they drive clear across the country, I want you to stay with them. If you need more money, I'll find a way to get it to you. Can you do that?"

"Yes, ma'am," he said.

"And you can get hold of a car?" I asked him.

"Yes, ma'am," he said.

"Well, that's fine," I told him. "Is there some way I can reach you by phone?"

He gave me the number of a woman in the building. "She'll knock on my door," Murphy said. "If I'm not here, she'll find me."

Well, I called the night before you left, Meredith, and Murphy wasn't there. The woman said she'd find him, and an hour later I called back again.

Murphy answered, and what do you think? He was drunk.

"I'm going to trust you," I said. I was already crying. "You get a car," I said. "Tell me you can get a car."

"Yes, ma'am," he said.

"You wait down the block from here," I said, and I gave him my father's number in North Carolina. "You call there," I told him. "Just tell him where they are. That's all."

The next thing I did was reserve a seat on the Greyhound bus to Raleigh. I called my father to say I was coming for a visit, and I told him to expect Murphy's call.

"What's going on there, Cathy?" my father asked.

"I'll see you soon enough," I said. "Don't worry." Then I hung up.

Well, as you know, Murphy never called. I figured he'd simply gotten drunk with the money I'd given him or hadn't found a car. I felt so hopeless already that when I was finally home, fifteen hours after setting off from New Orleans, and my father said he hadn't heard from anyone, I could only laugh like a lunatic in some asylum. I laughed at the thought that I'd grown so desperate as to place my trust in such a one as Murphy.

The whole way on the bus I worried I'd made a mistake, leaving so soon. I worried your father might somehow find his heart changed and turn around and go home. Now I can at least put that worry aside. Even in the face of disaster, he kept to his course. How long will it be, I wonder, before he starts to think of this child inside me, wondering if it's a girl or a boy, wondering if maybe it is his child after all and which of his features will appear in its face, wondering what name I will choose.

If it's a boy, Meredith, I will name him after your father. That's how much I want him to know. If it's a girl, I'll give her my mother's name, which was Elizabeth Ann. It's a pretty name, I think.

I long for you to see this child, Meredith, and I think you will.

Although you'll get this letter after my father's operation, I wish you'd pray for him anyway. God may have done so to mine, but I just don't think he could turn away from a voice as sweet as yours.

This may be no way to end this letter, but I have one more request of you. Please leave this somewhere your father will find it. He'll read it if you do. I'm certain of that.

And when you get to this point, Thomas, don't let your shame cause you to stop reading. At least read this, as much as it makes me feel like a damn fool to write it: you've got a wife who spent seven years at your side and did nothing but love you every moment. Now that love has taken root in her and is growing. You decide what that means. You're the only one who can.

10

I ADMIT I have gone and let grown women guide me to the
most foolish of behavior, but never did I entertain the notion
of a twelve-year-old child pushing me so far beyond that any
no-good Joe on the street with half a mind could point a finger
at me to say, *That old nigger has taken three giant steps past
foolish to end up square in the middle of dumb.* Yes, it was
well past foolish to think swimming in the Pontchartrain was
the worst I could expect. That was the wick dipped in wax
before it's lit, I see now.

I stood in that window to feel the wind of an ice-cold Friday morning rattling the panes and just watched as that child
climbed into Mr. Thomas's car and near-buried herself under
that heap of clothes. In the two moments it took to steal my
attention from the plans I was laying out for myself, I figured
the child might just be searching for something she'd lost, a
dropped dollar bill or a left-hand mitten or some twelve-year-
old's secret belongings. But when she didn't raise herself from
where she'd hidden, I thought, *Well, Murphy, here's a matter
for your direct attention.*

And I did head straight over to Mr. Thomas with a mind
to tell him what I'd just seen. I found him changing into his

clothes in the bedroom, so I knocked on the open door before entering.

"Murphy," Mr. Thomas said, "you're just the man I need."

When I stepped through the doorway I found Mr. Thomas sitting on the side of the bed and holding his sock out to me with the top rolled down and white foot powder already spread around inside. Mr. Thomas, I should point out, could manage to reach the foot on his good leg just fine, but when it came to putting a sock on the foot beneath his bad one, he was helpless to do it. As a boy and, if my memory's right, as a young man, he'd been able to accomplish the task himself, but as a fully grown man he could not. His body wouldn't bend enough in the middle to manage.

It was a piddling thought, I guess, but I'd wondered before how he'd managed getting that sock on those times when he found himself alone. What about those years between Miss Barbara's passing and finding Miss Catherine? How'd he manage then?

For the life of me, I don't know, and I swear I almost asked that morning as I kneeled before the man's bed and slipped that sock over his foot and spied the arrow-shaped scars that ran up and down his leg like a pig's tracks through the mud. You see such a thing, and you just don't mind lending your assistance on that score. Of course, any nigger who witnessed the act of me kneeling before this man might want a word or two with me for going to such extremes for a white man's comfort, but the truth is I knew Mr. Thomas felt worse about asking than I could ever feel on being asked.

I'd performed this service probably going on a hundred times in my life, as when Mr. Thomas would have somewhere to get to early in the morning in Mandeville and not want to disturb Miss Catherine's sleep, but it didn't occur to me until this particular morning that a man such as Mr. Thomas could want a woman's company for even so simple a reason as to have someone at hand who wouldn't make him feel the least bit of discomfort over such a request as he had to make day in and day out, someone who would perform this service not from feeling sorry for the man — which was my thought no matter how I tried to rearrange it in my head — but out of a pure and simple feeling.

Well, I finished in two seconds flat and stood up and Mr. Thomas said, "I guess you ought to get going," using that weary voice he'd used all week, as though he was damn near giving up on his own life and everyone else's. But then he put his hands back behind him on the bed and bounced himself up, making himself look like a happy child the way he shot to his feet. I knew it was the only way for the man to get himself upright, hurling his body in the air and counting on his strength to keep himself well balanced when he landed, but it looked like a child's doing anyhow.

"You be careful with that car," Mr. Thomas said once he'd caught his breath, and he gave me a quiet laugh and a handshake. "I don't want them fishing you out of the water again."

"I'm not going near the water, believe me, Mr. Thomas," I said. "Your car will be fine because Murphy will be fine, I'll make damn sure."

Mr. Thomas laughed, then put a hand on my shoulder. "You'll go to Natchitoches?" he said.

"I'd appreciate the opportunity," I answered.

"That's fine," he said.

I'd shared with Mr. Thomas that aspect of my plan, saying I'd learned of a relative there I wouldn't mind paying a visit to. He was my mother's cousin, I told Mr. Thomas, adding that he was now old and infirm, which had been true ten years before. Now he was dead.

My mother's cousin, the good Reverend So-and-so Pugh, had landed in north Louisiana from Georgia as a Baptist minister, taking on a congregation ten miles outside of town composed mostly of tenant farmers and, during the summertime, nigger migrants. It was through the good reverend, when he'd traveled once through Mandeville on his way to a Baptist conference in New Orleans, that I'd learned years before of the rumors about Mollie Moore Eagen's misfortune, if that was in all truth the woman who on two occasions shuffled her feet through the church door with a child in her arms but did not speak to a soul except, the second time, to the good reverend, asking for the child's baptism.

The good reverend, as I said, was my mother's cousin. In my mother's last days, when she was sick in bed, he came down once or twice, always just a stop on his way somewhere else, and he would sit by her bed and let her go on and on about the kind love of the Lord. He gave as good as he got, telling her of the Lord's promise of eternal life in a place without tears or sorrow or strife, and I guess I have to give the man credit for whatever comfort my mother took from his words. Even so, he was a man I'd never liked, even as a boy. To Miss Mollie Moore, or whoever it was asking for her child's baptism, he told me he replied, "We only baptize, good sister, when a child can himself profess a commitment, but we'd be happy to share in the years' triumphant march," or some such nonsense. The woman, as you would expect, turned away in silence, without even saying if the child she was carrying was a boy or a girl.

Three weeks later the woman and child were found dead, my mother's cousin heard, though he said he knew nothing more of the circumstances. Both were buried by the Catholic parish, not by the good reverend's congregation. I asked him, without seeming too interested, to provide me with whatever other information could be found.

"You think you might have had the acquaintance of this poor woman?" the good reverend asked.

"I might," I said, but I was not about to offer any more explanation than that.

Either there was no more news of the woman or the information never reached me or the good reverend had other, more important matters at hand. What did finally reach me, through the pages of the *Times-Picayune* and written up in one of those special small-print obituary boxes you paid a handsome sum for, was the news that the good reverend had passed away. I later heard, though this was surely not contained in that obituary box, that my mother's cousin had passed from shotgun pellets that either he himself or someone else scattered all over the side of his head. He was sick with cancer in any case, and I heard something along the lines of him arranging the killing himself, eager to see his pain exchanged for a first fine glimpse of heaven.

That was one more sad story, at least to me, if not to the good reverend smiling down from heaven, and I did feel some discomfort, even considering my dislike, over denying to Mr. Thomas this man's passing for the sake of what I longed to learn. But when you're in for a dime, you're in for a dollar, and I didn't want to cast into Mr. Thomas's mind a single doubt on the good intentions I'd professed.

Well, maybe that's why I just didn't mention to Mr. Thomas the sight I'd seen through the window. I'd deal with that myself rather than delay or jeopardize my whole endeavor.

"You call if there's a problem," Mr. Thomas said, and he shook my hand again.

"There won't be, I'll make sure," I told him, knowing full well that a problem was already lying buried beneath a pile of clothes on the floor of his damn car. I turned around and near-whistled my way down the stairs and out the door, as blind and happy as a just-freed nigger.

As soon as I stepped off that porch, though, I felt something in the cold wind that struck my face. It may be nothing for a man to place a dollar on a horse that's already gone and won his race, but walking in the direction of Mr. Thomas's car, I could have bet that I'd seen the last of the man, as if there had just been something between us, something between those two handshakes that was like a final farewell.

That's not a comfortable feeling when what you don't know is if you're staring straight in the face of your own or another man's misfortune. I can look back at that moment when I shook the man's hand the second time and say there was also something like a final bit of mercy in our exchange, as if he was doing me some greater favor than I would ever ascertain. Maybe just that final sight of him was the mercy I mean.

Of course, I have considered that the mercy might well have been my own to show. A week is not much time to care for two children, not for someone who spends his whole grown life doing so, but I'd taken some pride in knowing that looking after Miss Meredith and Mr. Lowell was what Mr. Thomas needed from me in exchange for the care he'd shown, arranging payment for my hospital stay and holding off the law and not mentioning so much as indirectly the two years I was gone, giving me a bed to lie down on and food to eat, the whole while never placing any of my past sins before me like a dead rat served up on a plate. It's true we faced each other that week one hundred times like two brothers aiming to put all past disagreements aside but knowing the whole time so much of the secret heart beating inside the other's chest that we could, with a mind to and half the chance, shoot our hands out right through the other's ribs and squeeze the life out like that heart was nothing more than a wide-eyed fish just hooked.

Mr. Thomas didn't even set about trying to hide the pitiful sadness that had overtaken him so. Two days that week, when the children were off at school, he'd asked me to ride with him out to the house he'd quit when he left Miss Catherine, and of course I obliged. I wasn't sure what he wanted me to do, so I spent much of my time watching television in the family room while Mr. Thomas made his way through the house filling boxes with this and that, mostly Miss Catherine's belongings as best as I could tell. On the television I watched the soap opera shows, all about life in towns scrubbed so squeaky white they wouldn't know a nigger from the doorknob turning in their hands. Every once in a while Mr. Thomas would call to me and I'd follow his voice until I found him, then he'd point to something up on some shelf he couldn't reach or he'd want me to help him drag a box up near the front door.

The second day, when the front room and hall were filled with boxes, I couldn't stop myself from asking Mr. Thomas about his intentions. "Where's this going?" I asked, wondering if he planned to ship it all out to Miss Catherine in North Carolina or maybe bring it to Magazine Street so he'd have it handy to break his heart with over and over.

Mr. Thomas looked at me then for a moment that lasted too

long for my own comfort. Then, as if the thought had just come to him, he said, "They're for you, Murphy. I think I'd like you to have them."

"Mr. Thomas," I began, wondering what he thought I could do with a woman's things, her clothes and recipe books and pretty picture frames and such. But I stopped myself, realizing that of course he just wanted them off his hands and didn't care what was done with them. "I'll take care of it," I told him. "I'll see they're put to good use."

Mr. Thomas nodded his head and went back to his business of packing, and I sat down again in front of the television. I figured I could make more than a few dollars hauling Miss Catherine's things over to Magazine Street and offering them for sale, but when I pictured Miss Meredith and Mr. Lowell spying those items on the shelf, I realized I couldn't do it. What would those children think if they found Miss Catherine's belongings fixed with price tags and gathering dust? I figured I'd be better off letting the money run through my fingers and just pour out those belongings into the wide Mississippi.

If Mr. Thomas offering me those boxes hadn't been enough for me to wonder if he'd dug himself too deep a hole to see out of, what he did when we were set to leave the house that second day made me know for sure he had.

Once he'd closed and locked the door and the both of us were standing out front, he looked back and said, "I've got a favor I'd like to ask of you, Murphy."

Now the last time I'd been asked to undertake a favor for this family, I'd ended up taking my swim in the Pontchartrain, so I was not eager for the chance at another. Even so, given ten thousand guesses, I never could have landed where Mr. Thomas's thoughts had taken him.

He pulled a cigarette from out his pocket and lit it. "I'd like you to take this house off my hands, Murphy," he said. "That's what I'd like you to do."

As serious as Mr. Thomas might have looked that moment, I just had to laugh. I got a quick flash of myself standing out front of the house in a fancy bathrobe to fetch the morning's

Times-Picayune and waving hello to all the white folks standing out in front of their own to do the same. *Good morning,*
friendly folks. I'm your neighbor.

Well, I laughed and laughed.

Mr. Thomas, I guess, caught my meaning, and he stopped
me with an ice-cold look.

"I understand what I'm doing, Murphy," he told me. "I don't
expect you to live here. You couldn't even pay so much as
the water bill, I know that." He let some smoke glide out his
mouth into the cold air. "And I don't expect you could live on
your own for so much as a week without falling apart at the
seams. We've seen enough of that already, don't you think?"

Mr. Thomas stared at me a moment and then softened his
tone. "I've been thinking of a way to compensate you for all
the years you've given to this family. I thought this house
would do it." He lifted his hand and pointed the cigarette at
me, I don't know why. "You could sell it, Murphy. You'd make
enough to last you. It may be you'll have to find a way to make
it on your own. You understand?"

I looked at Mr. Thomas and knew he was going about adding
up the sum of my parts in his own head, reaching his hand too
close for comfort near the beating of my heart, and I admit I
felt some anger that he'd chosen this moment to do such a
thing. Why didn't he just clear the air between us, go ahead and
put words to all the hate he felt for me for doing what I'd done
so many years before? Instead, he was setting about making
me a charity case, another nigger in need of careful stitching,
which was worse.

For one sad moment I wished he could talk to me nigger to
nigger, one black man to another. I wished he could find whatever it was in himself of his mother's color that she'd passed
down to him, no matter her absence, and let that rule the roost.

I swear I looked at Mr. Thomas right then and thought of the
way his father and I bound those statues so, all wrapped up in
blankets and rope tied so tight you needed a good long knife to
go about the untying. How is it, at the moment the man was
offering me the chance at more money than I'd seen my entire

life, I wanted nothing more than to drag him back inside that house and put an end to his sad life, to tie him up like one of those goddamned statues, leaving him to suffocate in his holy white?

If that's a nigger's pride, so be it. If that was all I had left in me, then what's done is done. There's no way to fight it. But what the nigger's pride does for him is greater than any white man will ever know. The nigger puts his hand out and smiles and shakes the man's hand and says, *I appreciate it mightily, sir.* The nigger accepts the kind offer of charity but all the while hangs on, like he's hanging on to the side of a cliff, to the notion that at any moment, and just as quick as snatching an apple pie off a windowsill, he could grab the white man's neck in his hands, feel the pulsing of blood against his fingertips, and put a quick and easy end to him.

I know it might seem here I'm talking only of hate, of some rage burning in my heart, but I know for a fact that in regard to Mr. Thomas and his father before him and his two children after him, I'm talking also of the feeling that keeps my hands still and lets me laugh and shake my head and when Mr. Thomas says I couldn't care for myself for even one week makes me look him straight in the eye and admit it. And that's what I did. "Well, I guess that's all true," I said to Mr. Thomas, that simple.

Truth, my own mother liked to tell me, is the words you speak when you've run out of all others, and patience is what you have when you know you've already gone and waited too long. Love, she'd say, stretching out the sound of the word like it had stuck smoothly on her lips and would not let go, is finding a dark corner where you hide every ounce of your pride and never mean to return.

I used to laugh at the woman so, an evil, misunderstanding, unforgiving laugh. I didn't know.

Well, it might not be said here by those who think they know better that I'm speaking of something along the lines of that word that stuck smoothly on my mother's lips, but I believe I am. In addition to being an old worn-out nigger, I told myself there and then, I am this man's friend. I am. Facing up to that fact took more of my strength than strangling him.

Well, Mr. Thomas and I headed over and climbed into the car as though we were set to lead the way on a grand and sad funeral procession, as though we had a flower-covered corpse riding along in the back seat it wouldn't do to disturb. Even so, I could tell Mr. Thomas was heading back to Magazine Street feeling some sense of relief, feeling considerably better, it seemed to me, than he'd felt in some time. I'd wondered all week if he'd ever take the chance to address not just his personal charges against me but the subject of Miss Catherine and their particular disagreement.

As we passed the City Park and the statue of one General P. G. T. Beauregard up on his horse and the clock made all of shrubs and flowers and two giant iron spokes, Mr. Thomas took a long deep breath and proceeded to say that all this foul-tasting soup as he'd been spooning for some time now had been stirred up by Miss Catherine finding out something about him that wasn't so much true in the way she understood it but was true in its own way nevertheless.

I stopped Mr. Thomas there and then, just long enough to say that while I wasn't following him at just that moment, he should feel free to keep going and eventually I'd catch up. As we passed that clock, I looked at how it had been built up on the side of a small hill, with the statue towering above it and traffic circling around, and I made note of the fact that not once in the hundreds of times I'd thought to check when I went by had those iron spokes ever indicated the correct time.

I'd seen the city's nigger gardeners tending to those shrubs and flowers, the sight of which always reminded me of my father, kneeling down and leaning over and reaching with that certain care that any garden requires, a care even my father knew I would never possess. How was it, I wondered, that no one ever instructed those men to take a moment to set the iron spokes right and provide the citizens of this city with the proper time?

I guess it was all the thoughts I'd been thinking of Mr. Thomas at the house, wanting to do him violence and such, that provided me with a new consideration. Maybe it was all those nigger gardeners who purposefully kept the time wrong, who made damn sure those iron spokes were never lined up properly with the Roman numbers shaped from crape myrtle bush. In any case, I nearly laughed at the thought. What I said to Mr. Thomas, though, was that he should keep talking and I'd surely catch up.

"That's what I've done all through this, Murphy," Mr. Thomas said. "I've tried to catch up with myself. I've tried to look at where I'm going only after I've gotten there. Do you understand?"

Before I could so much as lift my head to nod, Mr. Thomas went on, and I had one of my brief flashes of Mollie Moore, the way she talked her blue streak without so much as a pause to catch her breath.

"Cathy's pregnant," Mr. Thomas went on. "She's pregnant, yes. But the only thing I can keep straight in my head is how I've never longed for my father's presence as much as I have these last two weeks. Not that we ever spoke of such things as this. We never had occasion to, I guess. But I feel as though he'd somehow enable me to see straight. He'd make me understand this."

Rather than tell Mr. Thomas that I still wasn't quite in line with his thinking, I just let him go on. I put my hands on my knees and looked out at the street and kept my mouth shut, just waiting and waiting for him to deliver the only true question in whatever manner he chose: *Why'd you go and do what you did, Murphy?*

"Catherine thinks I've been with another woman," Mr. Thomas said instead, and I damn near shook my head over the sad goings-on and misunderstandings stemming from this world of unholy flesh and blood, but then Mr. Thomas came forth with a laugh that wasn't exactly that but was something different, like it was the sun trying hard to find something bright to shine down on but coming up on absolutely nothing. "Well, I have been with another woman," Mr. Thomas said. "Now I have. It's true."

No matter what folks might say, there is nothing so uncomfortable as one man listening to another speak of such a thing as lying down with a woman, knowing all the while the man speaking is picturing in his head not the rush of feelings he might have felt at that moment but the same sickening turning and twisting a body would make when wrecked by the worst kind of illness. Yes, just those words and I saw in my head Mollie Moore turning and twisting, her pleasing shape bent and twisted so that I felt myself growing sick. How old a woman she would be now, I told myself, old and bent with age like me and all used up, not at all the woman whose features I'd studied and touched.

Would I have loved her still? Would that body being old and stretched with age still feel the same as it had a lifetime before? Yes, it would, I told myself, and I felt near sick again but this time at my own loss, at what I'd missed.

So I was ever more grateful Mr. Thomas did not follow the track of just exactly what he'd gone and done. He'd be speaking one thing and I'd be thinking another. I'd be thinking Mollie Moore.

Instead Mr. Thomas took a breath and said, "What Catherine thinks is that it's a woman, another woman, who is the reason that I don't claim this child she's carrying. That's not the case, Murphy, though God knows I wish it was that simple."

Mr. Thomas kept his eyes on the road, as if he was seeing in the lines of the street, in all those tar patches where the street had cracked and been sealed over, something of his own life. Of course it didn't surprise me that two years after my hearing Miss Catherine say how she wanted a child so and Mr. Thomas didn't, this had become the axe that split the wood.

"Is it my child?" Mr. Thomas said. He looked at me like I was the one to answer that question, and I was sure I saw in his face the very anger and rage that a moment before, standing outside that house, I'd hoped to summon from his soul. Now it scared me, like he was the one about to grab hold of me.

"This is the truth, as best as I know it," Mr. Thomas said, calming himself down. "I feel so confused I can't say for sure whether that child is mine or not. I can even understand Cathy's going and finding another man to give her what she wanted. I would have done the same, I believe. I have now."

Mr. Thomas looked like he might begin to cry, his voice rising and falling as if he could no longer keep it under his own control. "I know this," he said. "I know I didn't want to leave this child. Do you understand? That's what I felt. That's what I feel. I didn't want this child to know me and then one day have me gone. And I knew I would leave her, Murphy. I knew it."

"Like your own mother," I dared to say. It just popped out of my mouth, and I felt with my hands my own legs shaking. I was leading Mr. Thomas down the very path I already feared he would go. I put my hand up to my chest and wondered if this was the moment my heart would quit. I'd have been glad of it, I swear I would have.

But Mr. Thomas acted as if he didn't hear me. Maybe he didn't. "How is it that I knew I would leave her?" he said. "Where is it that I thought I would go? Why in God's name with a good mother for my children would I know that I wouldn't stay with this woman, that I'd think there was something else for me, someone with more than a child's understanding? I don't understand it. I swear I don't. Did I never love this woman at all, Murphy?"

It was not for me to answer that question, I knew, though I did think how at that moment Mr. Thomas was saying things his own mother might well have said had she looked at herself long and straight enough to do it.

"She is no more than a child, Murphy," Mr. Thomas said. "She has a child's hope, a child's forgiveness, a child's sense of what is right and wrong in this world. She's like my father, only he made himself that way to shut everything else out. That's not enough. I wish it was, but it's not."

I wanted then to ask Mr. Thomas one simple question. I tried to put it out of my mind but couldn't. Just my thinking of the question made it seem to grow inside my head.

Was this woman he'd now been with a nigger? What else

would this sad life, all this black and white mixed up in the man's head, have come to except for that? It should have been of no account, but that wasn't true. I knew it. I knew it more than anything else I'd known my whole life. I knew it from all my thoughts of Mollie Moore. I knew it from more than forty years of shaking hands with and standing next to one Lowell Henry Eagen, his skin as white as all those statues, though by the end covered with splotchy red, strawberry-colored patches on his neck and arms and on his back and under his arms; my skin the color of rain-soaked oak wood and, during the heat and sunshine of summer, mud; my hands and the very soles of my feet the pink-gone-to-brown of a horse's belly. How was it I'd lived going on seventy years and could get at nothing more than that, one color compared to another, everything else an awful mystery you knew was there but had no words for and could not in a million years offer so much as a single word of explanation for but knew nevertheless, knew with every ounce of bone and muscle and dark-colored, dark as a moonless night, skin?

Well, I didn't ask Mr. Thomas such a question as the color of this woman he'd lain down with. I might as well, I knew, ask about the world's creation. Mr. Thomas couldn't see that it wasn't Miss Catherine's being a child that bothered him so, that kept him from loving the woman the way he felt he should. No, it was his feeling that she'd never understand what it was to walk in his shoes, never understand what it meant to have such questions about his own life swimming around in his head every hour of the day and night. What if his skin had been a few shades darker? What if the world had given him no choice but to live a black man's life, set himself up in a black man's house and work a black man's job? What if he'd had no choice but to lay down with a black woman who in time would hand to him his own black children, and these children would then pay the same price for their blackness he'd have been asked to pay?

So I didn't ask the color of this woman. I rooted around until I ended up somewhere else, somewhere I could still take my own breath without feeling like there was no air left. I asked Mr. Thomas about his intentions. Was he planning on asking Miss Catherine back from North Carolina? Had he thought of that?

He looked at me then as if I'd not heard a word of what he'd said, the kind of look a mother gives a child when the child asks for something that not ten minutes before he was straight out denied.

"I don't know, Murphy," Mr. Thomas said. "I don't know what I'll do."

"You'll find out," I said, just to give the man some comfort. "The answer will come to you in time."

"I keep praying that's the case," Mr. Thomas said. "It hasn't yet, though."

"It will," I said. "You'll decide what's right." And I held hope up despite all my worries of what I knew of this world — that these two weeks would spread to months and then to years and Mr. Thomas would one day find himself an old man like me who'd spent a lifetime tending to sorrows of his own making.

It was at this moment Mr. Thomas spoke words that cut off all I'd just been thinking. "I'll tell you what Cathy thinks, Murphy, though I know she's wrong. I know she is." Mr. Thomas pounded his hands on the steering wheel. "What she thinks is that all this has to do with my mother's leaving, with her being a black woman who left her white husband, with my being uncertain about my own color."

In my head I said, *Yes, sir, and she's not the only one, believe me.*

"That's not true," Mr. Thomas said, angry now, as though I had indeed gone ahead and spoken. "It's not my mother who left me with so much confusion. I didn't know her. She wasn't real to me. Maybe I had dreams of her, the way Lowell and Meredith surely have dreams of Barbara. But those are just dreams. They're just the longings any children would have."

I wanted to say to Mr. Thomas that Miss Barbara's passing was a different animal completely from the skittish wolf of a mother who gets frightened so fully by her own reflection and what it tells her as to leave both husband and children. I didn't say it, of course. I didn't even have the chance.

"It's my father I keep thinking of," Mr. Thomas said. "Now go and tell me why that is, because that's the point where all my explanations stop, where I've got nothing but a great silent darkness when I start asking questions."

"Your father was a good man," I said to Mr. Thomas, and I heard Mollie Moore's voice in my head. "He was just wronged." I almost pointed out to Mr. Thomas how in addition it was his own mother who'd done the wronging, but I didn't trust myself from tacking on to that statement two more words, my own name.

"I know he was a good man," Mr. Thomas said. "I swear I feel sometimes he did such a fine job of storing away all his sorrow that he might as well have packed it in a suitcase and handed it to me. He might as well have said, 'Here, son, take this with you. I've got no use for it.' "

"No one's got use for it, Mr. Thomas," I said. "But that don't mean it won't cling to you nevertheless."

"He should have done better," Mr. Thomas said, screaming now, the car swerving this way and that under his shaking hands.

I held on and said, "Done better at what?"

"Just better," Mr. Thomas said. "Better."

I wondered then if it could truly be all so simple as Mr. Thomas's feeling as if it was in his father's pain that all his answers lay, that if he choked that ghost of Lowell Henry Eagen just long enough and hard, if he tore that man apart to the spittling tissue clear down to the bones, he'd find the answer to the whole great universe, an answer as simple as that one word Mr. Thomas said over and over again. If I had not known before that moment, I knew now that it's the very feeling of loss, not what's been lost, that shapes a life. It was true for me, too. I knew it was. It wasn't Mollie Moore I wanted still through all those years, it was getting rid of the feeling that I'd lost her.

Now I felt like it was me Mr. Thomas had been tearing at so forcefully. It was my own body that hurt.

Mr. Thomas drove on then without speaking another word. When we pulled up to the house and Mr. Thomas was ready to let me out the car so he could drive off again, I guess to see whoever this woman was that was tending to his pain in all the wrong ways, like she was wrapping dirty bandages across each and every one of Mr. Thomas's wounds, he acted as if all that had just passed really hadn't. He told me of Miss Catherine's letters and said he'd like for me to kindly go get them if I would.

I looked at him in such a way as he knew I was wondering why he didn't go and get those letters himself. The look he gave me back, though he didn't say a word, told me his answer. The man didn't trust himself to come back. He figured if the pain he felt could let him leave his wife and the child she was carrying, he could just as easily find himself leaving behind his own two dear children already born and half raised, and that was more fear than any man could dare to face.

It's a dark world, I decided, darker than any nigger's or white man's nightmare vision. That's the point all that talking had brought me to, that it's a dark world and we can do no more than help to hand the other along in all that darkness, blind leading the blind.

"I'll get those letters for you," I said to Mr. Thomas. "I'd be happy to."

Mr. Thomas nodded his head and drove off with as solemn a face as the Lord Jesus Christ must have had when he knew that all that was left to him was the dying part.

Well, it was my own mercy for the man in not pushing him to get those letters. That's part of what I felt a few days later in the cold wind that struck my face as I looked back at the falling-down house on Magazine Street and knew this was the last of Mr. Thomas Eagen I'd ever witness. I'd shown my own mercy for the man. I had.

But then the wind that had struck me just quit as suddenly as someone shutting off a fan, and I continued on to Mr. Thomas's car, where Miss Meredith was waiting under all those clothes. I figured there'd be no harm in driving a block or two with the child still hidden, but then I thought better of it and said enough under my breath to let her know I was aware of her presence.

Now why didn't I make of Miss Meredith the demand that she exit the car directly? Why was I bent so on feeding the flames instead of putting an end to them?

Well, I could see clear enough that it was a piece of this child's own life I was going off to retrieve as much as my own or Mr. Thomas's, and I didn't see the harm in tending to all of that at once. At the same time, I'd be providing Mr. Thomas with a friendly phone call informing him that his only daughter had been a stowaway making a secret passage in pursuit of news from Miss Catherine. That would make the man think about what matters in this world.

And I thought then of some words, boy to man and then back, that had passed between us so many years before. There were times when Mr. Thomas was growing up that his father asked me to drive his only son here or there, to the Catholic parish basketball games or on some school assignment or to the house of some friend. I'm speaking of before the accident ruined Mr. Thomas's leg, when he still had the choice of riding in the back of the truck, a choice he always made, clinging to the side and letting the wind rip through his hair. He'd call my name and I'd look out the side mirror, and there he'd be leaning half out of the truck and smiling a sunshine smile, hell-bent on getting my goat.

"Get yourself back, you crazy half-minded boy," I'd yell out the window, playing along but meaning it as well. Mr. Thomas would keep right on, pretending not to hear.

Then one time when I had to make a turn, I saw through the mirror Mr. Thomas's two hands slip and his body shoot forward so I was left looking at his middle instead of his head. If it wasn't for the belt buckle catching hold on the side and holding Mr. Thomas up like a seesaw, I swear he would have sailed clear over and out onto the road.

Once he'd managed to pull himself back in, I turned the

truck to the side, stopped short, and gave Mr. Thomas the one and only tongue-lashing he ever witnessed from out my mouth. Well, when I was done with my cursing and fearful warnings, Mr. Thomas, who couldn't have been more than ten years old, said to me that he would tell his father what I'd done. "You can't say such things to me," the boy said. "You're not allowed."

I knew sure enough what this child was up to. He was telling me that a nigger couldn't talk to him in such a manner without paying the white man's price.

I wanted to strike out at the boy there and then, but I did not. I said, "Your father doesn't give a good goddamn about such thoughts as you're thinking, Mr. Thomas Eagen, so you put them out your head. They won't serve you well in this life, I promise you." Then I grabbed his collar and marched him up to the front of the truck and told him he had a choice. "You sit up here from now on or you travel shank's mare," I told him. "It's your choice."

Well, Mr. Thomas paused a moment in his fear but then stepped directly into that truck and took his seat, and we continued on our way. I don't know for sure if what I'd said made him do it, but he looked over at me and made a kind of pronouncement, like he was expressing some thought that had recently taken root in his head.

"My mother was a nigger," Mr. Thomas said.

Well, I tried not to miss a beat, no matter my surprise. "Yes, she was," I said right back. "A proud one."

Mr. Thomas kept staring at me, like he'd spied a strange animal nosing around in the yard. "Are you a proud nigger, too?" he asked. No matter the words he chose, I knew that Mr. Thomas now meant no offense, that he was playing like a parrot on my shoulder. But there was also something he was after in his question, something the boy was trying to understand but didn't even know he was.

Mr. Thomas asked again. "Are you a proud nigger, Murphy?" he said.

"Not as proud as your mother was," I answered, and while I said those words only for Mr. Thomas's benefit, so he could think of his mother as a woman of some account, I knew there was more than enough truth to my reply to cause me my own discomfort.

"There's the right kind of proud and the wrong kind," I went on. "I've got some of both, I guess."

"I think I do, too," Mr. Thomas said, and not for the rest of his life did I hear any truer words from out his mouth than those he'd just spoken.

Well, I thought of all that for the first time in years and years when trying to decide what to do about Miss Meredith curled up under those clothes. I stopped the car once we were off Magazine Street, and I said for her to get out and come sit up front.

Once she did, I said, "We've got to address just what's going on here, Miss Meredith."

The child looked straight at me but didn't say a word.

I took a good long look before resuming the drive, wondering how much of her want Miss Meredith understood and how much she didn't. If it's true a man's understanding of the world is passed along to his child, I figured Miss Meredith didn't have much of a chance on that score. She might as well be hobbling along in the manner of her father, one hand out and running her fingers along the wall just to keep her balance, the way Mr. Thomas did when he first started walking again after the hospital. I remember how for weeks and weeks I had to take a damp washrag to those walls to wipe away the imprint of Mr. Thomas's fingers, shaking my head over both the boy's poor fortune and the strength he showed in setting his mind to such a task.

Well, I can excuse myself for the trouble caused by my decision on what to do about Miss Meredith's presence because I had her own interests in mind and not my own. I decided that telling her she couldn't take the ride to receive Miss Catherine's letters was like telling the boy Mr. Thomas he shouldn't try to walk. *Let things be,* you say, and you've done your best to wreck the child's spirit. So I decided the choice had to be Miss Meredith's, and she'd already chosen.

"Here's what we're going to do," I said, and Miss Meredith kept looking at me with her wide-open eyes, her mouth as silent as if someone had come along and stitched it shut. "We're going straight on to Mandeville, but we're calling your father from the house as soon as you've put two feet through the door. You're going to tell him straight out what you've done, only you're going to say you stayed hidden well past half of the drive. Then you made a noise and I thought there might be a rat making a nest among all those clothes and I pulled over, only to discover it was you."

Miss Meredith kept up her stare, and I felt so for her that I said, "I don't blame you for wanting to go, Miss Meredith. I'd have done the same, I imagine."

Still the child didn't utter a word, and I wondered for a moment if something might have happened when she was hidden under all those clothes, if her mind might have taken flight from the fear resulting from being covered up so.

It's a frightful thing, confronting a silent child. It flashed in my mind how all the noise of the world, the sounds made by animals and music and wind and footsteps and even angels singing heavenly hymns, if you believe such a thing — every one of them all rolled together is as nothing when compared to the simple voice of a child.

"I wish you'd speak up, Miss Meredith. Go ahead," I said, and I saw her eyes make just the smallest turn to fix on me. The child hadn't been looking at me that whole time, I realized, and I didn't know for sure if she'd heard so much as a word of what I'd said.

When I turned to look at what she'd been watching, what it was that had grabbed her attention, I saw it. Of course I did. Up in the sky and settling all around us, turning the world as quiet as Miss Meredith herself, was a snowfall.

Not in ten years or more had there been such a sight this far south in Louisiana, and it occurred to me that Miss Meredith might never her whole life have seen a true snowfall. Of course she was struck dumb. The sight of the world starting to get covered with that glorious white did the same to me, and as the two of us sat there side by side, my mind couldn't hold on to any thoughts beyond the feeling that there was something happening and our driving north, into more of that snow, was bound to rush us toward it.

Well, it turns out I was right, more right than I'd ever wish to be. I couldn't have known at that moment that this very evening I'd be walking through that snow with a bruised and beaten and bone-sore body, finding only with each new step into and under that snow the dirt roads that lead past chicken farms, the lights glowing in the coops like each has got a savior being born inside and canefields stripped bare and brown under all that white and shack houses sheltering nigger families whose only wish is to hang on through winter until there's more peaches and cotton to pick, more sugarcane to cut, those rundown shacks that look like they came straight from picture books with all that white clinging to their roofs.

One day more and I'd have paid an awful price for taking Miss Meredith along with me to Natchitoches, but after that I'd be putting one foot in front of the other with enough time in between to take a breath and feel my heart pounding so inside my body, getting as good a look as a man could ever want to get of the spot of earth where he'd be next, and having seen the last of Mr. Thomas Eagen and his children and his wife, I'd feel as cold as if I'd been packed one hundred years in ice but fine nevertheless, putting one foot in front of the other, Miss Mollie Moore Eagen finally behind me instead of ahead, feeling hungry and beaten up but looking down at my feet and reminding myself that they were carrying me forward at last.

I didn't know any of that, of course, when I was sitting there in that car with Miss Meredith and watching the snow. But I felt it somehow, I think. I did feel something. And that was enough to let me know that while I'd lived a long enough life to learn my lessons on the awful and frightful ways this world can be, I had at least one more lesson ahead.

"Let's us get going before this snow gets too bad, Miss Meredith," I said, and so we did.

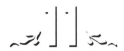

I WAS NOT, I knew, a dangerous child, not ever.

The car began to move, and I worried that Murphy meant to head all the way to Mandeville with no further acknowledgment of my presence, as if just by saying that he didn't know I was hiding there behind him he could make it true. But how could I spend two hours crouched in the darkness on the dirty floor of my father's Checker, clothes heaped over me like tattered, musty blankets?

I couldn't do it, I decided, so I tried to push myself up. But the car suddenly turned and I lost my balance, my right arm and then my shoulder slipping beneath the seat, my knees scraping on the grainy mat and locking beneath me. All I could feel was the car's engine, its vibrations through the floor, a steady rumbling. I smelled gasoline, exhaust from the engine, and felt dizzy, as though I were falling.

I lay there, desperate to get up but unable to move. Then I felt the car slow and come to a stop, and I heard Murphy order me to come sit up front.

Once I'd managed to pull my arm and shoulder out from under the seat, I pushed the clothes off me and swung open the door. When I stepped out of the car, I didn't see so much as feel the snow begin, pinpricks of ice on my lips and cheeks and eyelids, a quick, surprising chill in my hand when I ran my fingers through my hair.

I walked around the front of the Checker, afraid that Murphy might drive off once I was out of the way, leaving me to trudge off to school as if nothing had happened. Murphy waited, though, while I moved over to the passenger door, and only after I had climbed back into the car, after Murphy had begun to speak — his voice trembling, so that what I heard was the trembling and not his words — did I actually think, *Yes, it's snowing; this is snow.*

I thought then of Lowell and missed him, wishing he was there in the car with me. The year before, during our Christmas vacation, Lowell had spent a weekend camping with the family of a school friend, a round and happy boy named Felicien Lozes, at some park cabin in Mississippi, up somewhere near Jackson. It had rained all weekend in New Orleans, but further north they'd gotten snow — almost a foot of it, Lowell said — and he returned full of stories about snowball fights and icicle duels, the icicles plucked off tree branches and the low edge of the cabin roof. At dawn they spied above their cocked but unloaded shotguns brown rabbits and squirrels darting through the white woods — the easiest of targets, Lowell told me, as if he'd known what he was doing, as if he'd shot a gun a thousand times before, which of course he hadn't.

When Murphy said we ought to head on to Mandeville before the snow got too bad, I almost told him I'd decided that I didn't want to go, that I'd rather spend the day in school hoping the snow would continue and the whole city would end up covered in white; then Lowell and I would be free to spend what remained of the day playing along Magazine Street.

I had spent more time in the last two weeks in Lowell's presence than I could ever remember spending before, but he'd remained as dim to me as a shadow at sunset, his confident swagger among those on Magazine Street somehow unreal and insubstantial. At night, when he locked the door to his room, when he refused to respond to my knocking, I was desperate to know exactly what he was doing, simply to sit there with him and share his company.

Years later, when Lowell married, when he and his new wife moved from their small apartment in New Orleans to a house in Covington, I drove across the causeway to visit them, and Lowell pulled out from a taped cardboard box the sketches he'd drawn on Magazine Street, his portraits of the shop owners and the men who gathered at night beneath the streetlights to drink and laugh and tell stories. Seeing Lowell's sketches, I was struck first by how accomplished they were, then by how angry each of the portraits seemed. I wondered if these were true representations, if Lowell had seen something in these people's lives that I had not, or if the anger was actually his own.

How had I not come to know my brother, my twin, any better? I could, if I wanted, call to mind the smallest detail about him: his thick fingers and wide palms, which were, even when he was a boy, so much like my father's, so different from my own, or the way his left eye twitched ever so slightly when he wanted to suggest a bemused detachment from whatever was going on. But beyond the sight of him, his presence, what did I know?

I thought of how once, when we were carving jack-o'-lanterns for Halloween, I'd showed him what I had done. My pumpkin was carved with one eye slightly smaller than the other, the mouth curved up in a thin, almost imperceptible smile. "It's you," I said, and even as he shook his head to deny any resemblance, he gave me that very look.

"It's him, Catherine, isn't it?" I'd said, turning the pumpkin so she could see. Catherine's hands were wet and sticky from scooping out the pumpkins with a wooden spoon, but she laughed and brushed her wrist along the top of my head.

"Oh, Lowell, it is!" she said.

Only then did Lowell laugh, too.

"Thomas, come see," Catherine called, and my father wandered over from whatever he was doing. "Look at your son, the jack-o'-lantern," Catherine told him, and we all laughed.

I carried the pumpkin outside and my father reached down inside to light the candle. We stood back and admired it. "Thanks a lot, Meredith," Lowell said. He put his hand on my shoulder as if he meant to shove me, but he didn't. "That's really great," he said. "Just wait to see what I do to you with mine."

But I could tell he was happy to have us all standing there seeing his face in the glowing shape of the jack-o'-lantern. He said, "Let's go back inside. It's cold." But we didn't move. Lowell just stood beside me with his hands in his pockets, smiling, my father and Catherine behind us, my father's arm around Catherine's shoulder, pulling her close.

I was still thinking of Lowell, wondering what he would make of this snowy day, when Murphy started the car again and drove off. "Are you sure now you're feeling well enough for travel, Miss Meredith?" he asked, but I didn't look at him. I simply nodded and watched the snow fall all around us, melting as soon as it touched the street but accumulating on the lawns and the neutral ground and on the streetcar rails and the magnolia trees along St. Charles.

My father once told me that when he was a boy, they'd had a heavy snow in Mandeville, enough to cover the garden out back — enough, I imagined, to fill the pond around Saint Francis, the snow rising up above the green-stained hem of Saint Francis's robe until he seemed to be walking on top of a cloud, which is where I thought all the saints lived, their robes always bathed in streaks of sunlight and damp with a fine mist.

I asked my father how old he'd been when they'd had that snow, but he said he didn't remember.

"Were you little or big?" I asked.

"I was medium-size, I guess," my father said. He paused for a moment and then added, "I honestly don't remember how old, Lamb. I was in school. It was a school day, I remember that."

What I'd meant by my question, what I'd really wanted to know, was whether that snow had come before or after my father hurt his leg. I figured that surely all my father's childhood memories must include that piece of information, an asterisk beside each event to remind him whether the boy who'd done this or that had been healthy or lame.

Sitting in the car and heading for Mandeville, I wondered if I would divide my own memories so, with our leaving Catherine and ending up on Magazine Street forming as sharp a division as the break in the causeway when it collapsed. There was this side and that side, and no traveling between them.

When I finally turned to look at Murphy, he seemed frightened, as if he was thinking how angry my father would be to discover I'd gone with him.

"I'll tell him it was my fault, Murphy," I said. "I will."

Murphy looked quickly at me and then back at the road. "Yes, ma'am, you will," he said. "You'll tell Mr. Thomas in no uncertain terms that Murphy was unaware of your presence. You caught him by surprise, you'll say."

Murphy sounded so angry now that I told him I was sorry. "I'm not trying to get you in trouble," I said, and I curled my hands inside my duffle coat and felt my nails press against my palms.

"Trouble?" Murphy said, and he laughed, drumming his fingers on the steering wheel the way my father did while driving. "I've gotten such trouble on account of the Eagen family, more's not likely to make much difference. I'd say you've got such trouble filling up inside you, Miss Meredith, there's no helping it spilling over to others."

"I'm sorry anyway," I said, wondering if what Murphy said was actually true. My troubles, I thought, were just my father's spilling over to me, like the fancy fountain my grandfather had once made, one bowl standing above another, and that one above another, each wider than the one above to catch the overflowing water.

Murphy looked over at me and laughed again. "Go on," he said, "I'm just teasing. Don't pay me any mind."

Then he turned the car onto Broad Street, and we passed a pumping station with giant bright blue pipes curving up from beneath the road and into the walls. Those pipes, I knew, ran under the ground through the whole city, pulling water from the drains on every street whenever there was a heavy rain, sending the water through a series of canals into the Mississippi. The pumps never seemed to work very fast, though, and by the time the rain was done the streets were sometimes flooded, water rushing through neighborhoods and halfway up driveways like mountainside rivers. Lowell and I liked to stand out front of our house and feel the rush of water into the drain, the pull so strong we could look down and see the water curve around our legs like a rushing stream moving past stumps, leaves and twigs scratching our ankles to gather against the drain's metal grid.

My father had explained to us the reason that New Orleans needed its water pumped from the streets and into the Mississippi. Because the city was below sea level, he said, the water wouldn't run off anywhere but would instead just sit there; the ground was already too marshy and damp for the water to seep in. That was why houses were built on pilings the length of telephone poles hammered down into the earth. Otherwise, the houses would settle into the mud, walls separating from other walls, the floors leaning one way in one room, the other way in another. That was why the city's streets and sidewalks always sagged and cracked and then needed to be filled with tar, and it was why you couldn't just bury a body in the earth but had to set it in a marble or granite tomb. Otherwise, over the years and years, my father said, the water would gradually force the body to float back up to the surface. The bones would emerge from the mud like dinosaur fossils.

In the cemeteries near City Park and in the one where my mother was buried, everyone was laid to rest in that manner, the larger tombs lined with marble doors, each carved with a family member's name. Each of the cemeteries looked more like some ancient and abandoned miniature city than a place to lay the dead.

In the nigger cemeteries, though, there weren't any giant tombs or great marble squares, only headstones like the ones my grandfather made. Did they simply pull the bones out once they'd risen to the surface? I wondered if one day, when we visited my grandfather's grave, we'd come upon his headstone and see him there, his skeleton stretched out in the earth like a bas-relief, like the sculptures the ancient Greeks carved into the walls of their buildings.

Murphy turned the car onto Gentilly Boulevard, and I saw a house I recognized, a tiny white shotgun with green shutters and awnings that had belonged to a man named Jack whom my father once knew, another doctor who'd been something else before that, a lawyer or stockbroker or some other job having to do with money. Once, when my father and Jack disappeared together one night — gone, Catherine said, to watch some awful old western at the movies — Catherine had frowned and said, "I swear those two are cut from the same cloth." I didn't know exactly what that meant, but Jack was the only true friend I ever knew my father to have, the only man my father would stand next to and not give the impression there was somewhere else he'd rather be, some other, more important business that required his attention.

Early one summer evening just before twilight, we were all at Jack's house and he gave Lowell and me a ride in his tiny red sportscar, first one and then the other because the car only had two seats. When it was my turn, Jack raced down Elysian Fields all the way to Pontchartrain Beach, the tiny white lights on the roller coaster's scaffolding switching on just as we drove by. I pointed to the lights and Jack smiled, taking both hands off the steering wheel for a quick moment and laying them over his heart to suggest that he understood the magic a child would feel in witnessing such a moment as this.

As Jack headed back toward his house, the wind blew so hard against my face that I felt as if I couldn't breathe. Jack tried talking to me while he drove, leaning over and yelling toward my ear, but I couldn't hear him and he finally gave up.

I looked over as we raced past all the houses on Elysian Fields, each one exactly like the next, with giant sloped lawns cut in the middle by concrete steps that led up and up until you got to a screened-in front porch, nearly every house white, like Jack's. We passed Saint Roch's Church and Lawrence's Bakery, places where I'd been before, and then past the crowded red-brick Saint Bernard housing project with fans turning in every window, the light from inside flickering like a movie projector. I wanted to scream because Jack was going so fast, but instead I let the wind press my back and shoulders against the seat while my hair whipped against my head like a thick rope someone was tugging from behind me.

My father had told me that Jack was once a soldier in the Korean war. The only other thing I knew about him was what Catherine had said — that Jack had been married but that his wife had killed herself some years before. They hadn't had any children, she told me.

What happened to Jack's wife made me afraid of him, as if the pain he'd suffered had somehow left him dangerous, wholly unpredictable and mysterious, and I was relieved when he slowed down, turned the sportscar back into his driveway, and let me out.

"You're next, Cathy," Jack said, but she shook her head.

"I don't like those little things. They're like bugs," she said, and although she smiled, she seemed as afraid of Jack as I was.

Jack kept insisting, and Catherine kept saying no, and soon everyone was more than a little uncomfortable. "Some other time," Catherine stammered. "I promise."

My father, who'd been standing back and smiling during the whole discussion, finally stepped up and said, "Just leave her alone, Jack."

Jack revved the engine a few times and then turned the car off and raised his hands over his head. "I've dropped my weapon," he said to Cathy. "I'm unarmed."

"Thank you, Jack," she said, but her face was flushed as if she were embarrassed.

I didn't know what happened to Jack beyond the fact that he moved away until years later, when my father was living alone in Mandeville, a letter arrived from New York. My father didn't mention the letter. Maybe he thought that I wouldn't even remember Jack or that the letter would mean nothing to me.

But during one of my weekend visits, shortly before my father died, I saw the letter sitting on his desk, the envelope sliced open with the wooden duck's-head letter opener Lowell and I had given him as a birthday present thirty years before. I read the letter after my father went to bed.

In the letter Jack said that for no reason in particular, he often found himself thinking about my father and just wanted to catch him up on what had happened in his life the last few years — the women he almost married but didn't, the university hospital where he now worked, seeing patients and conducting research. At the end of the letter, Jack wrote, "Tell Cathy I've gone and bought a new MG and will take her for a spin when I come down your way again. Tell the girl I'm old and driving slow these days, so there's nothing to fear."

How was it that my father had never mentioned to Jack, no matter how occasional their correspondence, that he had not so much as laid eyes on Catherine in nearly twenty-five years? How could a man be struck so dumb about his own life?

It was only when reading this letter that it fully occurred to me how lonely both my father and Catherine must have been through all those years they were married and, for my father at least, all the years after. Why hadn't they had more friends? We'd lived, it seemed, in a house completely shut off from the world, and I didn't know how or why that had happened.

After reading Jack's letter to my father, I wanted to write back to him. "Come down here, would you?" I wanted to say. "He needs you." But of course I never wrote that letter. I knew that it was useless, that my father was well beyond saving by some old acquaintance who'd only want to make the casual investment of drinking a few beers and trading stories about the fine old times they'd had. If he couldn't be saved by his own grown-up child, who was willing to give him all the time and space in the world to talk himself through his life, then no one else was likely to be able to save him.

I stopped thinking about Jack as soon as Murphy turned the car onto the Chef Menteur Highway, which was almost empty except for giant trucks shooting past us as if the rough-faced drivers hadn't even noticed it was snowing. Murphy switched on the radio, listened for a moment, then switched it off again. "Are we going to pass most of this trip in silence, Miss Meredith?" he said.

"No," I said, but I'd been seeing in my head again that picture of Lowell and me standing there in the flooded street, looking down at ourselves like our feet had been replaced by the rush of water. What had been the exquisite pleasure there? What was it that made me feel again, just by thinking of it, the warm sun on our heads and necks and shoulders after hours and hours of rain, the cool water on our feet, Lowell's laughter, my own?

I missed Lowell, I knew that. I wanted him with me. I wanted at least to know where he was, what he was doing.

I turned to Murphy and said, "Can we go get my brother? We could pick him up at school. He'd go with us."

"Miss Meredith," Murphy said, angry again. "I'd be more than happy to turn around and bring you on home. I'd do it in two shakes of a lamb's tail. But that's it. I'm not prepared to tell Mr. Thomas that the both of you children were gone into hiding in back this car. Lies as tall as the Empire Building are certain to fall."

"Okay," I said. "Fine, keep going," trying to match Murphy's angry tone with my own.

"You watch yourself, Miss Meredith," Murphy said. "I've set about doing you a favor here, and it would be well for you to recognize it as such."

"I'm sorry," I said. "I didn't mean anything." I decided then that for the rest of the trip, I'd try not to think about anything — not Lowell, not Catherine's letters waiting for me in Mandeville, not my father's response when I called to tell him what I'd done.

Once we'd left the city and started passing the fishing camps along the lake, the snow got a little heavier and I could hear the sound of it crunching under the car tires. Besides the noise from the tires and the car's engine, the world had gone quiet, and I could hear each one of Murphy's raspy breaths, as if the simple act of breathing were difficult for him. The car windows frosted over, and Murphy pulled a white handkerchief from his back pocket — one of my father's handkerchiefs, I guessed, since he seemed to have hundreds — and wiped it across the windshield so he could see.

"It's warm in here, at least," he said, but he looked at me as if he'd asked a question.

"It is," I said. "It's fine."

After that, we rode for a while in silence. Murphy turned the radio back on, pushing one button and then the next as if he were playing a piano to the music. "Mr. Thomas is most certainly a character," he said, shaking his head. "He is."

"What's wrong with him?" I asked.

"I didn't mean to suggest there was anything wrong with Mr. Thomas, Miss Meredith," Murphy said. "I only meant he's got his own habits, like this radio's only having one station. That's all."

"I know," I said, "but there's something wrong with him, isn't there?"

"There's nothing wrong with Mr. Thomas beyond being lonely and scared," Murphy said. "That's all."

A song I thought I recognized was playing, although the truth is the songs that station played always sounded familiar to me. Unlike my father and Lowell, though, I never knew the songs' names. I would hear a particular trumpet blast or a certain spiraling sound from the clarinet or the way the drums clicked and crashed like wooden blocks behind the other instruments, and I'd think how I'd heard that before, but that was it. I didn't have names for what I knew.

Although this music always sounded happy, although it made me picture couples twirling on a dance floor, the women's dresses billowing up around them, there was something sad in it, too. It reminded me of my father, of his awful silence, of the confusion I felt in his presence, the way he could look so solid and powerful but also seem somehow off-balance, his feet turned out and his hand on my shoulder or Lowell's, as if he had a hard time just standing.

"Why's he scared?" I asked Murphy. "I don't understand."

"The same as you, I guess," Murphy said. "The same as anyone. You get scared when you're feeling you don't know what's going to happen next. That's always the case, I guess. You don't know, but sometimes you don't feel it. Sometimes you go along thinking you're the captain of the ship. You're not, but it's what you feel."

Murphy pulled out the handkerchief again and wiped the windshield, cursing under his breath. He set the handkerchief down on the dashboard. "Other times, the truth hits you," he said, "and you feel like a starved and thirsty rat on a sinking ship. He knows a good long drink is coming, but it's not the drink he wants."

Murphy gripped the steering wheel with both hands. "I'm sorry, Miss Meredith, about what's happened to your family," he said. "I know there's no finding comfort from that, but I want to say it."

"Why'd we leave?" I asked. "What did he tell you?"

"Mostly nothing," Murphy said. "A whole lot of nothing. He did try, though. The best I can tell is your father doesn't himself half understand his reasons."

"What do you think?" I asked.

"It doesn't much matter what I think," Murphy said.

"It matters to me," I said, and only by saying such a thing did I realize that it might be true. I felt as uncomfortable as I had watching Lowell get pulled close to Murphy's bed in the hospital and imagining it was me.

"I think a lot of things," Murphy said. "I think Miss Catherine probably knows better than anyone else what's at work with your father. Maybe that's all of what she's had to say in those letters."

"Do you think she would have left if we hadn't?" I asked. "Because that's what my father said. He said we had to leave because she would have if we didn't."

"I don't know about all that," Murphy said. "Let's just see what Miss Catherine says." Then he turned to me and said, "I can tell you this, Miss Meredith, and it's not just your father's lesson but my own as well. You'd be much better off paying attention in this world to what you've got than what you've lost."

"Okay," I said, but it seemed to me that if I set about making a list, the things I had wouldn't fill a single page while the things I'd lost would fill a hundred.

We spent the rest of the drive listening to the radio. I heard my father's voice in the music, his singing, the round stretch of vowels, the melody, his pauses. I thought of how he must have sung to us as tiny babies, and I imagined my eyes fixed on him, on the wonder of the sound in my ears, his lips moving, my eyes watching them move, the sound in my ears.

The snow let up, and I looked out the window. I was amazed at how beautiful everything could be. Once we were on the north side of the lake and curving back west toward Mandeville, there started to be pine-tree woods along the side of the road, the snow sifting through the needles whenever the wind picked up, the thin branches up top sagging and spilling the snow.

When we headed into town and crossed the railroad tracks, Murphy turned onto Sharp Street instead of going straight over to the lake. He slowed the car down and turned his head from side to side, looking at the rundown houses, the black-tar shingle roofs and tiny lawns, everything turned white from the snow. Sharp Street seemed cleaner and brighter than it had ever seemed before, with children playing in the snow, pulling each other along on flattened cardboard boxes and giant blankets, tumbling over one another and shouting.

"Will you look at all this?" Murphy said, clearly as amazed as I was by the brilliance of the scene, as if it were a beautiful picture painted in honor of our return. "Gone just two short years and they wash the whole damn place clean," he said, laughing and waving through the cloudy window at the children, who had reluctantly marched over to the curb to let my father's car pass.

Murphy turned back to me. "We'll go on," he said. "I know you're eager for those letters."

"Okay," I said, although I hadn't been thinking about Catherine's letters. Instead, I'd been wondering if Murphy felt like he belonged back here in Mandeville, living again in my grandfather's house, tracing a path up and down Sharp Street to make conversation on the porches and in the kitchens, peering through the screen doors to laugh with the families inside.

All of a sudden Murphy seemed impossibly old to me. None of the children playing in the street would even know who he was. They wouldn't remember my grandfather or my father. Of course they wouldn't remember my mother, the time when she and my father had just gotten married and she was not yet pregnant and they'd come visit my grandfather, who loved her.

I knew that he did. He'd told me so. He said she was the most beautiful woman he'd ever seen. "Like you," my grandfather once said, "your mother was all skin and bones, with a heart and soul containing nothing but a million best wishes for the world. You can't imagine how much she would have loved you, how much she did in that brief time before she passed away."

That made me cry, of course. "Barbara was," my grandfather started, but he couldn't even go on and I couldn't even listen. He held me and rocked me in his arms. I loved her, too, I knew, though that love was always interrupted by the reminder that I hadn't seen her except once, when she held me, when I was too little even to know I was being held.

And I loved my grandfather so, feeling that he and not my father was the one who carried my mother's memory with him. I wondered if those children on Sharp Street, as they grew older and began to wander away from their homes, would think of my grandfather's house and the overgrown garden out back as somehow mysterious and haunted. Would they sneak around at night through the garden the way I'd seen, from the upstairs window, the older kids do, drawn by whatever danger there was in clowning around in the presence of holy statues lit by the moon or shrouded by swaying willow branches?

Had I actually seen or only imagined the image that leapt into my head as Murphy and I drove up to the house: a boy and girl lying down on the ground together near the pond, embracing each other, their arms and legs entangled? I stand at the upstairs window, in the dark room, and look down on them the way my father looked down on me as my grandfather carried me inside, Lowell still splashing around in the warm water of the pond. Then the boy and girl see me or see something or hear some noise, and they are running off, away from the house, through the azalea bushes, under the willow tree, past the line of oaks. Only then, at that moment, do I realize what I have witnessed, what I or someone else or some imagined noise has interrupted, and I feel somehow ashamed.

It was the same feeling I later got when I discovered and then secretly read Catherine's letters, the ones she received in the mail, the ones she thought, I learned soon enough, that my father and not me was reading.

Today, with all these years to consider it, I don't make too much of my deception. It was not Catherine's suspicion over something so little that caused the mistrust between her and my father. That mistrust, I know, must have already been there. It was that mistrust that was the cause and not the result of her jumping to the conclusion that it was my father and not me or even Lowell who was reading her letters, hunting them out from the hiding places she designed in search of some unspoken and maybe damning secret.

How is it, though, that my father and Catherine had come to mistrust each other so? How is it that their years together, the love however great or small between them, had served to cast doubt on the other's character rather than cast all doubt outside?

It is not enough to believe that this mistrust was simply a conspiracy of circumstances, the result of the coincidence that Catherine had chosen to place blame for her privacy's invasion in the hands of the wrong person, her husband. If coincidence was involved, it was simply like the coincidence of the causeway's collapse, a catalyst, perhaps, for all that followed in its wake, but not the one true cause — no cause at all, in fact.

Well, I was sorry nevertheless for what I'd done in secretly reading all those letters to Catherine. Just inside the front door of my grandfather's house, scattered all across the floor, was all the mail that had arrived in our absence, weeks and weeks of bills and a few catalogues, but I spotted Catherine's envelope immediately, grabbed it, and left Murphy to pick up the rest.

"Don't mind me," Murphy said, groaning as he kneeled down before the mail, as I ran off to the living room to read what Catherine had written. She'd folded the two letters separately and numbered them so I'd know which to read first. Before I began, though, I pulled from the envelope the other thing Catherine had sent — a photograph of me and her mother that had been taken the one time we'd all gone to North Carolina to visit. There I was sitting outside in her mother's lap the way I remembered, my back arched against her shoulder as if I were trying to squirm away, both of us laughing, I imagine, at some silly noise Catherine's father was making to try to get us both to smile, the fields so bright behind us that Catherine's mother and I looked as if we weren't really there, as if some photographic trick had put the field behind us.

I didn't have to wonder why Catherine sent me this picture. I knew it was her way of reminding me of the family I'd gained through her, the family that not just death but also my father's ruinous will had set about dismantling.

I read and read and did not cry a single tear, though I had thought I would, not even when I was finished and realized there was at least one more letter to come and I'd probably gone and left that behind in New Orleans, since my father had called her and she now knew to send the next one to Magazine Street instead. So I wouldn't know until I went back what I'd thought I'd learn from her that very moment: why we'd left, why she'd gone to North Carolina, why anything.

And I didn't know why Catherine had told me some of what she did, like about the boy she'd left behind in North Carolina so many years before. But I do believe I understood something of what she must have felt with so much sadness as she wrote — that these letters of hers might well need to open up to me, like the slowest-budding flower, bit by bit through the years, revealing more and more of their meaning just at the point when I was able to understand it.

Even so, I felt as though I did understand the love that had gone into her words. I thought of all the times she'd put me to bed in the way she described, the two of us talking our way through the still night, making up names for the trees and stars. I felt as if I were waiting for the sight of something just like she'd seen on the highway, that old couple dancing in the shed somehow telling her that someday her life would be all right. I didn't know what that sight would be for me, but I believed one day it would come. I figured it might be something as simple as what Catherine had described at the start of her first letter, the reflection of a hundred stars and the moon in a tiny pond, the stars jumping from one spot to the next, the moon like a gold stone in the center. Just that would be enough to tell me what I wanted to know — that there was indeed a heaven above me and all my thoughts and feelings, like each sparrow in the air, had been accounted for somehow, each moment of love and of missing my mother and now of missing Catherine would become like those hundred stars, maybe more, so many that they'd cast a beautiful light down across the world.

I held Catherine's letters in my hand and swore to myself that I wouldn't miss that moment when it came. I'd pay attention. I'd notice. I'd be fine.

Murphy had left me alone while I was reading, but he'd stayed near and quiet just in case, I'm sure, I called to him, feeling overtaken by what I'd read. When I did call to him, I just said, "I'm done," and he stepped into the living room and took a good look.

"Miss Meredith?" he said, and I put down the letters in my lap.

"I'm fine," I told him. "She said she'd write more."

Murphy sat down on the sofa next to me. I didn't say anything, and Murphy just waited, tapping his foot on the floor, not in an impatient manner but in a way that suggested he was happy to wait, as if he were just running through a pleasant song in his head.

Still, I didn't feel the need to say anything, so Murphy finally did. "Years ago, Miss Meredith," he told me, "I used to wonder if ever there would be a time when I felt all grown up. You understand?"

"Yes," I said.

"I'm casting out a net here," he said, "but my guess is you thought maybe this would be the time for you, like you'd exchanged one set of clothes for another or found yourself living in what felt like a different skin."

"I don't know," I said, though I wondered if this was what I had thought, that the girl who began to read would be gone by the time the reading was done, replaced by someone else who didn't feel the same way anymore about even the slightest thing.

"Well, it never does happen," Murphy said, "and I swear it's the damnedest thing. Look at me, so old and shriveled. But if you cut through any part of me, I bet you'd see all the layers, each and every one, just like the oldest tree with the young one still wrapped inside. You understand all that, Miss Meredith?"

"I do," I said.

"Well, that's fine and good," Murphy said. "That's what counts." He pushed himself up from the sofa and clapped his hands against his hips and said, "What old Murphy needs now is a drink before we get started."

I thought Murphy meant that he was almost ready to head back to New Orleans. "What about calling my father?" I asked.

"We'll do that soon enough," Murphy said, and he headed off to the kitchen.

I folded Catherine's letters and put them back in the envelope along with the photograph she'd sent, then I walked through the house just to look around and remind myself of all that was there. It hadn't seemed strange to me until then that in the two years since my grandfather had died, my father hadn't so much as sorted through his belongings, separating what he wanted to save from what he didn't. All my grandfather's books were still on the shelves, his clothes still crowded in the closets, his shoes lined up in a row along the wall in his bedroom as if any minute he'd be ready to step into them. In the bathroom, my grandfather's shaving mug and razor sat on the sink, although maybe my father had used them when we'd come to visit. I didn't know.

It seemed to me that at least Catherine, if not my father, would have done something with all my grandfather's things, packed them away in neat boxes with labels on them the way she'd done with our clothes when Lowell and I outgrew them. But maybe my father had told her not to do anything. Maybe he'd figured all along he'd end up back in Mandeville and would just take my grandfather's possessions as his own, dressing himself in my grandfather's clothes, reading his books, putting the same razor that my grandfather had used to his face each morning.

If I had at all believed my father about why we'd left Catherine, about how we'd had to leave, I didn't believe him now. We'd left because my father wanted to leave, I decided, because he thought he'd find something in Mandeville that could not, no matter how he tried, include Catherine. I stood in the window and looked out at the garden covered with snow and thought that I had no choice but to love him, but I knew I blamed him, too. I blamed him for everything.

I went downstairs and found Murphy sitting in the kitchen with a drink in his hand. "I'm calling him," I said. I went to my grandfather's study, where the phone was, and picked up the receiver. I didn't know what I would tell my father, but I knew I had things to say. "Just guess where I am," I'd tell him, as though the very fact that he didn't know would be enough to hurt him. "I'm far, far away," I'd say.

But when I put the receiver to my ear, there was no sound. The phone was dead, either from the snow or, more likely, because my father had failed to pay the bill. Then I heard Murphy walking toward the study, and instead of hanging up I said into the receiver, "I'm fine. Murphy is too. We will."

Murphy stepped into the study. I looked at him, smiled, and then looked down again. "I love you, too, Daddy," I said. "I'll tell him."

I lowered the receiver slowly, worried that my hand would

begin to shake once it had lost the weight of the phone, then I looked up at Murphy.

"That was over fast," he said. "Mr. Thomas didn't care to speak to me?"

"He said he wasn't angry," I said. "He said he understood what I'd done."

"Miss Meredith?" Murphy said, and he walked over to me. I thought for sure he'd pick up the phone, but he didn't. He put a hand on top of my head and said, "Are you sure that's all?"

"He said we could stay here tonight because of the snow," I told Murphy, looking straight into his eyes. "He said we could come back tomorrow instead."

"What did he say about going to Natchitoches?" Murphy asked.

I didn't know what Murphy meant, if it was Murphy or my father who was supposed to go to Natchitoches. I kept looking straight at Murphy, though, noticing how his eyes seemed to be floating behind his glasses.

"He said it was fine," I answered, hoping that would work either way.

I winced, though, thinking Murphy would know now I'd lied, but he didn't seem to. He just stood in the doorway and looked back at me. "We should go soon, then," he said. "We should go while this snow's let up."

"Fine with me," I said. "Let's go."

I didn't know how I'd come to tell that lie, but I felt as proud of myself as I felt scared for doing so.

Now I was free to go to Natchitoches with Murphy, whatever the reason he wanted to go. I didn't even know where or how far Natchitoches was, except that it was somewhere north of Mandeville. Murphy poured himself another drink, and I put my duffle coat back on. "I'm going to go out back to the garden," I told Murphy. "I'll just be a minute. I'll meet you out front."

"Don't be too long, Miss Meredith. It's cold," Murphy said, but as I opened the back door and stepped out on the porch, I heard him call, "Would you include me in your prayer, Miss Meredith?"

"I will, Murphy," I said. "I already meant to."

I stepped out onto the snow-covered grass and made my way over to the pond and the statue of Saint Francis. The water wasn't frozen, but there was ice along the green edge of Saint Francis's robe and an inch of snow along his raised arm and the top of his head. I didn't want to say just a Hail Mary or Our Father, but no other prayer came to mind. So instead I just talked to the statue. I said, "Soon, when he finds out, my father is going to think I'm crazy, too."

Then I just stared at the statue, wanting it to answer by saying, "That's fine. It doesn't matter. Go in peace." The whole world was still quiet, as if it were not yet dawn and every creature on the earth were still asleep.

I stood another minute and felt a chill starting again on my face and in my fingers. "I'm going," I finally said, and turned to make my way around the house. I saw the footprints I'd left from the porch to this statue, and I thought of another thing Catherine had written, about the story her father had told, how he'd poured the gasoline over those anthills and left the brown circles he'd then claimed had been left by the moon.

Catherine's mother had believed him. She'd wanted it to be true. She'd wanted that sight of those brown circles in the green grass to be that one true moment for her, that one moment when the world was stretched out before her in all its great mystery. I wondered if Catherine's father had any idea what he'd ruined.

He didn't, I knew, and I walked around the side of my grandfather's house feeling so sorry for that woman, feeling she'd had her chance and missed it, feeling she'd had her chance only to watch it get stolen away.

I looked behind me and saw the arc of my footprints around the side of the house, leading to the garden and to Saint Francis, back to the porch and then inside to Catherine's letters, and then all the way back to New Orleans and Magazine Street and the causeway's collapse and to leaving Catherine, our clothes scattered across the lawn.

I won't miss it, I told myself. *I just won't.* Then I looked ahead and there was Murphy standing by my father's car, stomping his feet and shifting from side to side. "Come on, Miss Meredith," he called when he saw me coming. "It's cold."

I took my time, though. I didn't care. I was trying to remember everything, trying to follow my own footsteps back and back as far as I possibly could.

12

I CLIMBED BACK into the car, wondering if Murphy would want to know what I'd thought to pray for out back. I'd said I would pray for him but didn't. I was too full of thoughts for myself. Also, I didn't know what sort of prayer he thought he needed, forgiveness or healing or good fortune. But Murphy didn't bring up the subject of prayer. He just switched on the car's engine and asked if I might be hungry. "I'm not," I said.

"You'll need to eat in any case," Murphy told me, but I shook my head.

"I'm too cold," I lied. The truth was I felt too full of whatever it was that had come over me standing outside in the garden, something that seemed close to revelation though I had no idea what it was that had been revealed.

Go in peace, I kept thinking. *Go in peace.* Was that it?

"Maybe later," I said to Murphy, and he seemed content with that answer. He put the car into drive and slowly pulled away from my grandfather's house.

As we headed out of town and onto a highway I didn't recognize, I felt my body growing warm again, the feeling coming back to my hands and feet, though I hadn't noticed until then that they were numb. The lie I'd told, pretending to talk to my father as I'd done, was warming me as much as the heat building in the car. That lie felt good somehow. It felt as if just that were enough to give me strength, as though I'd finally found a way to cut myself off from the overflowing fountain of trouble my father had caused me, the spoiled and sickening water that had washed over me my whole life. I felt I was giving back to him now what he well deserved.

"How far away is Natchitoches?" I asked Murphy, surprised by my own voice, how bright and happy it sounded. Maybe now I was the dangerous child Murphy had claimed me to be, finding joy in my sad life the way you pluck certain feathers off some rare bird to prevent its flying off, spoiling a certain measure of its beauty so that you can continue to observe what remains.

No matter what Murphy had said, I did feel different. Everything felt different, new, newly discovered: the touch of my lips together, the cold air, thoughts of my mother, of my grandfather, of Catherine. What was it that they all shared beyond the strength of my affection?

Murphy said that it would, with all the snow, take almost two hours to get to Natchitoches.

"That's good," I said, wanting it to take as long as possible, weeks and weeks if that's what it would be, enough time for me to grow accustomed to myself.

It was almost noon. I figured my father wouldn't start missing me until after three o'clock, when school let out. I knew I wouldn't change my mind about the lie I'd told, but if I did I could always call my father from Natchitoches and just like that sweep aside the story I'd told Murphy.

It wasn't Murphy I'd wanted to deceive, though, and for a moment I did feel bad about that. If I called home from Natchitoches, I knew, my father was likely to be angrier at Murphy than at me unless I also explained exactly what I'd done — that I'd lied and that this was why Murphy had continued on from Mandeville without so much as a word to my father about my being along for the ride.

What I didn't know, what I learned only much later, was that school — not just mine but also Lowell's and every other one in New Orleans — had shut down because of the snow. Everyone had been sent home even before first period was set to end. Lowell had come looking for me on the front steps of Sacred Heart, thinking we could take the streetcar back to Magazine Street together but also, I'm sure, jumping at the chance to talk to the girls waiting inside the front gates, something that on any other day would have got him into trouble. When he didn't find me, he decided I'd already gone home ahead of him.

Of course, I wasn't there either, and neither was my father. After an hour or so of waiting, Lowell started worrying. He thought that maybe the two of us, my father and I, had gone off somewhere together, but he couldn't imagine where, since he knew that Murphy had my father's car and was gone to Mandeville.

Years later, and on more than one occasion, I asked Lowell to tell the story of how and where he managed to find my father that morning. It was not a story he wanted to tell, but I think he realized it meant more to me than to him and so told me anyway, though I had to push hard for details.

What Lowell has told me is that he went from shop to shop along Magazine Street asking if anyone had seen us, both of us together or just one. Someone — probably Evelyn, Lowell says, though he claims he doesn't remember — recognized the panic in his voice and saw the worry on his face and told him enough of what she knew to send him running off to Camp Street, three blocks away and ten blocks down, to a house sitting in the row of houses between Saint Patrick's Church on one corner and the Lighthouse for the Blind on the other.

Lowell says he wrote the exact address on a scrap of paper that he then slipped into his coat pocket, but when he got to the right block of Camp Street, the scrap of paper wasn't there and he couldn't remember the number. Instead of giving up, he knocked on one door and then the next, each time inquiring about my father.

I've tried to imagine Lowell setting out on this desperate mission, running down Camp Street through the snow blind and wild with fear. How was it that Lowell, so apparently un-shakable, had concluded so quickly that something was wrong? How was it that he felt my absence so certainly that he stepped up to strangers' doors, looked into their faces, and asked if they knew or had seen a Dr. Thomas Eagen, a man with glasses and a bad leg, with red and gray and sandy hair, his wayward father?

At the third or fourth house or maybe the fifth, Lowell says, the door opened and he immediately knew that the woman standing there — one hand on her hip and the other on the door, her hair pulled back behind her head, dressed in a loose white shirt and khaki pants, her feet bare, her face young, the woman thin, dark-eyed; this Lowell's complete and only de-scription — that this woman was the one my father was with.

How did you know? I've asked Lowell. What was it about her that made you know?

Lowell's answer is that he just knew, he doesn't know how or why. He says he looked just one moment at the woman and could tell that she knew, too — she knew why he was there, who he was. Lowell says he didn't have to utter so much as a single word. He just put a foot across the threshold and the woman stepped aside, one hand still on the door, pulling it open even more.

Lowell found my father in the living room, standing next to a bookshelf, a book in his hand, music playing quietly on some hidden stereo, everything as if my father were simply some proper gentleman making a polite and formal visit to some old friend.

I have to admit that I don't know for sure, not really, that there was anything more going on in that house than that. There's what Murphy believed, what Catherine must still be-lieve, but I don't know for sure, and I'm not inclined to con-demn my father for one ounce more than he truly deserves. What I do know is enough.

I have asked Lowell about the house, about everything. He says he remembers the pale wooden floors reflecting the light from a silver chandelier, nothing else.

"Lowell," my father said. There was no surprise in his voice, Lowell says. No shame or worry or shock or fear, just Lowell's name, pronounced as if — and I admit this is mine — my father were simply jogging his memory, confirming for himself that he did know what the name was and could say it.

"I can't find Meredith," Lowell told him.

My father, Lowell says, put the book he was holding back on the shelf and looked not at him but up at the chandelier, squinting his eyes at the light. For a few seconds, he didn't say anything. Then he lowered his eyes to look straight at Lowell and said, "She's with Murphy."

For a moment, because my father's voice was so calm, Lowell thought that this was something he had known all along, but then he said, "Oh, Jesus Christ," walked over to the phone sitting on a coffee table, picked it up, and dialed. This first call, I'm sure, was to Mandeville, to my grandfather's house, because my father immediately hung up and dialed again. He did the same a second time, hanging up immediately, and then dialed the phone again.

This time, when there was an answer, my father said, "Hello. My name is Thomas Eagen, and I'm trying to locate my daughter. Is there someone there who could help me?"

He waited a moment and then put his hand over the receiver. It was the police, Lowell figured, and he was feeling even more frightened than he had before. My father looked over at Lowell and told him to go home. "I'll be there as soon as I can," he said. "Everything's fine, son. We'll get hold of them."

Lowell turned and saw that the woman was standing behind him. She looked frightened, Lowell says. "Hello," Lowell says he told her as he walked past.

"Hello," she said back, stepping away from him, out of his path. "I'm sorry."

Lowell says he truly does not know what the woman meant by saying what she did. Was she expressing sympathy with his and my father's concern for me? Was she apologizing for being caught by him with my father?

When Lowell stepped out the door, it was still snowing, and he walked back to Magazine Street, went upstairs, and waited.

I had, of course, meant to hurt my father. I had meant to make him sick with worry. But it hadn't occurred to me that Lowell might worry, too. I had pictured him in school and then afterwards running around outside in the snow, as amazed by Magazine Street's sudden transformation as Murphy and I had been by the change to Sharp Street in Mandeville.

As Murphy drove northwest toward Natchitoches, the snow did not get worse, as I'd expected, but instead let up. The landscape changed to one of small, rolling hills and then slightly larger, sharper ones, and soon there was no snow anywhere, the landscape brown and green again, turned-under fields followed by thick, untouched woods.

I asked Murphy what it was he meant to do in Natchitoches, but he wouldn't tell me. "You'll see soon enough, Miss Meredith," he said, and he was silent for a moment. Then he said, "That's not a fair answer, I guess. The whole truth is I don't know what we'll find. It may be nothing."

"Give me a hint," I said, thinking I had a better chance of getting Murphy to talk by joking with him.

"I'll just say we're going to pay our respects, Miss Meredith," he said. "We'll have to see who's there to receive them."

"Who is it?" I asked. "Who are we calling on?"

"Mostly myself, I suspect," Murphy said, then he added, "That's enough, Miss Meredith, you hear? Let's just see first."

"Okay," I said, squirming a little to get comfortable in my seat. It was hot now in the car, so I slipped my coat off and threw it into the back seat.

I watched the road signs as we passed from one parish to the next, East and then West Feliciana, Pointe Coupee, Avoyelles, Rapides — names I'd heard from my father but places I'd never seen until now, not that there was much to see from this highway beyond rundown houses so close to the road it seemed you could just reach out through the window and touch them and also, every once in a while, larger houses that you could only spy for half a second because they were set back in the woods at the end of paved driveways that curved through the trees.

Murphy tried the radio, but we'd gone too far to pick up WWIW and he couldn't find any other stations except ones playing news or country-and-western music, neither of which Murphy wanted to hear. "One's always bad and the other's worse," he said, and though I laughed, Murphy didn't.

By the time we crossed into Natchitoches Parish, the snow had started again, heavier now than it had been before, and Murphy had to slow down and keep wiping the handkerchief across the windshield to keep it from clouding over. When we passed the sign for the town of Natchitoches, Murphy asked if I wanted to eat before we went about our business. He seemed nervous, tapping his fingers on the steering wheel, and I could tell he didn't want to stop. "Let's go ahead," I said. "I'm still not hungry."

I'd asked him if he'd been to Natchitoches before, and he said he had but only twice, and both times as a child. He drove around as if nothing about the city were familiar, heading down one street and back up the next the way my father had done in New Orleans after the causeway's collapse.

"What's wrong?" I asked, but Murphy didn't answer. He kept driving until finally he pointed up at a church steeple in the distance and said, "I bet that's it."

The church was a Catholic one standing on a corner at the end of the town's main street, which was lined with flat-roofed shops and tiny restaurants, an A&P and a car dealership that had a sagging rope of dusty plastic banners stretched out across the clamshell parking lot. The street was called Clear Lake Road, though we hadn't passed a lake or even the tiniest stream.

Murphy turned the corner, and behind the church was a cemetery that the road cut through. Murphy stopped the car and told me I should put on my coat. "This is where we're going, Miss Meredith," he said, and I kneeled on my seat and reached back for my coat. I now realized what Murphy had meant by saying we'd come to pay our respects, though I still didn't know whose grave it was we'd come to see. I thought it might be his father's, since Murphy had said once that his father had come down to Mandeville from somewhere in north

Louisiana. His mother, I knew, was buried in the same cemetery as my grandfather.

Murphy took my hand and we crossed the street, moving from the side where the white people were buried, directly behind the church, to the side reserved for blacks, both parts of the cemetery surrounded by chainlink fences with entrance gates bearing metal signs that said SAINT AUGUSTINE'S, 1905. The snow had formed a smooth cover on the ground in the cemetery, and we could barely hear our own footsteps as we walked from one row to the next.

I looked at the stones as we moved along, Murphy checking the graves on one side while I looked at the facing row, the two of us still holding hands. Most of the graves were worn concrete blocks, but some were cut marble, which they never were in the nigger cemeteries in New Orleans. Many of the stones had fallen over, though, toppled off their cracked bases either forward or back. It was as if someone had kicked them over and left the carved names facing up to the sky, though covered now with a mat of snow, or pressed down flat against the ground. I wondered if Murphy would end up, in his searching, having to set each of these stones upright, brushing off the snow or dirt to see if one had been carved with the name he hoped to find.

Except for us, the cemetery was empty. Although it was practically in ruins, there were fresh flowers and other kinds of decorations near many of the graves: a couple of Bibles, a baseball mitt, a rusted can filled with nails, even a navy blue shirt propped up against a stone, folded so that you could see the name Andrew stitched into the pocket.

"What's all this?" I asked Murphy. "Why's it here?"

Murphy shushed me. "Quiet, child," he said, but then he must have thought better of it because he said, "They're a way of people feeding their own good memories. It's how black folks sometimes set about remembering their dead. They put aside their pain for something better."

I wondered what I would put beside my mother's grave, since I had no memories of her. Maybe I'd put the photograph that Catherine had sent as a way to let my mother know her child had been loved. By my grandfather's stone I'd put one of the photographs he'd taken, one of a Saint Francis statue. He'd like that.

I figured I should keep an eye out for the name Warrington, and I did, though my mind kept running off to thoughts of my mother and grandfather, to the cemeteries in New Orleans and Mandeville where they were buried, picturing the snow falling there as well, thinking of how beautiful that would be, how I wished I could be in those other places to see it.

After a while, I let go of Murphy's hand and wandered around on my own, stopping at whatever graves caught my eye because of a particular stone's strange shape or color or because of the design carved into it. One had a cross wrapped by tiny roses, another a woman's sad and ghastly face, her two hands raised before her eyes. Though I'm sure the carved picture was supposed to suggest that the woman was praying, it looked more like she was about to lay her head in those hands and weep. Murphy just kept making his way through the cemetery, moving slowly from one row to the next, eyeing each and every stone as he moved past.

Watching him, I felt cold and tired and hungry all at once, and I tried to warm my hands by making fists in my coat pockets, clenching and unclenching my fingers. I hoped Murphy would find what he was looking for soon, so we could go eat something, then drive back to Mandeville. All the strength and energy I'd felt before, all the power I'd felt from my lie, had just disappeared, and the only thing I wanted now was to lie down in a bed in my grandfather's house, pull the covers over me, and go to sleep.

Then I saw Murphy begin to crouch and reach a hand down toward the ground, and I also heard at that very same moment the cemetery gate opening, the click and scrape of the metal latch. I turned to see a man in a police uniform. I watched him slowly close the gate behind him and stand there, looking not at me but at Murphy, who was now kneeling down in the snow, both hands on the ground, his head bowed.

"Are you okay, Murphy?" I called, and I ran over to him. "Are you okay?" I asked again, standing behind him, putting my hand on his back, feeling even through his coat the bony ridge of his spine. "Are you okay?" I kept saying.

When I looked at the stone in front of Murphy, I knew immediately, without even looking to see what name it bore, that my grandfather had carved it. It was a child's stone, a tiny pink marble block with a sleeping lamb on it, the lamb's legs curled beneath the body. The stone's edges were lined with crescent-shaped chips in the marble, something I'd seen my grandfather do in his shop a hundred times. With sharp, quick strokes of the hammer, he would twist the chisel in his left hand just as the hammer struck, the chips ending up scattered on the floor at his feet like a hundred crescent moons fallen from the sky.

A few feet behind this stone was another, also pink marble, its edges carved just as the tiny one had been, and I knew that it was my grandfather's, too, that he'd made it.

Only then, after that moment of recognition, did I read the names carved into the stones — the tiny one with only a single word, Comfort, carved in letters as thin as a line of thread, the other with my grandmother's name, Mollie Moore Eagen.

Then the man in the police uniform, a young man with a face so splotchy red I thought it had just now been frost-bitten by the cold, was standing next to me. I looked at him, but he was still looking at Murphy. "Get up," he said.

Those words must have startled Murphy, because he fell forward until his head rested in the snow. He turned his body and pushed himself up so that he was sitting, his head still bowed.

"He knew," Murphy said. "All that time the old man knew."

"Get up," the man said again, taking a step toward Murphy, but Murphy didn't get up. Instead, he slowly raised his head, putting a hand up to shade his eyes, and said, "Leave me alone."

"Stand up now, Mr. Nigger," the man said, suddenly angry. I saw him bend his arm so that his right hand now rested on his gun.

Even so, Murphy didn't move. "That's my child buried there, goddamnit," he said. "Don't ask me to stand."

Murphy's glasses were wet from falling in the snow, so I don't know if he even saw the man step forward to kick him. He didn't seem to see anything, not moving until the man's foot hit his stomach, the black boot disappearing into Murphy's black coat like they'd become the same thing.

Murphy fell on his side and pulled his knees up, groaning. Then the man kicked Murphy again, this time in the back, and again Murphy groaned, a hollow sound like a rush of wind in a rotted tree. He kicked Murphy again and again. I yelled then for the man to stop, afraid that he would keep kicking until all the air was out of Murphy's lungs and he was dead.

When I yelled, the man turned to look at me as if he'd forgotten I was there. "What are you doing with this nigger, little girl?" he asked me. "Did this nigger do you harm?"

I tried to think what I could say, feeling somehow that it was up to me and not the man himself to stop this. "He works for my father," I said. "Please don't hurt him any more."

The man seemed to relax for a moment, lowering his hand but looking down at Murphy instead of at me. "Is that your father's car out on the street?" he asked.

"Yes," I said.

"You from New Orleans?" he asked.

"Yes," I said again, not knowing what else to say, too afraid to say anything else.

"That car's reported as stolen," the man said, "by a nigger named Warrington from New Orleans, a nigger who just happened to have stolen another car two weeks ago and left it in the water. Is this nigger here named Warrington from New Orleans?"

The man put his boot against Murphy's back again but this time didn't kick him.

"Yes," I said, and by now I was crying, terrified. "That car's not stolen. It's my father's. It is. Please don't hurt him again."

The man looked at me for a moment and then crouched down, putting one hand on Murphy's back, the other at Murphy's neck, leaning his head down by Murphy's head, his mouth by Murphy's ear. He lifted Murphy's head and then pushed it down into the snow.

"Are you alive, Mr. Nigger?" the man whispered. Murphy turned his head but didn't say anything. "Is your name Warrington, Mr. Nigger?" the man asked.

"It is," Murphy said.

"You're under arrest for stealing," the man said. "Stand up now or I'll drag your skinny black ass in."

The man grabbed Murphy's shoulder and turned him so that now Murphy was lying on his back, his face wet with snow.

"He's old," I said. "Don't hurt him."

"Let me be," Murphy said to the man. "I'll try to stand."

He pushed himself up and sat there, his hands on his knees. He looked over at me and said, "I'm sorry, Miss Meredith."

"Murphy," I said.

"This is something you shouldn't have seen, Miss Meredith," he said.

Murphy ran his hands down across his shins and rubbed them together. "It's cold," he said. "It's cold, isn't it?"

And then, just as he was about to stand, his back still bent, his arms still down toward the ground, Murphy threw his body forward. He grabbed the police officer's legs and managed to trip him, and as he fell the man's head hit my shoulder and I fell, too.

I crawled through the snow to get out of the way. When I turned to look, Murphy had grabbed hold of the man's shoulders, and he was beating his head on the ground. I yelled, but Murphy kept going until the man had stopped struggling and I could see that his eyes were closed.

"Murphy," I said, crying, trying to stand up but slipping in the snow.

I watched Murphy take the man's gun and stand over him. "That's a nigger for you," Murphy said, his whole body shaking, the gun circling in his hand over and over as if he couldn't stop it.

"Oh God, Murphy," I said. He walked over to me, his eyes still on the man, and helped me up.

"Miss Meredith," Murphy said, and he put a hand on my head. "I'm sorry, Miss Meredith. I am."

I let Murphy pull me against his body, my face against his wet coat. I could feel him shaking. I wanted to ask what he'd meant by saying this was his child buried here but couldn't. "You'll be fine," Murphy said to me. "Miss Meredith, you'll be fine."

Then he stepped away from me and put his hands on my shoulders, gripping them tight through my coat. "Listen. I'm leaving you now," he said, his breath between his words thick and raspy. "I don't want to, I swear. This isn't my choice."

I shook my head but still couldn't say anything.

"You'll be fine," Murphy said. "This man's not dead. It doesn't much matter, but he's not. Look at him."

I looked over at the man and could see his chest rising and falling. "See," Murphy said. "He's not dead."

"Okay," I said.

"Just calm yourself," Murphy said.

"Okay," I said again, and I nodded my head.

Murphy leaned down. "I've got to leave now," he said, looking straight into my eyes through his streaked glasses. "Here's what you do. You walk over to the church and ask for a phone. You call your father. Tell him. You'll be fine. You understand?"

I shook my head again. What was I supposed to tell my father? Where would Murphy go?

"I've got to leave you now," Murphy said, "before this man's awake to the world and screaming *nigger* again. You understand?"

I just looked at Murphy. He let go of my shoulders and started walking away. I tried to follow him, but he wouldn't let me. "Stay here," he said, his voice angry. "Stay here and then go to that church. Call your father. He'll find a way to come get you. You'll be fine."

"I'm scared," I finally said. "I'm really scared."

"You'll be fine, I assure you," Murphy said. "I wanted to find out, and I did. That's all."

I was crying and crying, still terrified. I stood there and

watched Murphy leave, watched him walk to the cemetery gate, slowly open it, then close it behind him.

I watched him walk to my father's car, reach in his pocket for the keys, and put them down on the roof. I wanted to yell to him to take the car, but I couldn't.

I sat down in the snow then and cried. "Please help me," I said. I felt wild with terror, turning my head from side to side for someone to help me.

I was still sitting there, still crying, when I felt someone standing over me. It was the police officer. His hand was at the back of his head, and when he lowered it I saw the dark blood there. He looked at his hand and then wiped it across his pants, leaving black streaks across the gray cloth.

"The nigger's gone, I guess," he said, and I nodded. I looked down at the snow.

"Goddamn nigger," he said. "Goddamnit."

I still didn't look up, but I knew the man was looking down at me. "Let me ask you one thing, little girl," he said. "You're a goddamn nigger-lover, aren't you?"

"He didn't do anything," I said.

"That nigger about killed me," the man said.

I did look up then. "You deserved it," I said. "You did."

"What the fuck do you know, little girl?" the man said. Then he reached down and grabbed my shoulder and pulled me up. I turned to look at the two stones my grandfather had carved. I pulled away from the man and walked over to them and thought of what Murphy had said about this child being his own. I couldn't make any sense of it. I didn't know what he'd meant and would not know until my father arrived bearing Catherine's other two letters. Then I would.

"I've got to call to say he's loose," the man said. Then he paused for a second and changed the tone of his voice. "He's one dead nigger if we find him, you know," he said.

"You won't," I said.

I knew I was right. I knew for sure that no one would ever find Murphy again, that he would disappear as he'd done before, but this time no one, no matter how long they looked, would ever find him. He'd make sure.

I would miss Murphy, I knew. I would miss him now more than I would ever have imagined before. He'd taken care of me. He'd put his hands on my shoulders and sworn he didn't want to leave but had no choice. That was enough. It was.

And it was knowing that I would miss him, and not anything else, not fear or worry or exhaustion, that made me sink down again and lay my head in the cold snow and wish that this moment was the end.

I WAS RIGHT. I would not see Murphy again. My father would not, as he had that first time, go looking for him. The police would not look either, not really.

Sometimes I think that now, twenty-five years later, I should set out to find Murphy, complete for my own sake the ragged line of his life, discover how he died, where it was he thought to go when he left his life behind.

I used to tell myself that surely someone must have taken Murphy in, tended to him, handed his spirit along toward death in a kind and charitable manner. For years I liked to imagine Murphy situated with some happy family, with young children climbing up into his lap, the children laughing, Murphy laughing, too. It's what I needed to imagine.

Though I have given up on such thoughts now, I still believe there must have been, however much longer Murphy lived, one other person to whom he told his story. Given the opportunity, Murphy could not have resisted telling his story, beginning to end, over and over. He might have told the story only to some old drunk and only in some dark empty river warehouse or beneath a litter-strewn highway bridge, but that would be some other person nevertheless, someone capable of hearing the story, of recognizing its shape, both Murphy and his listener finding some comfort in the telling.

I hear that word, Comfort, and wonder still what my grandmother had been thinking to give her baby girl such a name. Had she thought, her whole life ruined, that this child she delivered might be the one to offer her some peace? Or maybe that name was simply one my grandfather gave to the child when he set about carving that tiny stone, not wanting to place an unmarked marble square in the ground at the spot where his wife's child lay. Maybe it's the name he'd wanted for his own daughter if he'd had one. It's a beautiful name, I think.

Somewhere in Louisiana, in some now-abandoned, overgrown Negro cemetery choked with weeds and crumbling stone, Murphy's body must have been laid in the ground, buried by the good graces of some Catholic parish. I do believe that. So I have thought sometimes to find him, to search for this grave, though I do not know where I would begin to look.

There is time for that yet, I guess, and through all these years I have kept my ears open for news of him. But those who knew Murphy and might have heard something of him have in recent years been dying as well: Evelyn of a tumor that began in her breast, Gabrielle at the age of sixty at the hands of an angry lover, other shop owners on Magazine Street, many of whom shut down and sold their shops years ago and then disappeared.

In Mandeville now, the dilapidated houses on Sharp Street are all gone — condemned, torn down, and replaced by the homes of those who commute each morning across the causeway to jobs in the business district of New Orleans. I don't know what happened to the families who had lived there for so many years, though there are other neighborhoods in Mandeville where they may now be, scattered among the town's other poor, the rotting houses there no better, indistinguishable, in fact, from the ones condemned and then torn down on Sharp Street.

We — my father, Lowell, and I — did not leave Magazine Street. I knew we would not, though my father never said so.

He did not even tell Lowell and me when he sold the house we'd left when we left Catherine. It was months later that I learned that the house had been bought by an order of nuns who'd grown too few in number to continue in their convent.

Lowell and I had gone to that convent once with Catherine to drop off clothes for the Cuban refugees that were then pouring into New Orleans. All I remember now are the giant-leaf fig trees that stood in a line behind a smoky brick building and the rich, sticky scent of the figs mixing with the musty smell of the old clothes, which had been thrown into cardboard boxes in the trees' shade. Young Cuban women moved silently from one box to the next while their children played in the sun on the convent grounds.

Once I learned that our house had been sold, I feared that my father would, without so much as a word, sell my grandfather's house as well, though he didn't.

For a long time the anger I felt about my father's silence found its focus in the suspicion that one day he would come across Murphy, spot him on some street corner or slumped on some porch step, as Catherine had done, and would not even mention it to me. I suspected that my father, seeing Murphy, would simply set his jaw and turn his head away, exactly as he'd done when his patients staggered and fell to the sidewalk on Magazine Street. I understand now his belief that he could not set about saving each one of these patients, but with Murphy, of course, it would have been different. There would have been more to my father's refusal.

I don't really believe that my father ever saw Murphy again, but I don't know for sure. I could not count on my father then, or during any of the remaining years of his life, to tell me.

As I said when I began, I wanted to talk and my father would not. It is this failure, really, and no other, for which I blame him now. It is this failure that, even with my father's death, I cannot find it in myself to forgive.

Saying this much, I must also say that my father did do his best to set the world straight again. If in the end he failed — and he did fail — it was because it was already too late. In this instance, I don't blame him. If there is indeed such a thing as fate, as circumstance taking a stranglehold on our best efforts, then it was this at work in arranging my father's final ruin.

As for the melancholy and regret that overtook me, that I have never truly shaken off, I don't know exactly what to say. When I think of it, I think not of my mother or father or Catherine but of Murphy, his back turned to me, his feet dragging through the snow in that cemetery in Natchitoches, the back of his coat streaked with damp lines as though he'd been beaten with a whip.

I understand better now the distance that lay between Murphy and me, the distance between black and white, but I felt then that I'd had a chance at something with Murphy, some sort of redemption, though I would not have known to call it that. I have sometimes wondered what Murphy would have done had I run after him and refused to leave his side, had I told him I needed his care because I could not ever again count on my father. Would he have left anyway, pushing me aside? Did he truly have, as he said when he left, no choice at all?

The story I have told, my story, would be best ended with Murphy's departure, I think, with my watching him disappear, with my knowing that I would not see him again. I recognized only then, in some dim and shadowy way, that my life would not ever again take on the shape it had once assumed. For me, at least, the rest has been little more than a dizzy unraveling.

Even when I realized that the letter Catherine had discovered, the letter she believed was evidence of my father's betrayal, was surely written not by some lover of my father's but by my grandmother so many years before, written to Murphy and left for him, though it was my grandfather who discovered it, my father who found it among my grandfather's possessions, I could do little more than close my eyes and lower my head and think of Murphy, of his loss, of the happiness stolen from him.

As for myself and my father and Catherine, for my grandfather and for Lowell — for all of us, the secrecy and confusion and misunderstanding contained in that letter feel to me, though perhaps they should not, like little more than an echo of this family's awful undoing rather than the undoing itself. For Murphy, though, that letter might have been a salvation. I wish it had been.

Today, twenty-five years later, at thirty-seven years old, I am a woman waiting for something, though I still cannot say what it is. I am ashamed to say it, but sometimes I feel I am simply waiting for the time when I give birth to my own child. Sometimes I think that would be enough.

Perhaps it has been wrong not to mention until now that this prospect, so immense and terrifying, has hovered above my words and taken root. Catherine confessed, in one of her letters, that her womb burned to carry a child. I understand.

Should I have mentioned, then, that no matter all the injuries I feel, I do believe that there will one day be a man who will love me and want this child, a man whom I will love as best as I can but one, I know, who will hear from me precious little of my life beyond its barest outline?

I do not mean to give that man this story, though it is meant for him and for that child. I will want both to know, though I feel somehow that despite my efforts, this is the final regret I will bear: that I will not tell them, that I will not be able to. I will want them to be warned, though, so I warn myself instead. In this manner, I will get the best of myself. I will give my child a good life. I will be a good wife and mother. If that sounds pitiful, I don't care. It's what I want.

I would like just to end here, give up, put this away, with thoughts of my eventual good fortune and happiness, with thoughts of a quiet, normal life, with the pleasant wanderings my mind sometimes takes when I lie down at night in my bed and drift toward sleep. But to end here, I know, would not be fair to my father. Throughout I have wanted to be fair to him, to his memory, no matter what I cannot forgive. Understand that it is for my own sake that I have wanted to be fair. I hope that's clear.

My father did see Catherine again. They spoke. They embraced. There was in their quiet conversation, I imagine, both compassion and regret. I do not know if they actually spoke of love, but I would like to think that they did. There had been, I believed, some measure of love between them, and I believe it still.

I will go back, then, and tell the rest of the story, no matter my reluctance, no matter my desire to be done with it, to think only of the day when I can put my hands on the tiny life swelling within me and believe that it will surely be enough, that there is some sort of certainty in this world, a touch that will always be gentle, one that will always speak of love.

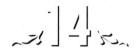

MY FATHER DID come to Natchitoches to get me. Because of his leg, he couldn't drive any car except his own, so he and Lowell were forced to take a Greyhound bus. They called a cab to take them from Magazine Street to Tulane Avenue and waited for an hour for the bus, delayed by the snow, to leave its terminal.

On the phone, when I called him from the police station, from the police captain's office, my father had asked only a few quick questions: Where are you? Where is Murphy? Are you hurt?

"I'm fine," I told him. "I am. Can you please get me now?"

"I will," my father said. "Are you sure you're okay?"

"I'm fine," I said again, and I did not cry.

"Meredith?" my father said.

"I'm fine," I said. "Really. Can you just come now?"

My father asked to speak to the police captain, and I handed over the phone. An officer led me out of the captain's office to the waiting room. I watched, through the glass window of his office, the captain speaking to my father, listening, speaking again. I could not hear anything of their conversation and so wondered what it was that my father thought to say. How much of his story that he had not said and would not say to me did he offer readily to this man? Was it less difficult to say to a stranger, "This began when I left my wife," and go on from there?

I waited silently the rest of that afternoon and into the evening for my father and Lowell to arrive, sitting in a metal folding chair, staring up at the blaring television in the corner of the waiting room, accepting the sandwich and soda that the police captain handed me and eating without so much as a single thought except that soon my father would be here and this would all be done.

Once, when my legs felt stiff from sitting so long, I did put my coat on and step outside. The snow had stopped. Beyond the parking lot, cars shot past the police station, their lights switched on. I had not noticed, in the fluorescent-lit, nearly windowless waiting room, that so many hours had passed, that now it was evening.

By the time my father and Lowell arrived, I had fallen asleep in my chair. I opened my eyes to see them standing before me. Although I hadn't heard him, I knew that my father had already pronounced my name and it was the sound of his voice that had woken me.

I stood up and my father walked toward me. He lifted me up into his arms. "I'm sorry," I said, and he didn't answer but simply held me.

"You're okay, Lamb," my father finally said. "You're okay." He put me down and I looked at Lowell, who offered me a questioning smile. I ran my hand across my eyes and smiled back, then Lowell lifted his hand and waved hello.

My father said he'd need to talk to the police captain a few moments. "I've got this for you," he said, and he reached into his coat, to an inside pocket, and pulled out a thick envelope, unopened. Inside were Catherine's two letters. They had arrived that morning, my father said, only hours after I had left with Murphy. He had discovered them on the floor in the front hall when he hurried back to Magazine Street after Lowell found him.

My father went to the police captain's office, and Lowell sat down next to me. I looked at him, wanting to tell him something of all that had happened, but he turned his eyes toward the television in the corner.

So I opened the envelope and began reading Catherine's letters. I did not cry. There was too much there to leave room for crying, too much that I struggled to understand, trying to find where each detail belonged in putting together all that had happened. This child, my grandmother's child, had been Murphy's. Catherine's child would be — was — my father's. My grandfather had been betrayed by his wife, Catherine by my father. Murphy had believed that my father knew that my grandfather had been betrayed; he did not. He had believed that my grandfather did not know. In the cemetery, Murphy learned that he did.

I thought then of Murphy, how that single moment when he found those gravestones had both confirmed and obliterated all he'd believed. How had it felt to learn all at once that he knew so much and had known so little? What sort of sorrow and shame did he bear?

And this child Catherine was carrying, my father's child? I did not know then and do not know now how much my father understood, how much he did or did not know, what he suspected and did not.

My father, done with the police captain's questions, did not ask to read Catherine's letters. Despite Catherine's final words, intended for my father, I did not offer the letters to him. Instead, I told him I would show him where Murphy and I had been. "I want you to see," I said.

"I don't need to see anything, Meredith," my father said. "It's okay. Let's go home."

"Please," I said. This one time, and perhaps never before and never again, my father somehow understood that my request, this single word, had been spoken in desperation, as if I were falling from the sky. If he did not reach now, that very moment, I would be lost forever. I would disappear, grow smaller and smaller before his eyes. He had to see, he somehow knew.

He did not know, of course, that I would lead him to his mother's grave, to her child's, to the two stones that my grandfather had carved. He did not know, I think, that he would see anything but some overgrown patch of earth that Murphy had meant to visit. But my father somehow understood this time that he should not deny me.

The police captain had sent someone to retrieve my father's car, and we drove back out to Clear Lake Road and turned at the corner of Saint Augustine's, its stained glass windows lit from inside and casting a faint light across the cemetery. I led my father and Lowell through the rows of stones, following the scattered footprints in the snow of Murphy's and my own and the police officer's coming and going.

Then we were standing before the two graves. I pointed, and my father leaned down to look. Lowell stood back, too afraid, too confused, to ask any questions. I stood back, too, watching my father shake his head from side to side. I thought of how he must have wondered through his childhood about my grandmother's leaving, imagining a million different explanations but not ever this one.

He slowly turned to me. "Murphy," he said, his voice shaking. He understood.

"Yes," I said, and that was it.

"What?" Lowell finally said, looking at my father.

"Later," I told Lowell. That word and my father's silence, his utter stillness, were enough to quiet him.

We all stood there, my father shaking his head over and over, making a noise that sounded like a surprised laugh but was not, was something different that I had never heard before.

"Meredith?" Lowell said, stepping next to me. "What's wrong?"

"Look," I said. "Go look. It's our grandmother." But Lowell did not move. He would not go near the two stones.

I wonder how it is that my father decided then what he would do. "Come on," he said, and he put his hands on our backs and guided us out of the cemetery. He stopped to close the gate behind us and then looked up for a moment at the church's stained glass window, a triptych of Christ: praying in the garden of Gethsemene, dying on the cross, rising from the dead.

What comfort, I wonder now, did my father find there? Did he think that moment of striking some great bargain — of offering his sustained, unwavering supplication in exchange for a certain measure of forgiveness and redemption, of a life regained?

Once we were in the car, my father told Lowell and me that we should try to sleep. But we could not sleep, of course. Outside of town, my father stopped at a service station, and while the attendant was filling the car with gas, he stepped inside and lit a cigarette and watched us through the window. When he came back to the car, I saw that he'd bought a road atlas, a thick leather-covered book that he folded like a newspaper under his arm. He turned on the light inside the car and propped the atlas on the steering wheel.

I knew then what my father was planning to do, but I asked him anyway. I wanted him to say it. "Are we going to see Catherine?" I said, and without looking up from the atlas, my father nodded.

"We are," he said.

I felt Lowell's leg tap against mine. Two taps. *Thank you.* It was a game we used to play when we were younger, trying to guess what the other one was saying with the taps.

I tapped back three times. *You're welcome.* Then three times again. *I love you.* Lowell did not know, could not guess what I meant, but that was okay. Neither of us could believe our great good fortune, that while we had lost Murphy, we would soon gain Catherine again.

I wanted to tell Lowell about Catherine's letters. I wanted to show him that there were things I could know that he did not, that Catherine had spoken to me in her letters not as if she were speaking to a child but as if she were writing to someone who could understand the sad, complicated workings of this world. I wanted him to know that she was carrying a child.

My father, though he didn't say so, did not want us to speak.

He reached over to both of us, put his hand on our heads. "Go to sleep," he said. "We've got a long drive."

I closed my eyes but for a long time could not sleep. I wondered what thoughts were running through my father's head. I wondered if he was reciting to himself the things he would say to Catherine. He would ask her to come back, I thought. He would say he was sorry. He would say that had he known about his mother, about Murphy, about this child, he would not have left, not ever. He would have believed all she'd told him. He believed it now. He would have loved her better. He would love their child.

Then I did sleep, for hours and hours, my head against Lowell's shoulder, and Lowell slept too, his head against mine. I woke with the first light of dawn, a thin strip on the horizon, and thought I heard my father singing, though it must have been simply the dream out of which I was waking. When I pushed myself up, waking Lowell as I did, I looked at my father and he was sitting there quietly, his mouth closed, both hands on the steering wheel.

"Where are we?" I asked.

My father looked over at me. "We're almost there," he said.

"We're in North Carolina?" Lowell asked, and my father nodded.

A few minutes later, we turned off the interstate at the sign for Chapel Hill, and we drove down a long highway dotted with tiny homes and trailers. It had snowed here, too, much more than in Louisiana, but the road was clear and it was not snowing now.

"What are we going to do?" Lowell asked my father.

"Not now," my father said. "We'll see."

He had put away the atlas and was now looking from side to side as though searching for whatever might be familiar, what he might remember from our trip five years before. We passed through the center of Chapel Hill and the university there and followed the signs for Pittsboro. It was only then, as we moved back into the country, passing farms now with giant barns and tobacco sheds, that the landscape became familiar to me. I thought again of Catherine's letters, of what she'd seen that night on the highway, the old man and woman dancing, the one hope for her life. Perhaps the moment I was waiting for, I thought, was simply the sight of her again, her kind face and the touch of her hands, her sweet blessing.

Then my father turned off the highway and onto the dirt road leading up to Catherine's father's house, the car moving past a line of trees and then cutting through the snow-covered fields.

We got out of the car and walked together to the door, and my father knocked. There was a light on inside, but no one answered.

When my father turned to look at Lowell and me, I said, "She's at the hospital. Her father's there."

My father looked at me as though I'd been touched with some mysterious power, but I said, "Her letters," and he immediately understood.

"How sick is he?" he asked. "Did she say?"

I recognized the hesitancy in his voice, as though he no longer knew how to speak to me because of Catherine's letters, because of what she might have written, what I might now know of him that he would not ever say.

"She said he'd be fine," I told my father. "He needed an operation on his heart."

My father looked concerned, so I told him again, "She said he'd be fine."

"Okay," my father said, but he just stood there as though he did not know what we should do, as though he had imagined this moment of our arrival for hours and hours and could not think now what it was we should do. He tried the door, but it was locked.

"We could go to the hospital," I said. "It's in Durham."

"No. Let's wait," my father said.

I thought he meant that we would stay outside or go back to the car, but instead he told Lowell and me to stay there on the porch and he headed around the side of the house. Lowell looked at me and smiled as though he was pleased by the thought that my father might break in to the house.

It didn't make sense, but I felt angry at Lowell. I felt angry because he did not understand, because of how little he knew.

"She's going to have a baby," I told him. Lowell just stared at me. He didn't believe me, I knew. He thought I was lying or had dreamed this story up the way I'd dreamed up the story that Catherine had tried to kill my father and that was why we'd left.

"She is," I said. "She told me so."

Before Lowell could say anything, the front door opened and my father was standing there. "The back door was unlocked," he said. "We'll wait inside."

Lowell turned to me as we stepped past my father. "You don't know that," he said.

"I do," I said. "You'll see."

My father did not ask what we were talking about. He took us to the kitchen and made us breakfast, hunting through the drawers and cabinets for pans and silverware. He made us scrambled eggs and poured us cereal and juice. "You need to eat," he said, putting my plate in front of me.

"I'm not hungry," I said.

"Please eat, Meredith," my father said. "Please just eat."

I did eat. I was hungry. I thought of Murphy then and prayed to myself that someone had by now offered him food, had given him shelter, tended to him.

"I miss Murphy," I said out loud, and I nearly cried again. Neither Lowell nor my father said anything, though. They didn't even look up from their plates to acknowledge what I'd said.

"Elizabeth Ann," I said, and my father did look up now. "She wants to name the baby Elizabeth Ann if it's a girl, after her mother," I said.

"Please be quiet, Meredith," my father said. "Please be quiet."

But I wouldn't. "If it's a boy, she wants to give him your name," I said. "Thomas Eagen." I began to cry.

"Don't, Meredith," my father said, but he did not get up or reach toward me. "Just don't," he said, angry, threatening me.

I stood up and ran to the front door and saw then the car heading toward the house. It was Catherine.

I didn't call to my father but stood there, watching the car pull up next to my father's car. Only when Catherine stepped out did I see the shock on her face. She was looking at my father's car. She did not, I could see, know what to do, and she turned around toward her father's car as though she might get back in and drive away.

And then I had flung the door open and I was running to her. She saw me and began crying but did not move.

When I reached her, when she pulled me up into her arms, held me against her body, I immediately knew — I swear I knew that very instant — that Catherine had lost the baby she'd been carrying, that something terrible had happened and that this was what it was. The baby had died inside her.

"Oh, Meredith, Meredith," she said, holding me, crying, but I knew.

"What happened to the baby?" I said.

"I miscarried," she said, still holding me, still crying. She didn't ask how I knew — feeling, I'm sure, that the loss she'd endured was so great that everyone, simply seeing her, must somehow already know. It was how I'd felt sometimes, thinking that people looked at me and thought, *This is a child whose mother died. I'm so sorry.*

When Catherine put me down, she said, "Where's your father?"

"Inside," I said. "Lowell's there, too."

I was holding Catherine's hand, marveling at how familiar it felt, sorry that she had lost the baby but feeling fine nevertheless, happy just to be there with her again.

"It's too cold out here for you," she said, because I'd run out without my coat. "Would you go get your father?" she asked me. "Would you tell him to come out?"

"You come, too," I said, but Catherine let go of my hand.

"I want to talk to him out here," she said. "Go run inside."

So I went in to get my father. He was standing at the kitchen sink washing our breakfast dishes. Lowell was still sitting at the table. The water was running. They hadn't heard me go outside.

"Catherine's here," I said, and my father turned to look at me. He continued looking but reached and turned off the faucet. I couldn't tell if he'd heard me or not.

"Catherine's here," I said again. "She's outside. She wants to see you."

"Stay here," my father said, and he walked past me. Lowell and I waited until he was out the door, then we ran to the living room and pulled back the curtains to see.

Catherine was leaning against her father's car, her hands deep in her coat pockets, and I thought for a moment of her story about Skinny Reed, the boy she'd left behind. The thought scared me, as though I'd brought to mind something I shouldn't be thinking.

My father stepped toward Catherine and said something, then Catherine pushed herself up off the car and put her arms around my father. He put his arms around her, too, and they stayed there for a long time, saying things to each other, things I wished for all the world I could hear. Then both of them were crying, and I guessed that Catherine had told him about the baby, what had happened. My father looked at Catherine and said something. She put her head down and shook it.

Then they turned, and together they started walking toward the house. Lowell and I stepped back from the window and walked to the kitchen. We waited there for my father and Catherine.

When they stepped into the room, Catherine said, "Oh, Lowell," and he went to her and let her put her arms around him. Once she'd let go of him, I walked over, too.

Catherine smiled down at me and put her hand on my head. "I've got something for you, Meredith," she said. "Come upstairs."

Once we'd stepped into Catherine's bedroom, she closed the door. "I got all your letters," I said.

"Your father told me," she said. She sat down on the bed and

I sat next to her, pushing myself up so I could fold my legs beneath me.

"You read those letters?" she said, and I nodded. "Well, I want to swear to you again it's all true."

"I know," I said, wondering what it was she had to give me.

"Because I've told you so much, I want to tell you this, too, okay?"

"Okay," I said.

"Your father's going to tell you something different, I imagine. He thinks that's easier for you. He thinks that's kinder. I've told him a million times that the truth's always kindest, but he means well. You should know he does. So don't tell him you know. Let him tell you whatever he wants. He needs to."

I nodded but felt frightened now. I looked at Catherine and waited for her to say what she wanted to say. I felt as if I knew what it would be.

"I'm not going back with you to New Orleans, Meredith. We decided that already. I'm going to stay here and take care of my father when he comes home. He'll be a while getting well. Your father will probably say that soon I'll be on my way down. He thinks you've both been through enough already and maybe the pain can get handed out like medicine, a little at a time." Catherine was crying now, and I was, too.

"I'm going to stay here for now," she said, and I nodded, thinking this was worse than before, thinking it had been better when we'd driven off and left Catherine sleeping in bed. That time, at least, I hadn't been asked to face her, say goodbye, look face-to-face at the life I was losing.

I leaned down and put my head in Catherine's lap, and she stroked my hair.

"Can't we stay?" I asked.

"I do love you, my precious, sweet child," she said.

"I love you, too," I whispered.

"You can't stay," she said. "Not right now. Your father and I both need the time to think this through."

I felt I knew that moment what turned out to be true, that Catherine would never come back to New Orleans, that whatever there was between her and my father had died as surely as that baby inside her. I knew she loved me, but I also knew that wasn't enough, that it never would be.

Catherine let me cry a while longer and then said, "I do have something for you. That wasn't just a story."

I sat up and she went to her dresser and pulled open the top drawer. "I brought these with me," she said, "I don't know why. I guess you could even say I stole them. But I'd like you to have them now."

She'd pulled a plastic bag out of her drawer, and before she even handed it to me I could see what was inside. It was all the tiny colored statues that Murphy had made and then left behind the first time he disappeared.

"They're silly things, I know," Catherine said as I pulled the statues out one by one and looked at them. "They're silly, but I thought you might be glad to have them."

"I am," I said, and I don't think Catherine knew how much I understood that moment — that Murphy had made these statues in the hope that one day he'd be able to give them to his child, that Catherine had taken them when she left because she'd thought she'd give them to her child. Now she'd given them to me because the hope for that child was gone.

I carried the bag down the stairs with me and slipped it into my coat pocket. I didn't know why, but I didn't want my father to know I had them; he might guess what I knew if he saw them.

We left Catherine then. She held Lowell and me again, and she put her arms around my father. "You'll all be fine," she said when we stepped out the door.

"We'll see you soon, Cathy," my father said, and Catherine looked at me and tried to smile, telling me with her eyes to be strong, telling me not to give away my father's lie.

"That's fine," Catherine said. "I'll see you soon, too." Then she closed the door. I cried and cried.

"What are we doing?" Lowell asked. My father was holding our hands as we walked back to the car.

"We're going home," my father said.

By home, of course, he meant Magazine Street, to the rooms above his office. It's where we stayed for years and years, until Lowell and I grew up and went off to college. It wasn't until Lowell had married and moved to Covington and my father wasn't feeling well that he finally moved to my grandfather's house in Mandeville. It was Lowell who insisted that he move. He'd be close by, Lowell told him. He'd have someone to take care of him.

I moved here to Magazine Street when my father went to Mandeville. My father gave me the house. He said it would make my life easier.

Now, since my father has died, I'll move to Mandeville, to my grandfather's house. It will be nice, no matter my discomfort, to be near Lowell and his family.

More than that, though, I can't help feeling that there's something there for me, something of that house that will help make me whole. I'll tend to my grandfather's garden, plant the roses I've always wanted, sleep in the bed at the back of the house so I can look out at night and see my grandfather's statues lit by the moonlight.

It's a slight and silly notion maybe, as silly as those miniature statues that I've lined up in the kitchen window, but I tell myself that if I keep tracing a line back through my life, I'll come to a point where there's a sudden, surprising moment of joy, some revelation that takes all my regret and washes it clean, a hallowed light as if from heaven telling me once again to go in peace, or maybe just some subtle sound I recognize and call my own, like the wind through branches or fallen leaves, or even the silence of an early snow. Something. Anything.